THE SWEET TEA ODYSSEY

OTHER TITLES BY CATHERINE MANN

Stand-Alones

Lightning in a Mason Jar

Hometown Heroes Series

Forever His Girl

In Too Deep

Pretend You're Mine

His North Star

This Time Around

THE SWEET TEA ODYSSEY

A Novel

CATHERINE MANN

LAKE UNION
PUBLISHING

This is a work of fiction. Names, characters, organizations, places, events, and incidents are either products of the author's imagination or are used fictitiously. Otherwise, any resemblance to actual persons, living or dead, is purely coincidental.

Published by Lake Union Publishing, Seattle

www.apub.com

EU product safety contact:
Amazon Media EU S. à r.l.
38, avenue John F. Kennedy, L-1855 Luxembourg
amazonpublishing-gpsr@amazon.com

ISBN-13: 9781662535871 (paperback)
ISBN-13: 9781662535888 (digital)

Cover design by Kathleen Lynch/Black Kat Design
Cover image: © Hibrida13, © Yana Iskayeva / Getty; © Margie Hurwich / ArcAngel

Printed in the United States of America

To my mama, Sandy Belle

CHAPTER ONE

Rosalynn

September 2026: Sullivan's Island, South Carolina

Rosalynn bit back a sigh of aggravation as, once again, her former husband spooned two heaping teaspoons of sugar into the unsweetened iced tea. Adding sugar *after* the brew cooled was just downright counterproductive. There was an art to making sweet tea that he'd never mastered.

Clinking his spoon against the tumbler, Seth sat across the table from her at the Realtor's office as they waited for the agent to bring the paperwork listing their Sullivan's Island dream home.

Clink.

Clink.

Clink.

Undissolved, those granules drifted through the amber liquid like grains in an hourglass counting down to the end of their time together. After twenty years of marriage, he still couldn't make a decent glass of Southern sweet tea, much less learn from his mistakes.

On the surface, Rosalynn Barnwell-Yates understood that sounded nitpicky, and she'd made her fair share of marital blunders. But the ongoing debate over something so simple as a pitcher of tea had been indicative of his lack of commitment to other elements of their relationship.

Like not draining their daughter Elsie's college savings account at a blackjack table.

Seth lifted his drink, wiry as ever in his polo shirt and khakis. Boat shoes. No socks. His style had remained unchanged since his frat boy days, when he'd charmed her at the University of South Carolina with his easygoing smile and overblown dreams. "Would you like some?"

She stifled a wince, reminded of old fraternity parties and beer with too much foam. "No, but thank you."

If only Seth had fessed up to his gambling addiction and sought help, maybe they could have found a path through to reconciliation. Instead he'd proved time and time again that he would spend his last dollar on a lotto card.

And lie about it.

She could have forgiven the lost money. But the refusal to seek help? That had broken her heart and ended their marriage. Irrevocably.

Their divorce was final as of last month. A massive hurdle tackled. They had only to divvy up what assets he hadn't gambled away. Not that there would be much left if they didn't manage to off-load their heavily mortgaged waterfront home. Rosalynn shrugged off the morbid thoughts and focused on the future. She still had her job as marketing director at a local arts center.

And most importantly, she had her daughter. Elsie. Her quirky and brilliant fairy child growing up too fast, with only one year left in high school.

Only one year left for Rosalynn to figure out how to replenish the college fund.

Once the Realtor finished tucking a business card in each of the two folders, Rosalynn could begin the search for a new house to start over with her teenager. A smaller place, yes, and unlikely to have even a partial water view, but all theirs. She intended to make the most of Elsie's last year at home before she left for college.

Rosalynn hauled her attention to the Realtor's voice.

Therese Copeland, a longtime friend and killer real estate agent, slid the folders across the rattan conference table edged in tiny shells. "Selling a waterfront home during hurricane season can be risky. Offers may come in at a lower price point. It's not too late to pause the process. If you could wait until after the New Year—"

"No," Rosalynn blurted.

"Well . . ." Seth hedged.

Typical. There'd been a time she had appreciated his refusal to let matters get complicated. "Our divorce decree states that we both do all we can to sell the property. Although, Seth, you're welcome to refinance the house in your name and buy me out."

Silence swelled inside, while waves rolled and crashed higher, louder outside. The tide surged ever so slightly. Nature's bellwether, an early warning of sorts for the incoming tropical storm. Unease lifted the hairs on her arms. She needed to wrap this up and check on her daughter. Rosalynn knew firsthand the stresses on a kid when parents divorced, even if her own mom had landed on a forever match the second time around.

Seth shook his head. A graying blond lock fell over his forehead. "Rosalynn's right. List the place. I already put a 'For Sale' sign out front on the way over."

He'd done what?

Therese gave Rosalynn a quick but unmistakable *I've got this, my friend* look. "Seth, I will need to replace that with one including our logo and contact info."

Seth waved away her concern. "Of course, of course. And if there's weather damage, we can sort that out with insurance. Even if we have to accept a lowball offer, surely Rosalynn and I will both pocket a bit of profit from the sale."

She'd made the down payment all those years ago, but saying as much would only gum up the works and delay moving on. No amount of money was worth prolonging the inevitable. Or worse yet, risking

Seth somehow tangling them up in more shared debt by taking out loans and signing up for credit cards without her consent.

Therese drummed her manicured nails along the paperwork, a gold starfish stenciled on her pointer. "Rosalynn? Anything you wish to add?"

"Let's move forward. Please." Her phone vibrated on the table, but she kept it face down. Work would have to wait. She didn't take many days off from the office. "Time to list."

The cell buzzed again. And again. Likely from her teenage daughter sending her drive-through order, texts being the primary way Elsie communicated with her lately. Rosalynn would buy out the whole menu if it would help, but so far, no amount of fast food seemed to break down the wall between them, which had grown even higher in the past few weeks.

Seth rested his hand on top of hers, his college ring shiny. "I'm glad you're interested in keeping the peace."

Rosalynn eased away and reached for one of the folders. "In the interest of peace, Elsie and I would appreciate some help securing the hurricane shutters on the house in case this tropical storm turns ugly."

Grimacing, he rubbed the back of his neck. "Sure, uh, I wish I could, but I've gotta baby my shoulder. It's that old college baseball injury acting up. I'm heading out after this. Road trip to Biloxi. You're both welcome to come along."

To a city with casino boats.

Had he always been this transparent and she hadn't paid attention? A question for another time.

"I'll pass. If we're done here, I need to head home to check on Elsie." As she tucked the paperwork into her bag, her phone vibrated again, rattling across the table and sliding from the edge. Leaning, she scooped the device up in midair just as her service dog popped to his feet, ready to assist.

Rosalynn motioned for him to wait as she tucked her cell into the canvas bag beside her thigh.

With a quick thanks and goodbye to Therese, Rosalynn gripped the handles on her wheelchair to roll back from the table, thankful to leave Seth behind as he took his time gathering his paperwork and finishing his tea. As she propelled the chair toward the door, her yellow Labrador retriever trotted alongside, nails clicking against the hardwood floors.

She'd had other service dogs over the years, and each time, she'd been unable to imagine a tighter bond than she'd experienced with that animal, more than that of a working relationship or a beloved pet. There was something special about Dusty, though. He wasn't necessarily the sharpest, but he'd stolen her heart with his goofy brown eyes and playful determination. His drive never to give up until he figured out what she needed touched her heart.

And had saved her butt on more than one occasion.

In the lobby, the teenage receptionist stood, fidgety and oversolicitous. "I'll open the door."

Sighing, Rosalynn shook her head. The girl meant well, but her unmistakable awkwardness about the wheelchair rubbed Rosalynn the wrong way on an already rough day. Why couldn't the receptionist have just asked if she needed help rather than assuming?

"Thanks, but Dusty's got it." She nodded toward the automatic door button and called to her dog, "Target."

Dusty reared onto his back legs and smacked the silver square with his front paws, full of enthusiasm for one of his favorite cues—he knew over seventy. The door swung open and let in a blast of muggy air. Rosalynn eased through onto the lengthy porch, and Dusty tipped his nose into the breeze, nostrils twitching.

Palmetto trees rustled in a pulsing rhythm from the tropical storm's outer bands. Each gust flung a fistful of raindrops. She wished she trusted the weatherperson's insistence that this would be a nothing-burger event. Aside from the damage a storm might wreak on her house sale, she hated the idea that it could tie her to her financially derelict ex for however much longer it took to clear the damage.

Her hand fell to rest on Dusty's noggin, gliding to stroke a silky ear between her fingers. Bottom line, she didn't have the emotional energy for an evacuation. Ending her marriage had taken its toll.

Right now, she wanted to go home and hang out on her dock while finishing off leftover barbecue. Heaven help her, she even craved her mother's hummingbird cake, but without the judgment or advice.

Fast food notwithstanding, best to get home to Elsie.

Pivoting the chair away from the door, she rolled toward the ramp jutting off to the side by the massive trash can overflowing with boxes and something rotting in the summer heat. Her nose scrunched at the stench. A powerful burst of wind lifted the garbage lid again and again, clanging each time it slammed closed. Another hefty gust nudged it forward . . .

Toppling the plastic bin right over onto the wooden ramp.

Frustration simmered. She eyed her dog, then the massive green bin blocking her exit. Moving it was beyond even Dusty's highly trained capabilities. Her accident at twelve years old, an incomplete spinal cord injury at her L2, had left Rosalynn with some sensation in her lower body and even the ability to stand for a few moments, but certainly not enough to tackle the roadblock ahead of her.

She blinked away tears, only from the gritty breeze stinging her eyes.

At least that's what she told herself. Surely not because of spending a horrible morning with her ex as they put their house on the market, a home renovated for her wheelchair needs as well. The last thing she wanted was to call *Seth* for help, even if he was close by. In fact, she wanted to be gone before he finished his subpar tea. But the parking lot was empty since the rest of the world was probably already home moving furniture off their porches since the last tropical storm had turned ugly with little warning. Bottom line, she needed help right now, and calling Seth to come on out was the most logical option.

Surrendering, she fished her cell from the bag tucked between her hip and the chair, almost toppling the pouch of dog treats in the process. Her cell screen logged eleven missed texts. But none from Elsie.

Rosalynn gripped her phone, thumbing open the string of unread messages, *all* of which were from her mother. She reached for Dusty again. At this rate, she would rub the fur right off his ears.

Mother-daughter relationships could be difficult. At least they were for her family, no matter how much they loved each other. Lillian Barnwell had earned her reputation as a legal powerhouse in DC and Virginia. If only she could approach family issues with a lighter touch. Especially since Rosalynn's accident during a ballet performance. Throughout that first year of recovery and beyond, her mom had been a fierce advocate, tackling obstacles from South Carolina all the way to the nation's capital. But Rosalynn wasn't a child anymore, and she didn't need her mother to reorganize her cabinets without asking or send Google searches about her doctors.

The phone chimed with another message.

A "lighter touch" definitely wasn't in her mother's DNA, especially today. According to at least three of the texts, Lillian had booked a flight from Alexandria, Virginia, to Charleston, South Carolina, and would Uber over to Sullivan's Island. No reason given other than that Elsie had reached out and they all needed to talk in person. Frustration and worry doubled on an already killer day. But she reminded herself not to borrow trouble, since it didn't take much to spin up her mother.

The speed of her travel plans shouldn't have been surprising. Lillian thought nothing of hitting the road at a moment's notice. Rosalynn could almost hear her mom's repeated refrain, *I'm always down for a road trip*. Not even the threat of a tropical storm possibly upgrading to a hurricane could deter Lillian when she went into Mama Bear mode.

Another ding echoed, vibrating the device.

No doubt about it. A storm of a whole different sort was blowing into town before sundown.

CHAPTER TWO

Lillian

March 1990: Charleston, South Carolina

Even before my life fell apart, I'd always been down for a road trip. And none had been more important than this one to Washington, DC.

The prep work filled me with as much excitement as the actual adventure. So much so, I could almost ignore the sadness over this being my last trip with Grady. I had stayed up late into the night after everyone else went to sleep. Racing around the kitchen like a chicken with her head cut off, I lined the bottom of the cooler with Ziploc bags of ice, pausing only long enough to shake the circulation back into my numb fingers. Anticipation built as I added in fried chicken legs, deviled eggs, a jar of peaches, and, of course, a jug of sweet tea.

Yes, in South Carolina, it's called sweet tea. We don't do sweetened tea. Or iced tea. It's *sweet tea*, an etymological quirk of our local language. Just as we might say "fixin' to" instead of "going to." "Hey" instead of "hello." Or "cut off the light" instead of "turn off the light."

My mama always insisted that words were important. And never have they been more crucial than now, with my thirteen-year-old daughter's future riding on a single piece of life-changing legislation. Words on paper could change the whole trajectory of my child's life.

As a paralegal, sure, I'd taken a stand on different issues in the past. But this was the first time I'd packed my cooler and a couple of homemade signs to march in a peaceful protest.

For my sweet Rosalynn? I would geld a mountain lion with a butter knife.

I added two more bags of ice on top before locking the lid down tight. If only I could seal away my emotions as easily. It had been a year for the record books. In the worst of ways.

Our lives had taken a tragic and unexpected detour fifteen months ago with Rosalynn's accident. The fall off a stage during a dance recital had nearly killed her. She'd spent three days in a coma. When she'd regained consciousness, our relief was soon tempered by the hard work ahead as she healed from a spinal fracture. The details felt overwhelming then as the surgeon tossed out technical terminology like little bombs exploding our everyday world.

My gaze skated toward the hallway and her closed bedroom door, and truth be told, I would have put a baby monitor in there to keep watch over her if I hadn't been certain she would throw it in the trash. There's no explaining the helplessness that swamped me from Rosalynn's initial diagnosis all the way to her being denied a spot on a school field trip to the zoo because of transportation issues. How could I accept there was nothing I could do to heal my daughter, who was tackling her recovery with a determination—a grit—that humbled me? Then I heard about a demonstration happening in Washington, DC, to promote awareness for individuals with disabilities. Finally, I could make a lasting difference for Rosalynn.

But I wasn't taking any chances. I'm superstitious. In big and small ways, like painting the porch ceiling blue so bad spirits would mistake it for the sky or water and keep on going.

Some might call my superstitious nature genetic. My mama never put her purse on the floor for fear of losing what little money she had left. And she always reminded the newly engaged to bury a bottle of bourbon upside down before the ceremony to keep the rain away. I had forgotten to honor that notion, and my drowned-rat photos from the day I married Grady Barnwell told the tale. The day our divorce became final earlier this week, however, the sun shone high and bright in the sky.

His gentle snore drifted from the living room, where he snoozed on the sofa since we no longer shared a bed. So far, we'd managed to hide the change from our daughter, chalking up his sleeping arrangements to long shifts at the fire station since we didn't want to reveal our split until after the protest march, a landmark event we were both committed to attending. Our marriage had always been rocky—with arguments about everything from money to his drinking. Truth be told, burying a bourbon bottle prior to our vows would have made for dark irony.

I forced myself to keep my eyes off his rugged body, too tall for the couch. I didn't have to look to know he had his arm thrown over his face to block out any light. How strange that such a quiet man could leave such a deep silence behind.

Best to stay busy and focus on the future. For this particular road trip, terrified of tempting fate, I stuck to my routine from years past and packed that cooler to the gills. I reached into the cabinet and filled a brown bag with paper towels, disposable plates, and plastic cups. No fast-food joints allowed on our odyssey. We would picnic at rest stops and camp, saving for unexpected medical bills. And one thing we'd learned above all this year—there were always unexpected medical bills.

Panic stirred in my belly over letting Rosalynn out of my sight, even though my mama assured me they had big plans for their time together while Grady and I were away. I double-checked my list on the counter with reminders for my mother. I moved my daughter's juice closer to the front of the refrigerator and taped a sticky note to the label before returning to road trip prep.

One mile marker at a time, one deviled egg after another, I would find a way to co-parent peacefully with Grady. But first I needed this trip to DC with him as a show of unity for our daughter so when we told her about the divorce, she would understand we were still a unified front looking out for her.

My marriage might have failed and I might have a mountain of obstacles ahead this week, but I also knew there was no force of nature stronger than a mother's need to protect her child.

Nothing would stop me from making my voice heard on her behalf.

CHAPTER THREE

Elsie

2026: Sullivan's Island, South Carolina

Elsie hated her life.

And the disaster of epic proportions was her own fault.

She flung a hair straightener into her suitcase on top of a pile of jean shorts, T-shirts, and flip-flops. She was a loser, like her dad. Probably due to something in her DNA. Or maybe she'd just picked up his loser ways.

Whatever the reason, she had to get out of South Carolina. ASAP. Unlike her father, she intended to do something to fix her epic mistake.

Besides, her mom didn't need the stress of Loser 2.0 under her roof. Rosalynn Barnwell-Yates had enough on her plate with her job, the move, the divorce, and yeah, the health stuff too. And her mom juggled all of it in a world that wasn't even built for her.

Elsie couldn't manage to make it through high school without wrecking her life. Now there was nothing left for her but to jump ship and start fresh. Hopefully with her grandmother's help. Elsie glanced at her phone, then checked her tablet too, but still saw just the one message from Grammie after their conversation.

Leaving today. We'll talk soon.

That was it. Nothing more. No mention of which flight she'd taken.

Or, more importantly, whether she'd told Rosalynn about Elsie's call.

Nerves gnawing her insides, she kept packing. She hauled her guitar case out from under the bed and skimmed her hand along the top with a reverence she didn't dare show anyone outside this room. She'd stumbled on the acoustic in the attic about a year ago, when her dad was packing up to leave and needed an extra suitcase. The strings had long since popped and the case's handle had broken right off. She thought maybe it used to be her grandfather's but wasn't sure.

Something about the faded stickers on that case called to her, promising music on *her* terms. A way to pour out her feelings during her parents' divorce. Emotions she still wasn't ready to share with anyone else. She'd tucked the instrument away in her bedroom and searched for YouTube videos on how to re-string the instrument, bringing it back to life in the privacy of her room.

She'd fought her mother so long and hard over a deep hatred for piano lessons and practice schedules. How could she admit her new hobby to anyone?

If somebody spilled the beans, a Rosalynn-generated practice schedule would land in Elsie's email by sunup, complete with the option to add to her digital calendar. And the question: *Would you like reminders ten, fifteen, or thirty minutes before the scheduled time?*

She would like *no* reminders. She just wanted to feel something without the weight of her mother's expectations. That kind of grind would squash the joy right out of the instrument when she really, really needed the outlet for the garbage going on in her life.

So she practiced in secret, self-taught with videos online when her mom was at work managing a whole arts center of professionals.

Her tablet vibrated from an incoming call with her best friend's ringtone. *My only friend left.*

Elsie set aside the guitar case, now secured with a bungee cord off her kayak. She snatched up the phone and hit the "Accept" button.

"Willow, I did it." She propped the device against two stacked pizza boxes. "I called Grammie this morning. I told her I can't live here anymore, and she's going to help. I'm packing now."

At least she hoped Grammie intended to plead her case. Her grandmother had promised to get the first available flight, but before they could talk more, Grammie had to hang up because of an incoming call from a doctor looking after her husband. Elsie's heart squeezed as she looked at the photo taped to her mirror, snapped when they'd made a special trip for her dippy piano recital. She stuffed down a twinge of guilt over taking Grammie away from Ace's bedside when he didn't have much longer left to live and reminded herself the stress would be so much worse for everybody if the truth came out. Besides, it wasn't like she'd *asked* Grammie to leave Ace and fly here. She'd just asked for some help.

Why hadn't Grammie called her back?

Willow Hererra stared at Elsie from the screen, brushing her damp hair as she sat cross-legged on her bed. "Wait, isn't this happening kinda fast? Don't you have to do legal stuff before you can go since you're not eighteen yet? My mom would call the cops in five minutes if I just up and left."

"I found a form online to emancipate myself." She kicked through a pile of laundry and stubbed her toe on one of Dusty's chewy bones on her way to the dresser.

She didn't dare think of how much she would miss that goofball.

"Don't you still have to go through the courts and stuff?"

"Grammie is a lawyer." She dumped a drawer of underwear into her suitcase. "She'll help me with the process."

"Are you sure you want to bring your grandmother into this?" Willow asked skeptically. "She's your mom's mom. The last time I sassed my mother, Grandma said she would 'yank a knot in my tail' if I ever did that again. And that was just for sassing. I don't wanna think about what she would have done if I threatened to leave."

"Mom and Grammie argue all the time." Lately Elsie had been too busy hiding from her mother to get in an argument. Her mom had a spooky Spider-Sense at figuring stuff out, and some secrets needed to stay buried. "I think Grammie will take my side."

"I wouldn't bet on that. There's a parent code with my mom and my grandmother. They might trash-talk each other, but nobody else can."

Anxiety left Elsie so lightheaded she tripped over a high-top sneaker. She sank onto the edge of the unmade bed, flopped onto her back, and grabbed the tablet. "I'm certain. Grammie's flying here to get me today."

Well, her grandmother was flying to the Charleston airport, but she hadn't specified if Elsie would be coming home with her.

Eyes wide, Willow paused brushing her hair. "In the middle of a hurricane?"

"It's a tropical storm."

"Every hurricane is at the start."

Elsie thumbed open the weather app on her phone just to confirm. "From what I see there's no change to the intensity. It's not even predicted to be a Category One."

Although the path *had* shifted for a direct hit to their coastal town. And the last tropical storm turned really fierce without much warning. Elsie glanced out her window, where the waves crested higher, some splashing over the dock. She was like a rotten-karma magnet.

"My parents aren't taking chances with our property. They are locking things down tight—we've been filling sandbags in case there's a storm surge and Mom got extra gas for the generator. I had to take a quick shower in case the power goes out." Willow darted her eyes toward her door. "I'm not going to be able to hide in my room much longer."

A rocking chair on the porch knocked ever so slightly against Elsie's window. She should probably start hauling stuff into the garage. Grammie always said a swaying rocking chair meant bad luck. "If they're so worried, why don't they just evacuate?"

"Dad says it's too tough to transport all the animals. He worries about getting stuck in a traffic jam with the horse trailer." The Herreras had two Thoroughbreds, four rescue dogs, and a three-legged cat. Lucky Willow. "We'll just hunker down here. I wouldn't count on your grandmother making it anytime soon."

Elsie smiled for the first time since that awful Monday a month ago, a.k.a. the worst day of her life, the cherry on the sundae of a crummy year. "I pity the person who tries to say no to Grammie."

"Are you, uh, going to tell them what's really going on with, well, you know . . ."

"No. Absolutely not. They'll call the school." Her throat tightened until she struggled to swallow. Her family's counselor called it a panic thing. "Then everyone will know what happened."

"I think you're right not to say anything. Your secret is safe with me. No matter what." Willow looked away again, then back at the screen. "Hey, my parents are hollering for me to help with the horses. Some, uh, people from the neighborhood have come over to help."

Some people.

Willow's friends.

Elsie's *former* friends, from before her life blew up.

"Sure, go ahead." She had packing to finish and a plan to make if Grammie didn't come through.

Although now, after talking to Willow, Elsie worried her grandmother might have another motive for coming, to gang up on her. The adults around here hadn't been all that trustworthy lately.

Willow hesitated. Her forehead furrowed like she really cared. "I'll call you later, though. Okay?"

Elsie's throat closed again. "Thanks. Go make those sandbags."

She disconnected, then hugged the iPad to her chest hard against the ache that wouldn't go away. More than a pain, it was a fear that grew heavier every day. She *had* to leave. She just couldn't bear going back to her high school for even one more minute. Walking down the hall, hearing the whispers and the laughs, feeling the eyes on her. Yesterday, she'd hidden in the library during lunch rather than go to the cafeteria and risk a day when even Willow wouldn't sit with her.

A tear trickled down her cheek and into her ear. Sniffling, she scrubbed her wrist under her nose. She'd never been popular, but she'd embraced being different, a part of a quirky pack of other misfits. Like science nerd Willow. Band geek Jareth. The artsy theater twins. Then there were the floaters who'd been booted out of the popular crowd, like mathlete Porter, who hung their heads as they asked to sit at the misfit table like it was a consolation prize. Elsie took pride in welcoming them, in being the better person.

Now *she* was a floater with nowhere safe to land. Worst of all, she'd been betrayed by one of those trusted few in her circle of friends. Someone who'd sold her out for a little piece of popularity, unleashing a storm of bullying that left her desperate to escape.

Please, Grammie. Please, Grammie. Please.

A vehicle rumbled outside, slowing. Her gut knotted, and she was afraid to hope. It was probably just her mom. Except it didn't sound like the van. The engine certainly didn't sound like her dad's convertible. Maybe it was a turnaround since they lived at the end of the street.

Flinging aside the tablet, she rolled from the bed and to her feet, peering out the window just as an unfamiliar sedan stopped out front. An Uber ID card was perched on the dash. The back door of the compact car swung open, and an arm extended holding a one-of-a-kind briefcase. The vintage piece was covered in needlepoint cabbage roses. A purse charm dangled from the handle, the kind with a frame for a family photo.

Grammie had arrived.

Elsie stuffed down the shame sweeping over her at the thought of her grandmother knowing the truth of why she needed to leave.

Or the humiliating prospect of Grammie seeing those naked photos, taken by someone threatening to ruin her life.

CHAPTER FOUR

Lillian

2026: Sullivan's Island, South Carolina

We Southerners are known for our grits. Cooked slowly with loads of butter and salt. Eaten plain or topped with the same sort of foods a Northerner might ladle over mashed potatoes.

People from outside our neck of the woods either love grits or hate them. No middle ground. Opinions are strong either way. Rather like the strong will of a Southern woman. Because yes, we are also known for our grit. At least, that's true for the women in my line.

So when Elsie called that morning insisting she intended to emancipate herself and live with me in Virginia, I didn't hesitate to book a ticket on the next flight out of Dulles International Airport to Charleston, South Carolina. Not an easy feat with an impending tropical storm. I said goodbye to my husband at the hospice facility with a hug and lined up a nurse's aide to assist him while I was gone.

However, as I've mentioned before, the women in my family aren't easily deterred, and I knew if Elsie had set her mind to this emancipation notion, she would succeed. Unless someone with a stronger will interceded.

Namely, me.

I did try to phone Rosalynn with a heads-up, but I couldn't get through and had to resort to generalized texts. We tended to do that sometimes—ignore calls from each other—when we needed a breather from the friction. She often accused me of micromanaging. Fair point. I would then suggest she was prickly. Also a fair point.

And so the cycle continued.

During my layover and after landing, I'd resorted to more of those texts and prayed Rosalynn received them in time to meet me at her house. I'd refrained from too many details, not that Elsie had given any hint of what was upsetting her. Too much can be misinterpreted in text exchanges—a generational thing, perhaps.

Like the whole notion of Ubers. I had a love-hate relationship with the app, but all the rental vehicles had already been spoken for, due to widespread panic about the weather. Flights had been canceled and stranded passengers had opted to drive out.

And that's how I ended up in a rideshare with a chauffeur named Bubba.

During our trek from the airport, with his little sedan buffeted by sporadic gusts, he'd told me how he started working for Uber because of the flexible hours during his chemo treatments. I couldn't tell if his story was real or manufactured for bigger tips. I decided to err on the side of compassion and added 25 percent to the bill.

It was hurricane season, after all, and I made my living fighting for underdogs.

I hefted my signature briefcase in one hand and lifted the handle on my small carry-on with the other. The muggy South Carolina weather swamped me with familiarity even after more than three decades of living just outside DC. The incoming storm swirled a briny wind full of mosquitoes seeking a safe place to latch on for dear life. The ocean roared a little louder. Waves crested a little higher.

Maybe that was why my granddaughter hadn't come out to greet me. Unless she wasn't here. After all, Rosalynn hadn't answered either.

Had they evacuated? If so, they'd left the windows unprotected and none of the porch furniture had been moved.

"Yoo-hoo . . . Elsie?" I called out.

Blinds parted in a far window, and I caught a glimpse of my granddaughter before the slats closed.

My rolling bag bumped along the grooves in the walkway as I trekked toward the front door with the welcome wreath undulating. Seeing my daughter's lovely clapboard home unprepared for the incoming storm fired an anger so deep in my belly I stopped walking. I had to gulp down three breaths of that salty air to rein in my temper.

Even with the For Sale sign out front bending in the wind, this was still Rosalynn's home. Her dream house on the water. The one-story bungalow was nestled on a gently sloping hill along an inland canal. Most of the other houses in the area were built on stilts. I'd offered to pay for an elevator if she wanted one of those homes, but this place had stolen her heart. So instead, as a housewarming gift, I'd paid for a stone seawall to offer additional protection against flooding. Rosalynn had drawn up plans for the planked walkways and the dock, both wheelchair accessible. When deciding to sell, she'd vowed she didn't mind downsizing to a house better suited for the day Elsie went to college. But dreams died hard.

And some dreams were the very best part. Like being a grandmother.

Elsie burst through the front door on bare feet.

"You made it." She ran to me with her arms outstretched, her brown hair flying loose and free like her mother's at that age, but with hints of gold she'd inherited from Seth.

I dropped my bags and hugged her hard. No one had been able to prepare me for how much I would love my grandchild. I'd spent Rosalynn's entire pregnancy worrying myself sick no matter how many times her obstetrician and neurologist assured us that with careful monitoring, she should be able to safely carry and deliver a baby. The physicians had been correct.

When Elsie had been placed in my arms, swaddled in that blanket with a pink knit cap on her head, I'd been gobsmacked by powerful emotions. My heart had swelled and I'd been utterly defenseless.

I still was.

Proof positive? Booking a plane ticket in the middle of an oncoming tropical storm at a single call from my grandchild.

I angled away and swept her hair from her face, trying to read her green eyes. "Elsie, what weren't you telling me on the phone?"

She glanced away and made a big show of picking up my briefcase, a vintage piece covered in needlepoint—a hobby I'd begun to pass the long hours in waiting rooms while Rosalynn finished PT and OT. It hadn't taken my daughter long to evict me from the sessions. She'd always been more overt in asserting herself, whereas Elsie could be an avoider by nature, like my own mother.

Elsie climbed the porch steps and set the case beside the rocker. "I can't believe you came so fast. After we hung up, I started to feel guilty for taking you away from Ace. I tried to call you back but couldn't get an answer."

My fist clenched around the roll bag. My husband was dying in the hospice facility. But he wasn't leaving the earth just yet, and he'd been emphatic that I needed to be in South Carolina. That said, I couldn't return to him fast enough.

"Ace is stable, and he insisted I come. And not a moment too soon. Now that I'm here, I can help you and your mother evacuate for the hurricane—"

"Tropical storm," Elsie interjected.

"For now. As my mama would have said, 'Hope for the best. Prepare for the worst.'" And my mind was chock-full of all the worst possibilities, the added risks and obstacles for Rosalynn if she was trapped in the middle of a natural disaster. I sat in the rocker and tugged off my pumps, switching them for gym shoes from my bag. "Open the garage door so we can haul out the plywood for the windows."

Which would give us time for a little conversation.

"Board up the house? On our own? You're kidding, right?"

"Hope for the best," I repeated. "Prepare for the worst."

"Maybe Dad could . . ." She shook her head. "Never mind."

She flipped open the cover on the garage's security pad and tapped out the code. The door rumbled open to reveal the cavernous space with kayaks on one side and boards stacked neatly against the other wall. I had wanted to gift Rosalynn with permanently affixed hurricane shutters, but my husband's COPD and lung transplant had cut our plans short for the extra expense.

A transplant that was now failing. My fingers clenched around my purse handle, right above the picture charm of our wedding photo, with Rosalynn beside us holding flowers.

A lifetime ago.

I swiped away a bead of perspiration and wished I had time to change, but I needed to scout the lay of the land with Elsie before Rosalynn arrived. "Back to my question. What's this I hear about emancipation?"

"Just what I said." She carried a box marked CLIPS for securing the boards. "I'm ready to move out. I took the practice GED online and passed it, so the real test should be a breeze. I won't need anything from you except help filing the emancipation paperwork—since you're a lawyer and all."

And since I was an attorney, I'd cross-examined enough lying witnesses in my career to recognize something in Elsie's phone conversation just didn't line up. Maybe I should have been more persistent in contacting Rosalynn, but that maternal instinct had nudged me to take a speedier, direct approach.

Yes, I understood my propensity to overcompensate had roots in that accident decades ago. But like most Southern matriarchs, I knew the world depended on me. After all, it wasn't micromanaging when assistance was needed.

I'm sure a counselor could have a field day with that notion. "Does this have something to do with your parents' divorce?"

"No," Elsie blurted. "Not at all."

The divorce was definitely a subject I'd needed to steer well clear of with my daughter. I'd negotiated high-profile, multimillion-dollar lobbying cases in the nation's capital. I'd been offered—and turned down—judgeships by administrations from both political parties. Most recently I had been approached to run for Congress, something that had never been anywhere on my life-goals bingo card. I told them no thank you. I preferred to be a free agent, taking up cases of my choosing.

None of that experience had come close to helping me with Rosalynn. Our mother-daughter tug-of-war had an extensive history long before her brutally misguided choice to marry Seth Yates, a spoiled frat boy who still hadn't cut his mama's apron strings.

My disapproval hadn't gone over well with Rosalynn. Now that they were divorced, my daughter had become even more defensive. I wanted to assure her that I didn't intend to say "I told you so." Except even that simple declaration would accomplish nothing other than giving airtime to "I told you so."

After a final yank to my shoelaces, I shoved to my feet, reaching behind me automatically to still the chair. "Why the rush to leave home? You could do a dual enrollment in a local college and still live at home, enjoy your senior year with your friends."

"I meant it when I said my leaving isn't about the divorce." Elsie dropped the box of clips in front of a three-panel picture window. "Although since Mom and Dad have split, if I go ahead and leave now, Mom can start over in her new house. We can all have a fresh start."

"What did your mother say about this plan?"

She stopped dead. "You didn't tell her already?"

Ah, that had been the point of her call. Elsie must have hoped to dodge broaching the subject. "No, apparently not. That's the reason I flew down. I only mentioned you'd reached out. But no specifics."

"Well, when you tell her," Elsie said, scuffing a toe through the sandy earth, "make sure you let her know I'm going to continue my education. I have my college fund."

"When *I* tell her? Think again, my dear." The kid had my heart, but that didn't mean I was a pushover. "Your mother should be here soon and we can hash this all out together."

Elsie went pale, backpedaling faster than a cat in a pile of fire ants. "I, uh, need to call a friend to see if school has been canceled. If Mom gets here before I'm done, feel free to go ahead and start that conversation without me."

My heart hurt for Elsie. Truly. I'd seen firsthand how the crumbling of my marriage had hurt Rosalynn, both before and after the accident. Elsie had apparently decided to handle her torn loyalties by leaving altogether.

But even as my heart hurt for her, an overwhelming relief swept over me too. I must have been wrong this morning when I'd worried Elsie's crisis involved something far darker.

CHAPTER FIVE

Rosalynn

2026: Sullivan's Island, South Carolina

Apparently, following her mom's superstitions had paid off for once. Rosalynn mentally thanked all her lucky horseshoes and those bowls of black-eyed peas as Therese dragged the trash can away from the wooden ramp.

Just as Rosalynn had been about to surrender and text Seth for help, Therese had come running outside, shouting for her to wait. Whatever the reason, the Realtor had relieved Rosalynn's stress level on one front at least.

The rumble of the rolling bin echoed the distant thunder. Wind gusted a plastic bag across the parking lot, inching her stress level back up a notch.

"Thank you, Therese," Rosalynn said as she propelled the chair forward. Dusty's nails tapped along the planks as he tucked into a perfect heel position alongside. "You came out at just the right moment. Or did you see me through the window?"

"Lucky coincidence." The real estate agent reached into the pocket of her linen shift, pulled out a business card, and passed it over. "I thought you might need this. It's a company that will board up your house if the storm strengthens. They're reasonably priced and easy to work with. They're totally trustworthy. I use them for the rental properties we manage."

Rosalynn refused to feel embarrassed over her ex-husband's shoddy behavior. Dusty rested his head on her knee in comfort, a cue he also used to relieve neuropathy pain. "Thanks, that's a great help."

"All a part of the job. Whatever I can do to make this house sale easier." Therese paused, stuffing her hands into her pockets, anchoring the dress from sweeping up at the hem. "I hope I'm not out of line in saying that you deserve better."

"Not out of line at all. I'm aware," she responded with a wry smile. "Thanks again. Stay safe in this weather."

She hoped the Realtor didn't take offense, but aside from the impending confrontation with her mother, Rosalynn couldn't get to the minivan fast enough, away from Seth inside gathering his paperwork and finishing his grainy tea. Hopefully he would procrastinate long enough for her to make her escape.

Of course she understood she wouldn't have Elsie without Seth—a platitude well-meaning people mentioned as if that somehow erased the pain of divorcing a man with a gambling addiction. Nothing could eradicate the guilt over having given her child such a sad excuse for a father.

How naive to have assumed that all men would be as honorable as her own dad. Memories of him flooded her as she activated the key fob, opening the side door and ramp on her minivan. The sound of him singing classic Carolina beach tunes teased. Each droplet carried by the breeze reminded her of him taking her kayaking *after* her accident. Her mother had nearly blown a gasket when she caught them returning to shore.

Once inside the specially modified van, Rosalynn tethered Dusty's seat belt harness before rewarding him with a piece of dog kibble. He gently took the pellet of food from her palm. She saved the high-value treats—like cheese or mini dog bones—for more challenging tasks so as not to risk him overeating. She smiled at the notion of Dusty barreling aside a slew of rolling trash cans for a chunk of cheddar.

She pushed the controls to rotate the driver's seat into position for her to transfer from her chair. Settled behind the steering wheel, engine purring, she checked her dog with the rearview mirror. "Hey, Dusty, I think *I* deserve a high-value treat for making it through this day, don't you? Maybe an ice cream sundae with Elsie."

Speaking of family . . . She sighed. She was used to her mother's bulldozer tactics, but flying into town during a storm seemed a little over the top.

Rosalynn tapped the Bluetooth button on her steering wheel as she pulled out of the parking lot. The charm hanging from her rearview mirror—a ballerina in a wheelchair—spun. "Siri, call Mom."

The ringtone filled the vehicle. Already, traffic was picking up, with most heading out of town. Her lane stayed sparse. Alarmingly so. Had the forecast worsened? She sped up. The need to check on her daughter increased along with the van's RPMs.

Her call shifted to voicemail and she disconnected. No need to leave yet another message for her mother. According to the original text, Lillian's plane should have landed. Unless her flight had been diverted for weather?

A quick call later, she'd secured the workers to board up her house later in the day, just to be safe. Half the businesses lining the street had already boarded up their windows. Some sported sandbags as a barrier against potential storm surge. Beachy storefronts gave way to clapboard and stucco houses in her out-of-the-way coastal community, barrier islands dotting the horizon. The carpet of reeds bowed in the wind. A pair of wading herons took flight, with a slower egret trailing behind.

Her property definitely followed the rule of "smallest house in a great neighborhood." The one-story wooden bungalow had been a fixer-upper, but with the open-concept floor plan, the sight lines had been stunning. And in gutting the rest, she'd been able to design a kitchen, a bathroom, and doorways to spec, from the doorway width to countertop height to adaptive equipment.

Beyond that, she'd made memories here bringing up her child. She, Seth, and Elsie had placed handprints in the concrete walkway. She and her daughter had fished off the dock, built sandcastles on the shore, and kayaked in the quiet cove.

Quite simply, this was home.

A picket fence surrounded the entire property so Dusty had room to stretch his legs. Planked walkways spidered outward, giving her easy access to the firepit and farther down to the marshy beach. Her new home would also meet her needs, but with less character.

Her gaze gravitated to Seth's janky For Sale sign flapping in the breeze. Pathetic. Just like him.

She'd been brought up to believe character trumped all else, a code taught to her by none other than her mother, who was currently hefting her porch furniture into the garage. Sheets of plywood lay in the yard. Rosalynn's mouth twitched with a grin at the thought of Elsie hauling those boards around at her grandmother's behest.

Heaven help anyone who said no to Lillian.

Rosalynn shifted her van into park in the driveway. She should have known her mother would never let something like a tropical storm keep her away. But it begged the question . . . Why now of all times?

Lillian dropped a rocking chair and shaded her eyes before waving. She looked none the worse for wear after her flight in her wrinkle-free business-casual slacks and blouse, her dark hair clipped back in a low ponytail. Rosalynn resisted the urge to smooth a hand over her roots, two months past due for a touch-up. She wagered a mental bet with herself on how long it would take her mom to comment. Like they didn't have bigger issues bearing down on her beach community.

"Mother," Rosalynn called out the open window. "What in the world brought you here? I don't want to sound rude, and I love you dearly, but it's mannerly to give a little notice before showing up."

"I tried to call," her mother said as she dragged the rocker into the garage before walking back to the porch. Lillian never stuck to one task at a time. The woman deserved a multitasker of the year award. Every year.

"Fair point," Rosalynn conceded, although her mother probably couldn't hear as she wrestled with a patio umbrella.

Where was Elsie hiding?

Rosalynn used the quiet minutes unbuckling her dog and transferring from the van to calm herself. She couldn't afford to let her anger at Seth bleed over into the conversation with her mother. First and foremost, she needed to get to the bottom of whatever had prompted Elsie to reach out—bypassing her own mother and father. Possibly because Elsie knew if she told her father, Seth would have come straight to Rosalynn. Whatever marital troubles she and Seth may have had, they'd been in agreement that parents needed to present a unified front.

Although that would make the subject of a drained college account tricky to navigate, an infuriating move she hadn't even told her mother about. Rosalynn didn't want to consider the notion that he may have used the money to pay off a bookie out to hurt him.

Or his family.

On the paved driveway, Rosalynn thumbed the key fob to retract the ramp and close the sliding side door. She unclipped Dusty's leash, releasing him to shake off, stretch his legs, and water a bush if needed.

"Free time, Dusty. Free time," Rosalynn said before turning toward her mother and extending her arms. "Hi, Mom."

Lillian wrapped her in a hug bearing the familiar scent of jasmine tinged with a hint of perspiration. "Hello, my sweet girl. Let's tuck into the garage, where we can hear each other better."

Grains of sand carried on the wind, along with the sounds of neighbors hammering boards in place.

"That bad, huh?" She wheeled toward the shady cavern and set the brakes beside the rockers.

"Well, it's not good." Her mom dropped into the chair with an exhausted sigh. "Elsie called me this morning. She said she wants to emancipate."

Every cell in Rosalynn's body went into full panic mode.

"Emancipate?" The word felt foreign on her tongue and in her stunned brain. Her mother must have misunderstood or overreacted. "Thank you for your concern and caring, but I suspect you've been roped in by a case of teenage dramatics. I seriously doubt Elsie wants to have herself legally declared an adult with all the responsibilities that entails."

"The lawyer part of me says otherwise." Lillian plucked a dog hair off the armrest.

"Okay, I'll speak to her." Rosalynn watched Dusty run zoomies around the yard, leaping over planked walkways like he was tackling an agility course. "You could have given me a little more time to answer your call or been more specific in your texts. Showing up out of the blue is overkill, even for you."

Lillian shrugged. "My girls needed me. So of course I came."

No need to argue when it wouldn't change a thing. Her mother was already here. "We love you too. Thank you for worrying. You have enough on your plate with caretaker duties. How's he doing?"

Her mom's fists clenched around the armrests, her chewed fingernails the only outward sign of her stress. "The doctors give him anywhere from four to six weeks. We're just trying to keep him off the ventilator for as long as possible."

"Oh, Mom . . ." She bit her lip to hold back the tears and rested a hand over her mother's, her mom's wedding band cold to the touch. "You shouldn't be wasting time here. I have things under control, truly. Workers will be arriving any minute to board up the house. Please, go home. Elsie and I will be up for a visit at the end of the month like we planned."

To say their goodbyes. Her throat went tight at the impending loss of such a loved member of their family.

Lillian slid her fingers free. "He and I agreed that I should come speak with you in person about Elsie. Let's get this matter settled so we can go."

"*We? We* can go where?" Rosalynn struggled to follow her mom's train of thought. "What are you talking about?"

"I won't be any good to *anyone* if I'm worried about you back here in the middle of a hurricane."

Rosalynn sagged back. Her mother had a tendency to use those legal powers outside of the courtroom when the mood suited her. "Mom, I'm not interested in debating with you. I'm not reckless. In case you've forgotten, I'm forty-nine years old. If the weather is upgraded from a tropical storm to a hurricane, even a Category One, Elsie and I will evacuate."

"Or you could just leave now, before things reach the crisis level. Remember when you got trapped in the bumper-to-bumper traffic when evacuating a couple of years ago? If you'd listened to me then, you and Seth wouldn't have been stuck in that evacuation shelter."

Their journey had become so bogged down by the bottlenecked interstate that they'd been forced to stop. They'd spent the night in a school gymnasium since there hadn't been any hotels left. She could still smell the mildew and feel the frustration over the lack of adequate accommodations, made all the worse by having to debate time and time again with the shelter manager that she had a legal right to keep Dusty with her. Having to transfer from her wheelchair to a Red Cross–issued cot wasn't exactly easy or comfortable.

Her mom wasn't wrong that leaving now could prevent a wealth of frustration. "Okay, I'll go. We can drop you off at the airport on our way out."

"We're going together. I wasn't able to get a rental car or a flight back."

A sense of inevitability crept over her. Regardless of the forecast, her mother wouldn't let up until they left town. Together. And to be fair, she didn't want to keep her mother away from home longer than necessary. "Has anyone ever told you that you're manipulative?"

"I'm determined."

"Understatement," Rosalynn teased gently.

Her only hope lay in that storm taking a complete turn away. Within the next couple of hours. All flights being restored ASAP. With a seat available for her mother.

Right.

She had a better chance at hitting the jackpot in the Powerball lottery. Which would never happen since even the idea of buying a ticket made her think of Seth. "Let's head inside and tackle the hurricane prep. Just in case."

Lillian shoved to her feet. "Just in case. When do your workmen arrive to board up?"

"They promised to be here by sundown and stay until they're finished," she said, waving the card. *Thank you, Therese.* "So let's focus on the inside and see what's going on with my wayward daughter."

She called Dusty to join them. The Labrador trotted alongside her, his tongue lolling as she entered the mudroom. At least the arts center where she worked had already announced weather closure for a week.

Rosalynn slung her bag to hook on to one of the pegs on a lengthy oar. Elsie's gym shoes rested on the dryer. A braided fleece rope hung from the dryer handle for Dusty to tug. Lillian tapped the twisted fabric on her way past.

Together, they moved through the laundry room and into the kitchen with an open-concept view. Decorating over time, she'd tried not to be a cliché with the beach decor. She loved the soothing vibe, with rustic white walls, blue furniture, and accents in various shades. Paintings of Lowcountry landscapes were all by local artists only, with the exception of a sandcastle watercolor from Elsie in the second grade—framed and double matted, displayed in a place of honor over the fireplace.

She tried to envision her home goods in a new house and came up short. Could that be a part of Elsie's unrest?

As if to mock her, Rosalynn's gaze landed on a suitcase—Elsie's—by the front door.

To evacuate or move out? A pang twinged in her gut. She'd been looking forward to having Elsie all to herself this year. "Mom, why don't you take a moment to freshen up from your trip before we set to work. I want to speak with Elsie on my own first."

While she appreciated that her mom's love for Elsie went so deep that she would drop everything to help, Rosalynn had also experienced how Lillian's love could become suffocating. Her need for control too often stifled independence.

And Elsie needed to own up to her choices rather than abdicate joining a tough conversation.

CHAPTER SIX

Elsie

2026: Sullivan's Island, South Carolina

Elsie knew she couldn't hide out in her bedroom forever, clutching her guitar but afraid to do more than go through the chords without strumming for fear of her mom overhearing. She'd only bolted here to call Willow back for advice on how to handle her mom and Grammie. And yes, maybe buy some time for them to talk things out between each other. Then she wouldn't have to explain and be interrogated.

Why hadn't she thought through her escape plan? Devised a PowerPoint slide deck like her mom would have done, to prove why this was a great idea. Instead, she'd just reacted in a way that probably made her train wreck of a life worse.

Now, without Willow's help, Elsie was on her own to figure out next steps since her friend hadn't answered. Willow had just texted about sweating out her body weight while hauling around sandbags.

A knock sounded on her door. "Elsie?"

Her mom.

Ugh.

Elsie shoved her guitar case back under the bed. The bungee cord snagged on the carpet, stopping her progress halfway. The case's neck still stuck out, sporting a faded bumper sticker for Charleston's Spoleto arts festival alongside a decal from the Silver Maple Campground.

She ground her teeth and kicked some laundry over the instrument before sitting on the edge of the bed. Fast. "It's open."

The door swung wide and her mother rolled inside, stopping short by the pile of clothes. "Elsie, I saw your suitcase by the door. What's this I hear about you sending out an SOS to your grandmother? Emancipation, Elsie? Really?"

Elsie's fists bunched the comforter. Betrayal stung, which was silly since she'd left Grammie out there with her mom anyway. Willow had been right about the parent code. "She was supposed to explain, but now you're both ganging up against me."

"Nobody's ganging up on anyone. She only told me what you should have. Don't you think I would have noticed when you didn't show up for supper?"

"That's not funny." She shot to her feet. "I don't want to talk about it right now. We need to board up the house. Where's Grammie?"

"She's taking a shower." Her mother backed away from the door, clearing the way. "If you're asking to haul around plywood, that tells me you're really trying to avoid talking to me. No such luck, kiddo. I've already reached out to a company to take care of it for us."

"That's good, I guess."

"I could use your help in the kitchen, though. I need to check the generator, make an inventory of the refrigerator, and sort through the laundry. We'll have time to talk while your grandmother changes her clothes."

Might as well surrender. Besides, in the kitchen she would have more avenues to bolt. "I could fill up bags of water for the freezer."

Freezing bags of water would give extra protection to the frozen goods in the event of a power outage. And with luck, this would be the last time she would have to mess with stupid stuff like that for a maybe-hurricane.

Her mother called Dusty to follow along, and together they tackled the clean clothes. The dog tugged at a cord to open the dryer door and on cue dropped towels onto Rosalynn's lap for her to fold. The smart goofball even climbed halfway in to retrieve a sock stuck to the back.

Elsie had never known a time when her mom didn't have a service animal. The one before Dusty had been a golden retriever named Scout. He'd been a stoic sort, not as goofy as Dusty. Even though she'd known not to interfere with Scout when he was working, Elsie used to sneak and toss toys for him to pick up. It had seemed like such a game then. Or maybe she'd been jealous of Scout, which felt silly now.

He'd been so completely fixated on her mom, even when he wasn't working. Dusty had a bit more spunk in him when he was on "free time."

Elsie glanced sideways at her mother, avoiding eye contact while gauging her expression. "Is Dad evacuating or staying?"

"He's heading out for Biloxi." She tugged a T-shirt right side out with extra focus. Her mom was rarely still, like being in motion helped quiet her mind.

Was she plotting her plan of attack for their conversation?

"I didn't realize he knows somebody there." Did he have a girlfriend? He'd sworn there wasn't anyone else, but still. Her confidence in the honesty of guys was currently underwater.

Her mom didn't answer. She never bad-mouthed Elsie's dad in front of her. Most folks would have shouted to the rooftops that he wasn't over here helping secure the house where his kid lived. Even if he wasn't cheating, he was bailing on them when they needed help. He only showed up to be the life of the party or if she was getting some kind of award that made him look good.

This one time, she'd been driving her mom somewhere and backed into another car. Elsie had been freaking out, worried that she'd somehow reinjured her mother. Her father was "too busy" to come help when the police arrived. He'd mumbled some BS about it sounding like Elsie had it well in hand and how proud he was of her.

While her parents weren't the cause of her need to leave Sullivan's Island, escaping her dad's sphere sure was an added bonus. Like getting a large order of fries in the drive-through when you'd ordered a regular-size meal.

Her mom cued Dusty to nose the dryer door closed, then pivoted to face her. "Elsie, it seems we need to talk about why you want to move out."

Dodging her mom's laser gaze, Elsie grabbed the box of gallon-size Ziploc bags and began filling one after another. "Since Grammie's already told you, there's nothing more to discuss."

She realized she sounded snippy, and none of this was her mother's fault. But she just couldn't keep from snapping at her mom.

"We could start with *why* you want to leave." Rosalynn inched closer. Dusty rested his head on her knee, a sure sign she was stressed.

The dog picked up on that stuff. Elsie wondered what it would be like to have somebody interpret her moods that way, where she wouldn't have to cough up the painful words.

She shrugged. "It's time to go. I'm ready to live on my own. Plenty of people graduate from high school when they're seventeen."

"That's not much of an answer. Don't you want to enjoy all the perks of your senior year?"

Perks? Elsie's grip slipped on a bag and water squirted out of the seal. She pinched the threads tighter together. "I'm bored at school, and I want to start college." Far, far away from South Carolina. "When you and Dad decided to get divorced, you both said I could choose who to live with. Well, I choose to live with Grammie."

Elsie stomped her way across the kitchen and yanked open the freezer.

A sigh hissed from Rosalynn. "Your grandmother wasn't on the list of options and you know it."

Like she really ever had a choice. Elsie stacked the water bags on top of three cartons of ice cream. Rocky road and mint chocolate chip for herself, and toffee pecan for her mother. She let the cold blast hit her face while she willed away tears.

Her mom wheeled closer. "You know you can talk to me about anything."

"If that was true, you wouldn't be flipping out right now." Elsie slammed the freezer closed.

"I'm only 'flipping out' because I don't understand why you want to leave."

Did her mom have to sound so reasonable? "Even if you won't let me graduate early, plenty of people live with their grandparents during their last year of school. A girl in the class ahead of me did that last year."

"Her dad was military and got transferred. She stayed to finish out the school year and graduate with her class."

Elsie fished out a box of mint cookies from the back of the fridge. "Still . . ."

Her mother quirked an eyebrow. "Well, you know what? We'll have plenty of time to talk in the car."

"What do you mean?"

"We're evacuating to Grammie's place." Her mom plucked the box of cookies from her hands. "These will make excellent snacks for the journey."

Say what? Was she actually letting her go to Alexandria with Grammie? Even if her mother didn't intend to let her stay, this was a step in the right direction. Good luck prying her out of there once she unpacked her bags.

Her grandmother applauded as she leaned against the archway between the kitchen and dining room. She'd changed into jeans and a short-sleeved turtleneck. Even with wet hair, smoothed into a perfect kind of bob, Grammie had a way of making casual seem put together. Kinda like the girls who made Elsie feel a mess.

Except around Grammie, she felt special. A thought to untangle another time.

Rosalynn opened the refrigerator. "I'll pack up the perishables to take with us on our road trip."

"Lovely," Lillian answered. "All three of us together. Four if you count Dusty—"

Elsie interrupted. "Five if you count Sheldon."

Grammie's eyes went wide. "Sheldon? Is that a friend?"

"He's my hermit crab."

Rosalynn let loose another hiss-sigh. "When did you buy a hermit crab?"

"This morning. I haven't picked him up from Willow yet, though."

Grammie patted her hand. "Possession is nine-tenths of the law, so for now, Sheldon needs to stay with Willow. I have to get back, and I'm not leaving you here with a hurricane bearing down."

Elsie chewed her bottom lip. "I definitely want to go, but Mom said we would only leave if it upgraded from a tropical storm . . ."

She'd wanted an ally in Grammie, but right now, her mom and grandmother looked more like a unified front against her.

"Check your weather app, my dear." Lillian shot her a side-eye. "And if you'll straighten up that attitude of yours a bit, I'll tell you all about a road trip I took to DC with your grandfather thirty-six years ago."

Elsie grappled for her phone in her back pocket and swiped her finger along the screen until she reached the weather app. She tapped the icon . . . and groaned. The storm had picked up speed and intensity since the last update, bearing down toward the South Carolina coastline.

She'd wanted to leave Sullivan's Island, but not like this. It was one thing to travel on a plane, and quite another to spend hours in the van with two of the toughest interrogators on the planet.

Two interrogators whom she loved and respected more than anybody. Even thinking about the looks on their faces if they discovered her secret made her sick to her stomach.

When this road trip began, she intended to fake-nap in the back seat, avoid conversation, and let them assume she was only leaving because of her parents' divorce.

CHAPTER SEVEN

LILLIAN

1990: Charleston, South Carolina

Why must men insist on starting road trips at the crack of dawn? Or in Grady's case, *before* sunrise?

I vowed that if I ever remarried, I would make a prenup that included a provision that no travel begins before nine in the morning. Not that I intended to walk down the aisle again. Which meant I would be able to make my own travel plans.

Eyes gritty, I swished mouthwash for the recommended sixty seconds while I tugged on my white tennis shoes to go with my jean jumper. The ultimate mom look. An identity I wore with pride.

At least I'd managed to snag a couple of hours of sleep after packing the cooler. I spit in the sink, ran the water, and grabbed my backpack on my way into the hall, pausing at Rosalynn's door. I surrendered to the need to peek in on her one more time before we left. Careful not to wake her, I tucked into the room still decorated with ballerina prints that she insisted on keeping even though they sometimes made her cry. An old pair of her slippers hung from a hook on the wall.

I adjusted her pink quilt under her chin and checked her feet to make sure she was wearing socks. Her body temp didn't regulate as well since the accident because of disruption of signals from her hypothalamus. One of the many crucial things I'd learned from the specialists and the stacks of medical journals by my bedside.

Sweeping her silky, dark hair back from her forehead, I pressed a kiss to her brow and whispered, "Love you, sugar."

"Love you, Mama," she murmured in a vulnerable way that her teenage self masked when awake.

Hitching my backpack onto one shoulder, I tapped the ballet slippers on my way out. I hadn't grown up in a home that could afford dance or music lessons. But my mother had done her best to provide cultural experiences however she could. As a school bus driver from the time I was three, Mom had volunteered for every shift to a concert, art museum, or theatrical performance, with me in tow.

During my pregnancy, I planned for the day my child could be a participant rather than just an observer as I'd been. We'd attended concerts in the park when she was a toddler. At three, I signed her up for gymnastics. Art classes came next with clay models and murals.

Then, when Rosalynn was five, I took her to a production of *The Nutcracker*. I'd packed my bag full of coloring activities and snacks to keep her entertained if she grew restless.

She never did.

With wide eyes, she'd stayed glued to the edge of the seat. My daughter had found her calling. From day one of dance lessons, while the teacher herded the rest of the class like a litter of boisterous puppies, my daughter pirouetted.

More importantly, Rosalynn sparkled. She had a gift that went far beyond the steps learned through repetition.

Until her accident.

Rosalynn's sadness had been so intense in those first weeks, with a seemingly endless flood of tears from the pain of the procedures and therapy. Then she'd realized she would never walk, never dance, again. Sadness had turned into depression.

I understood that my crusade to DC wouldn't change the past, but I had to do something.

Closing her door behind me, I trailed my fingers along the family pictures lining the corridor of our ranch home, purchased after the accident for its more accessible floor plan. From the kitchen, sounds drifted of my mother preparing us breakfast for the road, even though we'd assured her we could each make do with a banana and Pop-Tart. As the smell of coffee filled the air and the sound of frying eggs crackled, I was thankful she hadn't listened to me.

Outside, the morning still carried a chill as winter gave up its last gasp in Charleston. We were leaving the newer conversion van behind for my mother to drive Rosalynn to appointments. We would take the older minivan, the one we'd owned before the accident.

The back hatch was open and waiting for the last of my gear while Grady checked under the hood. We'd honed our travel routine over the years. My body went on autopilot.

"Hey, Grady, this is the last of my stuff." I tucked my backpack full of flyers alongside our rolled-up sleeping bags and tent. "Mom's cooking us breakfast."

"Della makes a mean fried egg sandwich," he answered.

I hated how we resorted to benign small talk these days.

He slammed the hood closed and clicked off the flashlight. His hair was slicked back, still wet, skimming the collar of his T-shirt. He kept it longer than most of his firefighter workmates, pushing the regulations to the very last millimeter possible in honor of the free-spirited deep-sea fisherman he'd once been, with dreams of owning a home and business on the water. Instead, we lived in a crowded landlocked subdivision.

Our gazes held for a moment, the silence awkward. In the past we could have sat in the same space for the longest stretch, hands linked in comfortable quiet without saying a word.

I backed away a step at a time. "Well, um, I'll tell Mom goodbye and get our food."

"Thanks. I'd like to hit the road before morning rush hour."

I bit down the urge to remind him that we could also avoid traffic if we left at nine. He was already stressed about taking time off work.

"Well, Grady, I'll skip my plans to churn butter before I go."

He grunted in response.

Sighing, I made my way back to the kitchen, where my mother was wrapping the egg sandwiches in foil to keep them warm. In a tracksuit, Della Avery wore her gray hair with pride, the spiraling curls unrestrained in broadcasting her survival. She'd been a military wife. Then a widow too young, a single mom with no degree and no work history.

I poured coffee into two insulated travel cups, adding a heaping spoon of sugar to Grady's and cream to mine. "Thank you, Mama."

"My pleasure. It's frustrating to stop for food thirty minutes after pulling out of the driveway."

Again, not a problem if the trip had started at nine. Not my mother's fault, though. "I don't mean just for the breakfast. Thank you for looking after Rosalynn and for everything else you've done this year. I don't know how we would have managed without you."

We'd asked my mother to move in with us so I could go back to work while she helped with Rosalynn's appointments. The decision made financial sense for all of us. I earned more as a paralegal than my mother did as a school bus driver. Plus, she'd been struggling to pay her bills. Without missing a beat, Mama had given thirty days' notice on her apartment, packed up her old Ford station wagon, and relocated to our home across town. Rosalynn started to smile again at the prospect of seeing Nana Della every day.

Della patted my cheek. "You would have been just fine. You come from a long line of strong women. I'm just doing for you the way my mother did for me, and the way you'll be there for Rosalynn and her child someday."

At the mention of children, my throat went tight. Grady and I had wanted three or four kids in the beginning. Since Rosalynn was a whoops pregnancy, we'd assumed we would have no trouble when the time came to add to our family.

Life hadn't worked out that way. I wondered if Grady would find someone else and have more children. I didn't quite know what to do with that thought. Especially now that things were already so strained between us.

"I made some banana bread too, since Grady has a sweet tooth. He's a good man, sugar. Like your daddy."

It stung hearing her talk about her perfect marriage to my father, usually followed by reminders of how a successful relationship required plenty of effort. As if I hadn't already worked my tail off to save my marriage before and after Rosalynn's accident. Grady had even stopped drinking, but it had been too late for us. If anything, her injury had held us together longer, as we hadn't wanted to do anything to hinder our child's recovery.

I pushed back those memories and focused on the here and now, on what I could control. "Thanks. I wrote down Rosalynn's entire schedule, and all the meals are prepared with labels in the refrigerator."

"We've got it." She shooed me away with her hands.

I stifled the defensive urge to explain myself. I'd yet to figure out how to stop being so prickly around my mom, but I vowed that my daughter and I would have a different, easier time.

"I just don't want you to overdo." Or for something to go wrong with Rosalynn. I jotted an extra note about cranberry juice on the dry-erase board, right under the medication schedule and a reminder about socks.

"I promise when y'all get home, I'll take the longest bubble bath ever." Smiling, she folded her arms over her chest. "You remind me so much of your father—always wanting to change the world."

I wished I had more memories of him. And the ones I did have? I couldn't be sure if those were real or just a product of hearing stories and seeing photos. "Have fun with our girl, and we'll be back before you know it."

"I never could protest when your dad was in the Navy. Well, I guess I could've, but he couldn't, and in those days what a wife did could reflect badly on the military member. Anyway, make sure you're heard."

My mom had found a megaphone at a thrift store and packed it in the van before anything else. "Absolutely. If there's press coverage, I'll do my best to give you a shout-out."

"Now that would make my year." My mother pressed a hand to her chest.

I hugged her hard, breathing in the scent of fried eggs and face cream. "I love you, Mama."

"I love you too, sugar." She pressed a kiss to my forehead as I'd done to Rosalynn's. "Now drive safe. Remember, your guardian angel doesn't fly faster than the speed limit."

"And I won't forget to lift my feet when we cross railroad tracks." Opinions varied on the reason for that superstition.

As I stepped outside, backing through the screen door, I balanced two thermoses of coffee, a stack of egg sandwiches, and two wrapped slices of banana bread. Not easy. Especially functioning on four hours of sleep.

Grady leaned against the front quarter panel checking his watch. Sheesh, the sun wasn't even up yet. Would it hurt him to try my way on this, just once?

Was I a micromanager, as my ex-husband always complained?

Well, I can tell you one thing. I wasn't sticking my head in the sand. And I most definitely wasn't holding back my daughter's recovery by overindulging her the way her father did.

We argued in those days. A lot. Over how to best care for Rosalynn—and everything else, for that matter. No matter how often I tried to tell myself that we were simply taking out our grief and frustration on each other, I also knew our marriage had been struggling before the accident. Our relationship had been built on the shaky foundation of a shotgun wedding when I was three months pregnant with Rosalynn. Then there'd been my friction with his mom. Plus his drinking.

And the most frustrating part of all? The attraction that had landed us in that speedy ceremony still burned hot when, for the first time in a year, we were absolutely alone together. Truth be told, we'd never had much time with just the two of us. A whirlwind courtship. Baby on the way. Bills piling up, which gave us both an excuse to become workaholics. Further avoiding each other because when together we argued over just about everything, from child-rearing to what brand of ketchup to buy.

How easy it would be to surrender to that temptation to avoid tougher subjects as we'd done in the past. However, more and more those encounters, while physically satisfying, only reminded us of the growing emotional void.

CHAPTER EIGHT

Rosalynn

2026: Sullivan's Island, South Carolina

Starting a road trip on limited sleep really stunk, but after packing through most of the night, they couldn't afford to waste time. Beyond the need to stay safe, the sooner she got this journey underway, the sooner she would have her daughter trapped with nowhere to hide.

Uh, rather, she would have her daughter and mother on a lovely "bonding" experience.

Waiting in the van, Rosalynn stared at her home, willing her mom and Elsie to hurry up. Headlights streamed into the garage. Otherwise, the dark hung thickly in the last gasps of night, all the murkier for the lack of stars in the cloudy sky. Even the streetlamps struggled to push through the haze. The tropical storm had shifted to a Category Two hurricane overnight, which meant winds of around ninety-six to one hundred and ten miles per hour. The weather app predicted another thirty-six to forty-eight hours before the hurricane made landfall, with a direct hit to her beach community.

Sure, she needed an open and honest conversation with her daughter, but she would have preferred one without the added layer of stress. The thought of Elsie wanting to leave early, even plotting behind her back, was devastating. A seismic shift in Rosalynn's world. And she couldn't help but feel she'd failed as a mother at a time when she was still reeling from a failed marriage. She'd assumed Elsie was okay with the divorce—well, as okay as any kid could be.

She'd assumed wrongly, and that stung. Her clenched fists went white-knuckled around the steering wheel as she thought of additional fallout when Elsie learned her college fund had evaporated at a blackjack table.

Rosalynn shook the blood back into her hands and adjusted the van's vents, set on low, just enough to circulate the air as the vehicle idled in the driveway. Rain pattered on the roof, heavier by the hour. The drumming crescendoed, drawing her already freaked-out nerves even tighter while her mother and daughter made one final sweep inside the house.

"Come on, come on, come on," she whispered, drawing a whimper from Dusty tethered behind her. The poor pup was curled up on his bed, tucked between a suitcase and the bench seat in the far back. "It's okay, boy. We'll be outta here soon."

Lightning crackled through the sky. Goose bumps lifted along her arms. A local police car drove slowly along the street, the PA system broadcasting a repeated warning to leave . . .

". . . for your own personal safety. If you choose not to evacuate, you do so at your own risk. Once weather conditions deteriorate and flooding conditions begin, officers may not be able to help you leave your home . . ."

The warning raised the hairs along her arms. Was this just an abundance of caution after the last scare, which brought unexpected flooding? Or— Her phone blared an alert as well that the storm was now strengthening to a Category Three. She struggled to breathe, while reminding herself of her grandmother's mantra. *Hope for the best. Prepare for the worst.*

All her windows were covered, even the front door. A few other houses along the road carried the same unwelcoming air, all boarded up. A memory floated to mind from the aftermath of another hurricane a few years ago, when the police spray-painted each boarded home after they'd cleared the house. How many alive. How many . . . not.

Many on her street had peeled out one after another during the night. Even her neighbors who usually rode out any storm were now hauling butt down the road in their Suburban, towing their sailboat. Elsie used to love afternoons out on the water with them, but lately, Rosalynn couldn't remember her daughter showing excitement over anything. Their SUV's headlights swept around the corner and away, dark swallowing her again other than the glow of the van's dashboard throwing a green haze onto the ballerina charm on her rearview mirror.

"Elsie," Rosalynn called out the window to her daughter, who looked like a pack mule carrying two overstuffed canvas bags. "We're running low on space. Everything's wedged in mighty tight and we need to go."

Her mother had insisted on packing Rosalynn's leg braces and walker, even though she could only use them for short distances, at times when she wasn't already completely exhausted.

"Uh, I'm just loading a few keepsakes in case our place gets whacked." Elsie slid the van's side door open and hefted the sacks in, both thudding beside Dusty, who was tethered in place. "I can stuff them under the back seat. I think I see a little room."

Her daughter sat on the floorboards before swinging her legs inside to push her feet against the sacks.

Rosalynn stifled a wince at the crunching sound. "It's a shame neither of us inherited my dad's talent for loading. Mom used to say it was like watching him play *Tetris*."

"*Tetris*?" Elsie pivoted back around, gathering her damp hair up into a messy bun and securing it with a scrunchie from her wrist. "It's that old video game, right?"

Nothing like a teenager to make a parent feel ancient. "Yes, where you stack blocks in a way that creates a full line without leaving empty spots—"

The drone of the police announcement wafted ominously in the distance, urgent even in its monotone repetition.

Lillian ducked through the rain wearing one of Rosalynn's floppy beach hats to protect her head as she carried a tote bag with two hands. "Great gravy, Elsie, what's in here? Bricks?"

"Grammie, that's just some stuff from my bathroom closet." She sprinted to take the sack from her grandmother. Elsie stacked the bags on the bench seat. "I mean it when I say that I'm not coming back. This will save you on shipping when I emancipate."

Rosalynn clenched her teeth to keep from speaking. They had the entire road trip to talk, discuss, negotiate. Easier said than done when she really just wanted to wring Elsie's neck.

Lillian clapped a hand on the borrowed beach hat. "I'll be finished in just a jiff. I'm going to fill a thermos with coffee."

"We'll be here where you left us. No hurry, though, because natural disasters are known for their predictability," Rosalynn said tightly. Her mother had never been known for moving fast in the morning, but come on, these were special circumstances. Opening the maps app on her cell, she checked the route and winced at the multiple alerts for stretches with slow moving traffic. Time for a backup plan.

As a crow flew, it wasn't that far. Normally, they could push through the drive in a day, but she was booking a hotel, just in case. She suspected the more direct path up through Florence and Fayetteville would have higher traffic and worse weather. Fayetteville could also prove problematic if the Cape Fear River overflowed. Swooping over, driving through Columbia and Charlotte instead, would add miles but hopefully prove to be an easier trip.

Provided nothing went wrong.

Elsie reached to stroke Dusty's ear. "I'll miss you most of all, Cowardly Lion."

"I can hear you." Rosalynn didn't bother looking up from her phone, sighing at all the stalled-traffic alerts on the map. "Could you run back in and tell Grammie to hurry up?"

"Fine," Elsie said with a huff and slouch. "I need to get my pillow anyway. So I can sleep rather than listen to you try and talk me out of leaving. Unless you want me to drive? I'll stay awake for that."

"I'll take it under consideration." Unlikely. An evacuation route didn't offer the best driving conditions for a teen. Especially a moody one intent on rebellion.

As Elsie jumped out of the van, Lillian emerged from the garage, a thermos in one hand, her cell phone in the other on speaker. "Thank you for returning my call so early, Mr. Nguyen."

Ah, Benjamin Nguyen. The facility manager at the hospice center. Rosalynn tipped her head to listen, her heart squeezing with worry.

"No problem," the deep voice rumbled. "You said I could return your message early. I saw on the news it's looking rather rough down there. I hope you're somewhere safe."

"We're evacuating now, but I was worried about cell connections and want to get an update before we hit the road. What's his blood pressure? And his O_2 stats? Has there been any improvement since last night?" She passed the thermos to Rosalynn, seemingly oblivious to the wind tugging off her hat or the rain dotting her blouse.

Shoulders hunched as she ducked back into the garage, Lillian looked . . . vulnerable. Which kept Rosalynn from shouting at her mom to quit dawdling and get in the car. She couldn't think of a time she'd ever seen her mother that way. Not even in those early days after the accident. She always had a metaphorical sword on her back, within reach and ready for battle. She'd navigated the labyrinth of a whole new medical world with dogged determination. Lillian had kept a smile on her face, the steel magnolia kind that reminded everyone she had a notepad within reach at all times. She kept track of everything. Including where to lodge complaints if something went awry.

Rosalynn's father, though?

Grady had been a basket case from the moment she'd regained consciousness in the hospital. He'd tried to hide it, but she'd seen otherwise, and truth be told, it had freaked her out a little. Like a week after her first surgery, when she'd woken in the middle of the night when her pain medication wore off. She'd caught her father crying on her mother's shoulder.

As an adult, Rosalynn could better understand her parents' reactions and feelings of helplessness. But as a teen? She'd struggled with how to tell them when she hurt or when she wanted to scream at the universe because of the hardware in her spine that would never give her back the ability to dance.

However the last thing she wanted was to make her father cry again. And the thought of her mom chewing out another staff member was scary and embarrassing.

Did Elsie feel the same about her parents? Embarrassed? Could that be why she wanted to leave?

Her daughter came back into view as she trotted through the garage again, carrying a guitar case, the edge of her pillow in her teeth. She swooped the case over her head as she sprinted through the rain to the van. Elsie leaned in and opened her mouth, dropping the pillow.

Frowning, Rosalynn asked, "Where did you find the guitar? I thought you hated music lessons."

"I just saw it in the attic and thought it looked like a keepsake." She climbed into the van and propped the case on the bench seat like an extra passenger.

The acoustic had been Rosalynn's father's. She recognized the stickers all too well, especially the fire department emblem smack dab in the middle. Nostalgia swelled. Strains of him singing wove through her memory. A Willie Nelson–style "Always on My Mind" or Van Morrison's "Have I Told You Lately." Closer to the time of her injury, he'd stopped playing almost altogether. No more love songs.

Back then, she'd felt responsible for the strain in her parents' relationship from carting her around to so many rehearsals and performances. Afterward, there had been the stress of surgeries and recovery. Wash. Rinse. Repeat.

Rosalynn asked, "Would you like to take lessons?"

Her daughter certainly had inherited Grady's musical talent, even if she'd ripped up every piano practice schedule Rosalynn printed out.

"Nah," Elsie said quickly, taking her place beside the sticker-covered case. "Maybe a tree will fall on the place and we can all start over with a big, fat insurance check."

Rosalynn's gut lurched. It was one thing to grieve over selling her house. It was another altogether to think of the home she'd renovated with such care being wiped away.

The sun started to rise, throwing a muddy glow through the storm clouds. Was that a funnel cloud pushing downward toward the water?

Deep breaths. One crisis at a time. "You'll forgive me if I prefer a different outcome."

"I only meant for a tree to fall onto a part of our house, say, maybe over the living room, right onto the piano. I wasn't wishing ill will on anybody else." She slouched into her seat and opened the guitar case. She reached inside. "I brought a keepsake for you too."

Elsie lifted up a brass ballerina holding a tiny nutcracker soldier. A lump settled in Rosalynn's throat. The twelve-inch statue had been a gift from her parents the year before her injury, dancing the part she'd dreamed of since she first slid on ballet slippers. "Thank you. That was thoughtful."

And it was kind. Even if the sight of it squeezed her heart so hard it hurt.

Her gaze skated toward her mother still huddled in the garage taking her call. Headlights from the van illuminated every line of worry on her face. A fresh wave of guilt hit that her troubles with Elsie had taken Lillian from her beloved husband's bedside, stealing even a couple of days from their last weeks together.

Tears welled and Rosalynn swiped her hands across her face, stifling frustration that Elsie hadn't considered Lillian's grief. Instead, the teen had piled on more worry. Why couldn't Elsie have waited just a little longer, until their scheduled trip to Grammie's place in Virginia?

Enough delaying. She leaned out the window again. "Mom, come on. You can finish the call while I drive."

Her mother tucked her phone into her pocket and sprinted toward the van, grumbling, "You're just like your father. So impatient on road trips."

"Well, getting out of here before the hurricane makes landfall really could be a matter of life and death." Rosalynn thumbed the remote for the garage door as her mom ducked into the passenger seat. She and her mother had agreed to take turns driving since her adaptive van could be driven by someone else with the flip of a switch.

Lillian tugged her seat belt in place. "See, I was right about evacuating. Elsie girl. I can't wait to tell you all about my first trek to DC thirty-six years ago."

Groaning, Elsie pulled the pillow over her head.

"Elsie?" Rosalynn called out in an attempt to smooth over her daughter's rudeness. "All buckled in?"

"Yeah," Elsie said, her voice muffled by the cushion.

That funnel cloud in the distance still reached toward the water, then retreated upward, like a yo-yo. Reminding her how many threats her home faced beyond just the force of the hurricane's wind. Tornadoes. Storm surge. Flooding. Falling debris. Even lightning fires. Her mind threatened to spiral into a well of panic as dangerous as the waterspouts teasing a prelude.

Exhaling hard, Rosalynn backed out of her driveway, then stole one last glance at her home as if she could safeguard it through sheer force of will. Nana Della's voice echoed in her mind.

Don't worry about the mule. Just load the wagon.

Rosalynn shifted the van into drive and left behind her home for quite possibly the last time.

CHAPTER NINE

Elsie

2026: Columbia, South Carolina

When Elsie had asked Grammie to rescue her, she'd envisioned a nice flight together. Like when Grammie and Ace had taken her to Disney, a trip that included airport food and a hotel with room service.

Instead, she'd been stuck in the back seat of the van for over six hours with a gassy dog. She really wanted another life. "Who fed Dusty peanut butter?"

Grammie twisted to look over her shoulder. "Oh no. I thought he could have some." She pivoted toward Rosalynn again. "Your other service dogs could have some peanut butter for a special treat. I smeared a couple of tablespoons on his KONG when I buckled him into the van."

Rosalynn changed lanes in the crawling traffic as if that might somehow make a difference when most of the time they ended up at a standstill. Although others had it worse. Like the church bus that was parked on the side of the road with a hood up, steaming engine, and soaked driver tinkering with the motor. The lanes going in the opposite direction were nearly empty, other than trucks from the power company and school buses assisting with evacuation.

"Dusty has a sensitive stomach, but he'll be okay." Rosalynn lowered the window an inch, only to wince as rain dripped inside. "You could check the emergency pet supply kit for probiotic pouches. We probably just need an extra break or two."

"For gas?" Groaning, Elsie slid down in her seat and tugged the neck of her T-shirt to cover her nose. "Don't say 'gas.' Can we please, please pull over soon?"

In five hours, they'd only gone a little over a hundred miles and stopped once. At this rate, she would graduate from high school before they made it to Grammie's house. Up ahead, a family stood under an umbrella while their father changed a tire. Which only made her mood worse thinking about her own dad bailing when they needed him. Had he always been this much of a loser?

There'd been one evacuation when her parents fought over the route and they'd ended up in a shelter, but before that, she remembered a time they'd spent the night in a hotel that had seemed fancy to her. Although what did she know? Her criteria had consisted of a pool, unlimited doughnuts for breakfast, and jumping on the mattress.

While nudging Dusty's dog bed tighter against his bottom with her foot, she typed out another text to Willow. What r u doing?

Willow answered, Eating ice cream sundaes so it won't melt if the power goes out.

Elsie typed, Lucky. I'm stuck drinking old Gatorades and eating a pimento cheese sandwich.

She could have sworn during other evacuations there had been at least one Happy Meal. She certainly didn't recall the bumper-to-bumper traffic. Or the long lines at the gas station or drive-through restaurants.

For some reason, her mom and grandmother were a surprisingly unified front on avoiding carryout food and sticking to the boring dreck in the cooler.

She would kill for an order of fries. Super-size.

Dots lit up the screen with Willow typing. Dad drilled holes in the plywood so we can watch the storm.

That sounded pretty scary, actually. I heard the cops say to go or they couldn't promise to help. Are you okay? How bad is it there?

Willow replied, Tough to say. It's already dark inside because the windows are covered. The wind is loud.

Elsie typed, Should you leave? Your dad could stay but the rest of you could go with your mom.

Typing dots scrolled and scrolled, like for a long answer, pausing like she was deleting, then simply: The roads are flooded.

Fear for her friend made that pimento cheese sandwich churn in her stomach. Elsie took in the heavy clouds overhead. The sky seemed more like sunset than noon. Did everybody else leave town? Our old crew, I mean.

The text box stayed blank for about a dozen heartbeats before the typing dots appeared again. Porter's family left with their boat. They're driving out west to a lake. Jareth went with them even though his parents are staying.

Once upon a time, she would have known that about her neighbor. She wanted to rage at Jareth for bailing out on their friendship since middle school. Most of all she wanted to kick the snot out of Porter and embarrass him the way he was humiliating her. She'd thought he liked her. He'd even talked her into taking a couple of underwear photos of herself. He'd asked for more—with her wearing less—but she'd said no.

So he'd found another way to get the images he wanted that were the price he had to pay for an entrée into a cool crowd. The idiot didn't even realize they were just using him, mocking him.

Mocking her. So far, he'd only shared one, but he'd shown her the others. He swore he wouldn't share the rest as long as she gave him a hand job . . . which she totally was not going to do . . .

Panic tightened her throat. Gulping Gatorade only made the bite of her sandwich swell more until she coughed, nearly choking.

"Elsie," her mother called, her eyes concerned in the rearview mirror, the ballerina charm swaying. "Are you okay?"

Not even close. But not because of the bread lodged in her windpipe. She downed another swallow until she could breathe again. Wouldn't that have made for a pathetic line on her loser tombstone? *Here lies Elsie Yates. Murdered by a pimento cheese sandwich and a traitorous ex-boyfriend.*

Her mother met her eyes in the mirror again. "Now that we're all together, Elsie, would you like to tell us what's going on?"

Nope. Elsie took an extra sip of the sports drink to buy herself a moment to think. "I want to move in with Grammie. End of story."

"Then my answer is no," Rosalynn said firmly.

"What? Really, Mom?" Elsie flopped back, arms crossed. "This is why I called Grammie. Grammie, help me. She's so stubborn."

Rosalynn snorted on a laugh. "I could say the same about you—"

Grammie interrupted, "Maybe we shouldn't be discussing this just yet, when we're all exhausted." She rested a hand on her daughter's shoulder. "Your father used to insist on starting trips before the crack of dawn, which just made everyone cranky for the rest of the day. We can talk at the hotel tonight or in the morning after a good night's sleep. Did you forward the confirmation to me?"

Silence echoed in the van other than Dusty snoring—at least she hoped he was snoring—and the patter of rain on the roof. Elsie spun her drink bottle in the holder until finally her mom spoke up. "Yes, Mother, I sent it to you. But at this rate, I'm not sure when we'll get there. I underestimated the traffic."

Two cop cars whipped past, along the shoulder, followed by an ambulance, all three with sirens blaring. This was the second time an accident had slowed their progress. Although it felt petty to resent the delay when somebody was hurt up ahead.

Her phone vibrated against her leg. She checked to see if Willow was calling. But nope. It was her dad. Totally not what she needed right now. Elsie tapped the red "Ignore" button.

Then she heard her mother's cell ring. Her mom frowned but ignored it, keeping her hands on the wheel.

Grammie's device chimed next. "Elsie, your dad's trying to reach you. Could you call him back?"

"Uh, I'm texting with Willow." Only she wasn't, because she couldn't think about the horror show of her life back home. That made her more nauseated than Dusty's peanut butter farts.

"Please," her mother pressed. "Isn't it wonderful phones have become so advanced that we can do multiple things on them at one time? Like text our friends and our parents."

"Fine, Mom. I'll text him—"

"Call him," her mother insisted.

"Rosalynn," Grammie said softly, "are you sure that's the best—"

"Mom . . ." Rosalynn cut her off.

Interesting.

Maybe Grammie might not be so unified on that parental front after all. "I'll message him that I'm fine and that I'll call him back later. We need to stop for gas soon anyway, right?"

Grammie adjusted her glasses as she scrolled on her phone. "Google Maps indicates the traffic jam isn't going to ease for a while. There's a truck stop at the next exit a mile farther. By the time we finish, maybe the wreck will have cleared and we can switch over driving."

Another detour.

Great.

Elsie didn't bother offering to take a stint behind the wheel again. She didn't want to rock the boat when there were snacks ahead that didn't come out of a cooler. She had $283 in her wallet that she'd been saving from babysitting for when she got to Grammie's so she didn't have to bug her for the little stuff. Just until she could convince her mom and dad to let her cash out her college fund.

Her mouth watered at the thought of a bag of Takis and a Dr Pepper, although the country truck stop looked like more of a boiled peanuts and barbecue kind of place. Based on the overflowing parking lot, they weren't the only ones waiting out the backlog from the wreck. A twinge of worry hit her at how long it had been for her mom since their last stop. Her mother had to be careful to make frequent bathroom breaks to prevent UTIs, which could be quite common for people with spinal cord injuries. And potentially dangerous. Rosalynn downplayed her needs so often, it was too easy for others to forget.

Grammie called over her shoulder, arm extended with a credit card, "Elsie, would you please pump the gas while Rosalynn and I head inside? I need to get a cup of ice for my sweet tea."

"Sure." Elsie flung aside her seat belt and plucked the card from between Grammie's fingers. "No problem."

She scrambled over Dusty on her way to the pump. A big sign read HURRICANE RATIONING.

After paying and selecting the fuel grade, she slouched back against the van while her mom and Dusty unloaded. The country truck stop with a café had an extended porch with enough swaying rocking chairs to keep Grammie occupied for a good ten minutes steadying them all.

Exiting the store with big Styrofoam cups of slushies, a chorus of kids called out things like "look at the doggy" and "I wanna pet him." One even lunged toward Dusty's path, before tripping over his shoelaces and splattering half his icy drink on the sidewalk.

Karma.

Their behavior wasn't surprising, but was annoying all the same. All her fear and frustration swelled to the surface and Elsie hollered at them, "The dog is working. Don't you see his cape?"

Shouting at children probably wasn't the smartest move.

Grammie pivoted back around while Rosalynn busied herself with passing extra treats to Dusty so he wouldn't be distracted—or try to lick up the spilled drink. Once the kids ducked into their SUV, Grammie waved Rosalynn and Dusty on into the truck stop and strode back toward the fuel pump.

Elsie winced. She needed Grammie on her good side. Still, she wanted to defend herself. No matter where they went, people commented on Dusty. Loudly. Some even asked to pet him in spite of the bright red letters on his cape that declared Service Dog. Do Not Pet. As if the rules somehow didn't apply to them.

Aside from the fact all those delays interfered with her mom's shopping, Elsie had resented those trips to the movies or a fast-food restaurant where she and her mother couldn't just enjoy their time together without being interrupted. Her mom would pass over a printed card with websites and info. But some individuals just didn't take the hint and kept asking question after question while Rosalynn's food grew cold.

A few people even got downright mad, insisting they were just complimenting the dog. It made Elsie want to become a service animal trainer and teach extra skills, like tying together the shoelaces of jerks who were disrespectful and broke the rules.

And sure enough, there came one now, addressing Grammie. "That dog reminds me of our Labrador. We should get her a vest so we can take her wherever we want."

Uh-oh.

Grammie's shoulders went back, a sure sign she was two seconds away from reciting excerpts from the Americans with Disabilities Act. Most folks still didn't understand and just talked about their friend getting "credentials" off the internet.

Apparently, Grammie's steely glare was enough to send the person scurrying off. Thank heaven, because once Lillian dug her heels in, there was no sidetracking her, even if it meant getting drenched out here in the middle of a storm.

Umbrella in hand, Grammie pivoted back toward Elsie. "Are you okay, sugar?"

Elsie rubbed her thumb along the lever of the gas pump. "Sorry, Grammie. I didn't mean to lose it. I need to work on perfecting your death stare. It works better."

"The look comes with time and too much practice. You need a few more wrinkles around your eyes before it can be truly effective." Leaning against the van, Grammie closed her umbrella and shook off the water. "I understand the urge to protect her even when she's fully capable of defending herself."

The rain pattered on the canopy covering the fuel pumps, ticking away the seconds while Elsie tried to figure out how to answer. How could she explain the mess she'd made of her life that could hurt her mom even more if those photos got out?

Grammie tapped the toe of her sneaker against Elsie's ankle boot. "Did I ever tell you about when your grandfather and I first talked about getting your mom a service dog? The conversation didn't go as well as I intended. Timing is everything, and mine stunk."

CHAPTER TEN

LILLIAN

1990: I-95 in North Carolina

“You passed the exit,” I shouted, twisting in my seat and looking back at the interstate sign. Well, not exactly *shouted*, because that would’ve been rude.

Okay, maybe I did raise my voice. But the small space made it sound louder. Echoes and all. As previously noted, I am not a morning person and I had spilled my coffee on the floorboards, soaking one corner of our atlas. I’d sopped up the mess with my favorite cozy fleece blanket—which I needed because the heater was on the fritz and the North Carolina March morning had been chilly.

Not an auspicious start for our road trip.

Gripping the wheel, Grady shot me an exasperated look, the kind *new* couples in love didn’t use. “You said for me to take the next off-ramp.”

“Right.” I forced my tone to stay low and patient this time. “And you drove by it.”

A tic started in the corner of his eye. “I’m taking the *next* one like you told me. It would help if you cited a mile marker.”

His criticism would've been easier to take if I weren't so exhausted from waking up at the crack of dawn. "I would, if you didn't pass a truck every time we get close to a mile marker, effectively blocking any chance of reading it."

"I can't drive *and* read the map."

"Then maybe I should drive and you can have the atlas," I snapped, before pointing frantically. "Turn. Turn! Turn here so we can reroute. You're about to miss it."

He veered sharply across the lanes, sliding through holes in the traffic like a NASCAR driver. Horns blared. He powered up the off-ramp, the minivan's engine roaring. Pine trees passed in a blur.

Swerving, he pulled over onto the shoulder and nailed the brakes. I jerked back in my seat with the force.

He swiveled to face me, irritation stamped all over his stubbled jaw. "What did I do to make you mad?"

Breathing?

Existing?

"You're barking at me when I'm doing the best I can to give directions, and I'm so tired I can barely keep my eyes open."

"You're the one who wanted to go on this expedition when it's all we can do to hold down the fort at home."

The accusation caught me off guard. His rejection of our trip, of this cause that meant so much to me, hurt. Divorce was the most painful experience of my life, second only to the day of my daughter's accident. But because of my child, I needed to find a path to peace on this journey, for Rosalynn's sake. And at that moment, I didn't trust myself not to say things I would regret. I grabbed my purse and yanked open the passenger door.

"Lillian? Where are you going?"

A part of me delighted at the shock in his voice.

"To find coffee." I hopped from the van, my gym shoes hitting the asphalt. I slammed the door and started marching along the roadside, eyes focused on the rural gas station at the top of the hill. Heaven help us all if they didn't have piping-hot java.

No more than a few seconds later, I heard footsteps behind me, running, growing closer. Grady jogged up beside me. "Lillian, get back in the van."

Seriously? He was issuing orders?

Completely the wrong tactic. I walked faster. "I'll meet you at the truck stop."

He sprinted around in front, stopping me in my tracks. "This isn't safe."

"It isn't safe for you if I stay in the van."

An eighteen-wheeler drove past, air horn blaring. The wind vortex stirred grit and gravel that bit into my skin, hurting almost as much as his presence, a reminder of our failed love.

I stepped into the ankle-high grass, where gnats promptly gnawed at my ankles. "If you didn't want to go to DC, why bother? My mother and I could have driven together and you could have stayed home with Rosalynn."

"You made it clear I'd be a crummy dad if I didn't do this." A hint of vulnerability glinted in his brown eyes.

"I never said any such thing. You're not being fair."

"And neither are you, starting this argument on the side of the road." He touched my elbow lightly, the simple contact somehow more stirring than an overt caress. "Come on, Lillian, before someone thinks I'm kidnapping you and throws me in jail. Then we'll never make it to DC in time."

I should have jerked away, but I couldn't scrounge up the will. I'd loved him and hated him. And honestly, I hated him most when he was so calm while I was melting down with anger. I also wanted him, my broad-shouldered ex-husband with his smoldering eyes and gentle hands.

In the back of my mind, I understood that when emotions ran high, too often we'd resorted to make-up sex to avoid larger issues.

How easy it would be to simply kiss him and ignore the fact he'd just admitted to pacifying me with this trip, as if he didn't understand how much this cause meant to me. I needed to be involved in the change, for our daughter, yes, but also for so many others. I ached to be counted in the collective voice. Would he have come with me if Rosalynn weren't a part of the cause?

Probably not. Another symptom of how we'd only stayed together for our child.

"Truce," I said with a weary sigh. "But I still need coffee."

"Understood," he answered with a curt nod, motioning the way toward our vehicle.

Hitching my bag onto my shoulder, I trekked back to the van, all too aware of how close I'd come to wrecking our ceasefire. I was also so very aware that we would be sleeping in close quarters at the end of the day.

And there weren't enough good luck charms in my Southern arsenal to guarantee I would make the wise choice when we crawled into our tent together.

CHAPTER ELEVEN

Lillian

1990: Fayetteville, North Carolina

The next hour of the trip passed in a tense silence, interrupted only by me giving Grady directions in between sips of sludgy coffee from the gas station. By the time we reached a rest stop for lunch, we'd settled into an uneasy truce.

Like so many arguments in our past, we stuffed it down and moved ahead.

Pumping quarters into a rest-stop pay phone, I wished we could afford one of those cellular car phones. Whenever I was out with Rosalynn, I worried about being able to contact help in an emergency. And on a more superficial level, I just wanted to check in with my mother more often.

Like every half hour.

Maybe that made me one of those helicopter parents, a term I'd heard recently. But when the worst happened to your child in the blink of an eye, looking away became all but impossible. I couldn't imagine a time I wouldn't hover right over her, ready to make the world's quickest emergency landing.

The call threatened to drop for lack of funds, and I was tempted to accept it as a blessing. Guilt made me pump coins back into the phone in spite of the not-so-subtle pressure from my mom about getting a dog. She had been talking nonstop about a newspaper article she'd read featuring service dogs and how if the Americans with Disabilities Act was passed, assistance animals would be more welcome in public spaces.

She continued to pressure me when I'd made it clear I couldn't add anything more to my overflowing plate. Certainly not the care and training of a dog.

But since my mother was doing me a favor, I didn't hang up. Instead, I grabbed some quarters and added more minutes to our conversation. "Okay, Mom, we're good now. We don't have much longer to chat, though, before I need to get back on the road."

A fib, but a kinder one. Phone tucked under my chin, I watched as Grady set out our picnic lunch under a fat tree. Traffic had been heavy, but we'd still made decent time, stopping just outside Fayetteville, North Carolina—the home of vinegar-based barbecue versus *South* Carolina's mustard-based sauce. An important cultural difference that starts heated debates.

"Tell me what you and Rosalynn have been doing."

"Well," my mother said, "we finished her bird-watching research project. She was especially excited about her drawings of a ruby-throated hummingbird and a wood thrush."

"Wow, way to go." A bluebird swooped under the covered walkway like a howdy-do from the report. "That wasn't due until next week after break."

"It doesn't hurt to finish up early. That'll just leave us free to do other things."

I thought about the time I completed my sixth-grade diorama of a swamp ecosystem alone because Mom needed to drive an extra shift to pay for my braces. I'd walked to the dollar store on my own to buy a pack of plastic critters. I was glad for Rosalynn, but I also wished Della's life could have been easier so we could have made memories like that.

"That's nice, Mom. Maybe the teacher will give her extra credit. I hope she didn't make you do all the work."

"She's an independent little student."

Not surprising since Rosalynn had spent much of the past year being homeschooled while recovering from operations, including a corpectomy that removed part of her vertebrae to relieve pressure on the nerves. Her spine was now fused with hardware, although she faced the possibility of surgical revision later down the road as she grew.

The deep desire for that mobile phone increased. "You're checking her for pressure sores, right? And following the medications schedule? Her muscle spasms can be excruciating if you don't catch them right away."

I'd been unprepared for the neuropathy and spasms. I'd wrongly assumed that the paralysis meant no sensation at all. The injury in her lower lumbar region—the L2, to be precise—had been a partial spinal cord injury, rather than a complete severing of the nerves. She retained some feeling in the fronts of her thighs and in her hip flexors and abductors.

Her specialists had mentioned the possibility of her carrying a pregnancy to term. But I could barely think beyond the end of each day, much less years into the future. She was my child, and envisioning her as an adult . . . That meant I wouldn't have a say in keeping her safe. "I hope you're not wearing yourself out."

"Lillian, you've only been gone a few hours."

"I know, but . . . lifting her has become more challenging as she's grown." Rosalynn could stand for brief periods of time, and the physical therapists were working on helping her extend those moments. The doctors had said her hip flexion and knee extension were weak due to quadricep and iliopsoas muscle involvement. But they were cautiously optimistic she could one day use braces or a walker for shorter distances to help with independence.

Man, I wished I'd paid more attention in biology class, but I'd sure gotten a crash course in anatomy this past year.

"Hey Mom, is Rosalynn free to talk? I'd really like to hear her voice, and I'm about to run out of change."

"Of course," my mother reassured me. "She's putting her plate in the sink, then she'll be right over."

"Thank you again for holding down the home front this week." I didn't know how we would have managed without her. I just wished we could pamper her somehow. My mom had worked so hard for so many years.

"And you'll give some thought to what we talked about earlier?" Her voice dropped to a whisper. "About investigating the possibility of a . . . Well, you know what? I put some flyers in your purse."

About service dogs. I should have known she wouldn't let go of the subject that easily, even though I had told her I wasn't ready when she'd mentioned it again—and again.

Thank heaven Della hadn't spoken the actual words "service dog" out loud this time with Rosalynn right beside her. "I saw them, Mom."

"Have you shown them to Grady?" I snuck a glance at him as he paused unpacking our meal to scoop up a wayward Frisbee.

He soared it back toward two teens a few yards away with athletic ease. The whole rest stop was tailor-made to pick at the scabs on my heart. From a family of six parked at a table to a couple chasing a toddler sprinting away from their blanket.

And most painful to see, the older man and woman holding hands as they returned to their land-barge-size sedan. What magic had they discovered to weather life's storms? Or had they found each other in their later years, lucky to have gotten happily ever after the second go-round?

"I haven't." In fact, I hadn't brought up the subject at all to him. This trip was about peace, after all. Not introducing more issues to wade through.

"Here's Rosalynn."

"Hey, Mom." My daughter's voice reached to me through the sound waves, making me ache to see her. "Where are you and Dad? Are you still on track to get there tonight?"

I clutched the phone harder. "We're making good time. We're having a picnic lunch outside of Fayetteville. If all goes well, we'll reach the campground in Alexandria before dark." Sharing a tent. Just the two of us. "Are you being good for Nana Della?"

My mother had planned on being called Granny, but Rosalynn had a mind of her own from the moment she could talk, labeling her "Nana Della." I refused to think of what grandparent name I might have wanted for myself, not if it meant any risk to my daughter.

"Of course. I'm thirteen, not three," she said with a dramatic sigh. "Since we finished the homework, we went to Blockbuster and rented a couple of movies—*Batman* and *Honey, I Shrunk the Kids*. We're going to roll coins while we watch, you know, for Nana Della's 'laundromat ministry.'"

Once a week, my mom hung out in the nearby Suds and Duds offering to pay for people's washing since she remembered how tight finances could be for those who couldn't afford a washer and dryer. Even on vacations, Della would thumb through the yellow pages and track down the nearest laundromat to help everyone from college students to the unhoused.

Our washer had broken when I was ten, and Mom had to save up for eight months to buy a replacement. We collected cans and bottles to turn in for cash. She kept a jar on the counter at all times for loose change. Walking past a nickel on the sidewalk was a crime in Della's eyes.

We spent every Saturday pumping quarters into the washer, then taking the clothes home wet to save money. Being poor left a mark.

See a penny, pick it up, all the day you'll have good luck . . .

"Sounds fun," I said. "Sorry I wasn't there to help with your school project."

"That's okay. Nana Della has an adventure planned for us tomorrow—"

"Shhh." Della's voice cut her short, then came on the line again. "Lillian, we have to go before she spoils our surprise. Y'all drive safe now and we'll check in with you again tomorrow."

The call disconnected, and it was all I could do not to crawl right through the line to demand more information.

Grady's warm hand on my shoulder stopped me. He held up a bag of Skittles from the vending machine. "I realize we said no unnecessary expenses, but this is my way of saying thanks for getting on the road before sunup."

His gesture and smile reminded me of the Grady from when we first married, before the daily grind of life, bills, and routine. Before he'd started drinking and I'd grown bitter. He'd stopped drinking, but I hadn't found my way through the bitterness back to trust.

Forcing a smile, I plucked the Skittles from his hand. "Thank you. I wish I could say I woke up with a joyful heart."

He chuckled, the sound deep and familiar. "You're welcome. The Skittles and I acknowledge your sacrifice." With a palm on my lower back, he steered me toward our picnic table. "What did your mother say?"

"Rosalynn finished her homework early, so they're watching a couple of movies." I was tempted to tear into the bag of Skittles now, but lunch waited. Money had been tight for too long when I was growing up for me to waste food.

"What else? Because something's got you irritated." He waited until I sat before taking his place at the picnic table.

"There's a price to pay for my mother's help, and that fee is always listening to her advice." I scooped our cups through the ice in the chest, then filled them with sweet tea.

"That's nothing new," he said dryly before tearing into a fried chicken leg.

"It's just more irritating lately. She says Rosalynn needs a service dog."

"Huh . . ." His forehead furrowed.

"Yep, a service dog. I can see her point, but I don't need anything more on my plate." My heart squeezed, and I looked down to keep my eyes from tearing up. A robin foraged along the ground for a worm. "If a service dog would help her, I realize I should consider it. But for some reason, I'm resistant, which makes me feel guilty for not being able to loosen control . . ."

I paused, sneaking a glance at him through my lashes. My need to oversee details had only increased since Rosalynn's accident, a frequent point of contention in our arguments.

"Cut yourself some slack," he said in a surprising break from our past interactions. "I hear service animals require a lot of training. I don't know that a thirteen-year-old could keep their skills up to speed without a boatload of support from everyone else in the house." He added four deviled eggs to his plate.

His favorites. I'd stayed up late making them for him in hope of easing the day. Like he'd done with the Skittles.

"That's what I was thinking. And would the organizations that train these dogs even place one with someone as young as Rosalynn? How do I figure out what group is legit and which ones will scam us? Even though this proposed legislation mentions service dog access, how do we know that would even stay in the final bill? We would have this highly trained animal that we couldn't take out in public spaces."

"We can talk to the physical therapist—"

"That's easy for you to say since I'll be the one cleaning up after the animal since you're moving out."

He quirked an eyebrow at me before he went back to twisting open the jar of peaches. "This isn't something we need to solve today."

Was he making a dig at me for being a control freak? He'd done so in the past. "I guess you're right," I said even though my frustration grew. "I'm getting ahead of myself."

Grady rested a tanned hand over mine on the splintery table. "I know we disagree on a lot of things when it comes to Rosalynn's care. But I do see how hard you work to give our daughter everything she needs."

I decided to overlook the part of his words that noted the disagreements, since those would be a tough third passenger riding along with us.

"From what I've heard, Grady, there aren't even many service dogs available." It took everything in me not to flip my hand over and link fingers with him as I would have done in the past. Besides, I already knew that kind of gesture was just a stopgap until our next big argument. "I wouldn't want to take one from someone who needs it more. *We* are here for our daughter."

He quirked an eyebrow. "I thought the idea would be to give Rosalynn more independence. Especially as she gets older and wants to go places alone with her friends. Or out on a date. What about when she goes to college?"

My insides chilled.

I pulled my hand from under his and busied myself with dishing up a spoonful of peaches for each of us, instinctively knowing what size helping he would prefer. I tried not to consider how much of my life I'd invested in thinking about this man's preferences and needs, only to have mine brushed aside. Skittles notwithstanding. "Perhaps that would be the time to investigate."

Although the prospect of her leaving home scared me all the way to my toes.

"I thought the whole purpose of this trip was to open options and opportunity for our daughter. Or are you just arguing because I'm the one who is bringing it up?"

I ground my teeth. "So much for talking to her physical therapist. Apparently, it's already a done deal in your mind since you're the one who gives in to her every request."

Like how he'd bought her the latest albums from both Kylie Minogue and New Kids on the Block, even though he and I had agreed we would take her shopping together as a family treat *after* her exams. If Rosalynn got wind of the dog notion, of course she would want one before we could wade through the logistics.

Grady's jaw went tight. "That's a bit out of line, don't you think? Besides, technically, the suggestion came from your mother."

"Okay, fair enough," I conceded, snagging a fork from the basket and spearing a peach quarter. "Let's take this discussion down a notch. The last thing I want is to fly off the handle. This trip is supposed to be about the two of us finding a middle ground for parenting Rosalynn . . . before we . . ."

"Tell her we're divorced?" he said gently, before leaning forward, elbows on the table. "Or we could just live in the same house until she's eighteen."

His casual suggestion froze me mid-bite. I set my spoon down carefully and chewed the mouthful of syrupy-sweet peaches. Tree branches rustled overhead, stirred by the spring breeze sweeping away the remnants of winter. If only we could have had such a cleansing wind to revitalize our lives.

Grady's throat moved in a slow swallow, his brown eyes darkening. Intense. Aware. "Lillian . . ."

His voice, more of a question, hung between us and I struggled for the right words, difficult to do when I wasn't sure what I wanted.

A buzzing sounded in my ear an instant before . . .

The Frisbee landed in the middle of our table, snapping the thread between us. A flicker of frustration chased through Grady's eyes before he scooped up the plastic disc and stood to fling it back to the teens.

Exhaling—hard—I snatched up my Skittles. Forget about the sweetness of the peaches, because I needed a much stronger sugar hit before we waded into all the ways marriage had shattered my illusions. All the times Grady had made me regret the day I'd put his ring on my finger. He hadn't been a violent drunk, but he had been so very cold, those walls growing thicker with each alcohol-drenched year.

"Grady, we should pack up and get back on the road," I said, shoving to my feet and dusting myself off. If I was going to be labeled controlling, I might as well enjoy the perks of steering my own destiny. "My turn to drive."

CHAPTER TWELVE

Rosalynn

2026: High Point, North Carolina

Rosalynn hated crying uncle, but her body was done for the day.

As much as she wanted to make it to their hotel, or even to her mother's house without stopping, the detours had put them behind schedule. They were only a little past the halfway point—High Point, to be precise—and the sun was beginning to set. Even with her mom driving now, Rosalynn just couldn't tough it out any longer. Maybe it was lack of sleep, or stress, or the combination of both, but she was more than simply depleted, with the neuropathy pain burning along her legs, firing nerves in a pins and needles sensation. She knew from experience if she didn't rest soon, the stinging would become excruciating.

Frustration fired just as hotly.

From the passenger seat, she studied Google Maps, searching for the best path forward when it felt like most of the journey had been detour upon detour, while trying to stick to major roads in case they had car trouble. Had it not been for the evacuation traffic, they could have already made it to the hospice facility outside DC.

Rosalynn stifled a wince while sneaking a glance at her mother behind the wheel. Lillian hummed along to tunes from her playlist of classics, currently rocking out to Paula Abdul's "Straight Up." She would have expected her mom to be more of a "Wind Beneath My Wings" sort based on all her song choices when she'd toted Rosalynn to so many appointments as a teen.

Could Lillian have selected inspirational tunes back then for Rosalynn's sake? Or had her mom needed that inspiration for herself during those difficult days? Food for thought, and heaven knew there was plenty of thinking time today. The weather had eased, if not the traffic. Apparently, the other evacuees heading north had the same thoughts on skirting west rather than driving up the coastline.

Then others, like Seth, had gone in a whole different direction. He'd made it to Biloxi in record time, according to Elsie. She'd said he was already at the pool with a burger. Rosalynn suspected he might have meant at the pool *table* for a game. His betting wasn't exclusive to cards or slots.

Was failing in marriage genetic? Or even learned behavior? Her parents' marriage had certainly been fiery. She couldn't recall many happy couple moments from them before her accident and certainly not in the year following all the way up to their divorce, although they had been more careful to keep their voices lowered.

What memories would Elsie have from growing up? Would she remember family trips to Congaree National Park? Or would all the good be eclipsed by a father who drained her college fund to feed his addiction?

Rosalynn flipped her sun visor down, using the mirror to see Elsie in the back. "How are you and Dusty doing?"

Elsie glanced up from her phone. "Better now that it's stopped raining and I can crack the window."

"Good to hear," Rosalynn said, searching for a way to engage her daughter. "You should write one of your poems about our evacuation experience and set it to music."

Lillian lifted a hand. "Maybe even a protest poem about our experience battling the traffic. Tell about the people having their manners peeled away by exhaustion and worry. Or obstacles others face, especially those with less money, who have fewer options to leave."

Elsie slouched lower in her seat. "I'm not a poet. Or a bigwig legal advocate. I'll leave that to you, Grammie."

Sighing, Rosalynn pursed her lips in frustration. Leave it to her mom to steer the way Elsie should express herself rather than just letting her own voice shine through. She wanted to tell her kid that living with Lillian wouldn't be the picnic full of freedom she seemed to expect.

Rosalynn tried again. "I'm not looking for perfection. Just you, speaking—or singing—about your experience."

Silence stretched in the van, broken only by revving engines and the occasional honked horn.

"Oh well," Lillian said. "Isn't there already a song called 'Hurricane' by Bob Dylan? That fits better with the hurricane being a metaphor for injustice."

And just like that, Rosalynn thought of how to lighten the mood, to create a memory, springboarding off one of her own. Hopefully, it would also distract her from the increasing pain in her legs. "Remember how Dad used to play that word game with song titles? Elsie, it went like this. Name a song, then find another tune with one word that's the same."

Lillian smiled. "I'd forgotten about that. I'll start by spinning off Bob Dylan's 'Hurricane' by choosing 'Rock You Like a *Hurricane*' by the Scorpions."

"Wow, Mom," Rosalynn said, applauding. "That was a surprise. How about 'We Will *Rock* You' by Queen."

Lillian added, "'I Love Rock 'n Roll' by Joan Jett."

Already the mood lifted. Perhaps that had been her father's goal during those tense times. Rosalynn chewed her bottom lip, then snapped her fingers. "'I Will Always Love You' by Dolly Parton or Whitney Houston, take your pick."

Lillian's smile dimmed for a moment. "'Will You *Love* Me Tomorrow' by the Shirelles."

"Ohhh." Rosalynn danced her hands through the air, singing the title. "'The Power of Love' by Huey Lewis and the News."

Elsie groaned from the back. "Huey Lewis and the *what*? I've never even heard of half of these."

Rosalynn clapped a hand to her chest in horror. "Clearly, we need to improve your music education. I should have done better as an arts director."

Lillian nodded thoughtfully. "I'll stick closer to your era . . . So, playing off the word 'love' from the last title, how about '*Love* Story'? Or better yet, '*Lover*'—those are songs by Taylor Swift, right? Did I ever tell you about the time—"

"Ewww." Elsie gagged, flopping to the side but unable to hide her smile. "Stop. Please."

Laughter swirled through the van, like a spring breeze. A welcome relief after so long dodging the land mines of Elsie's moods since the divorce became final.

A Taylor Swift song drifted over the speakers, "Shake It Off," and Lillian cranked the volume until all three of them were dancing in their seats. Rosalynn welcomed the distraction from the pain, shaking away the stress of the day and whatever else weighed each of them down. Three generations of women connected through the joy as one Taylor Swift song segued into another. Rosalynn had missed moments like these with her daughter, and with her mother too, for that matter. The lilt of the mood came as close to soaring across a stage as she'd felt since her accident.

Could times like this be enough to persuade Elsie to stay? To remind her that they were a family who loved each other even through the rough patches? Rosalynn wanted her daughter to see how hard she was trying during a painful transition. But it was just that. A transition to a new beginning.

The music swelled, and Dusty's tail thumped a percussive beat. Lillian swayed as she inched the van forward in the bumper-to-bumper traffic. Then tapped the brakes. Accelerated. Stopped. Almost as if the rhythm of the traffic matched the song.

Advanced.

Then jolted.

Hard.

Rosalynn's arms shot out and she bit her tongue. Bags and gear slid forward along the floorboards. The blast of horns echoed outside while Lillian gasped and Elsie squeaked in surprise behind her. The ballerina charm on the rearview mirror spun and the music played on as the realization settled.

Their van had been rear-ended.

CHAPTER THIRTEEN

Elsie

2026: Nowheresville, North Carolina

Elsie jerked forward, then slammed back against the seat. Her head swam in confusion. The guitar case tumbled against her, smacking her on the cheek. *Ouch.* The ballerina statue rolled off the seat and onto Dusty. His yelp jolted her, clearing her mind.

They'd been in a wreck. Someone had rear-ended them.

She spared only a passing glance over her shoulder—seeing that a massive SUV had all but crawled up their backside—then focused forward on poor Dusty. She yanked her seat belt off, the *ding, ding, ding* chime announcing she'd unbuckled as she launched onto her knees by his side.

Her mom called out, her hands pressed to the dash. "Elsie? Dusty?"

"Totally okay. I was belted in." She ran her hands over the dog's face and his haunches, squeezing gently. "Dusty seems fine too. Grammie?"

"All in one piece." Lillian ran shaky fingers through her hair. "Rosalynn? Are you sure you're all right?"

Elsie froze. Why hadn't she considered the added risk for her mom?

"Mom?" Elsie scrambled toward the front of the van.

Her mother reached back with one hand, waving her away. "Buckle up so we can get off the road before someone else hits us." She turned toward Grammie. "Mom, if you can ease ahead a few more feet to the off-ramp, the shoulder is wide enough for me to maneuver out if we have to call a tow truck."

Outside the vehicle, other cars were beginning to inch around and forward. Behind them, a teenage boy emerged from the driver's side of the SUV, wearing running shorts and a football jersey. He looked kinda like Porter with floppy, dark hair and an easy smile that seemed caring—well, if Porter had been an athlete instead of mathlete. The boy's father—who was *not* in Biloxi—stepped from the passenger side.

Elsie jammed her seat belt buckle back in place.

The too-cool teen jogged up to Lillian's window. "Is everybody okay? Ma'am, I'm so sorry. It all happened so fast."

His father stopped behind him, cupping his son's shoulder. "Everybody in there all right? I'm Chester. This is my son Chet Junior. I've already called the police."

Grammie clicked off the music.

"Well," her grandmother said in that overly polite tone that usually meant she intended to level anyone who stood in her way. "We're alive and there's no blood that I can see. Beyond that, I can't attest."

Grammie. Ever the lawyer.

"That's a relief," Chester answered, shoving his hands in the pockets of his khaki shorts. His polo shirt sported a golf club logo. "My son was driving while I caught a quick nap. We are evacuating out of Beaufort. I see you've got South Carolina plates. Let's both pull our vehicles off the road so we can catch our breath and exchange information."

As the duo jogged back to the SUV, Elsie shoved her feet into her shoes and checked her cell for SOS alerts from Willow about weather—or about photo leaks to people at school. No messages. There'd been a time when she and her friends had group text threads that blew up the phone. They would have wanted all the details of her wreck, flooding her with everything they'd googled about possible injuries.

Now none of them cared what happened to her. They'd brushed her off since the blowup with Porter, like somehow her poor decision-making might be contagious. Or like people would think they'd done the same thing if they hung out with her. Grammie would have called it "guilt by association."

Only Willow still spoke to her. A true friend.

The van tires crunched as they eased up to the off-ramp with the extra asphalt for Rosalynn's wheelchair so she wouldn't get stuck in the grass. The massive SUV trailed behind them with a bird dog sticking his spotted head out the window. Their front grille was crumpled in a snarl.

Ugh. How much damage had been done to the van? Her pulse hammered faster. Would they be stuck here searching for a rental vehicle? And would they even be able to find one her mother could drive?

A twinge pinched her heart harder than the seat belt. She needed a breather from . . . everything. "Mom, is it okay if I take Dusty for a walk while y'all sort this out?"

"Please, and thanks," Rosalynn said in a tight voice. "That'll make it easier to maneuver outside so we can all check ourselves over a little more thoroughly. Just stay within eyesight."

Lillian shifted into park and Elsie made fast work of clicking the leash onto Dusty's collar, the one with palmetto trees that she'd bought him for Christmas. She leaped out the side door, her feet slipping, her head swimming. Palming the side of the van, she steadied herself before leading Dusty to the grass, footsteps crunching the underbrush. He trotted alongside her, but his head kept swiveling toward Rosalynn.

"She'll be out soon, Dusty, then we're all going to have a bunch of together time." While he lifted a leg beside a tree, she walked to the end of the leash to sneak a look at the back of the conversion van.

Crumpled like a used lunch sack.

Were they going to be able to get the hatch open? Probably, but just barely, and they might well have to bungee cord it closed again.

Cars inched past, the traffic jam made all the worse by rubbernecking. She wanted to yell at the passersby to take a picture, since the ripple effect would make her family wait even longer. But photos were a bit triggering for her right now, so she bit her tongue.

Chester and Chet were huddled together talking, the father's hand on his son's shoulder again. Elsie's Spider-Sense tingled—she was getting better at reading two-faced people lately—and she inched closer, wriggling her fingers for Dusty. He nosed his way through the grass, sniffing. She tipped her ear toward the father-son duo.

Snippets carried on the wind, spotty from the roar of engines and Grammie slamming her door closed.

"—maybe it's her fault?" Chester asked.

"She was kinda driving like a granny," Chet answered. "I mean, sheesh, she couldn't even pull straight off the road. She came all the way up here."

Whoa. They'd better pray Grammie hadn't heard that part.

But Elsie did, and she'd had enough of people not being called out for the rotten things they did and said. She stomped over, Dusty sniffing his way alongside. "What did you say about my grandmother?"

"Oh, uh . . ." Chet scratched behind his ear. "Just that she kept going so slow and tapping the brakes every other second, it was kinda confusing to follow."

Lillian strode closer, her gaze taking in the damage to both vehicles. "I was tapping the brakes to get you to back off. Because when one car rear-ends another car, the fault is with the car following."

Go, Grammie.

Elsie jabbed a finger in Chet's direction. "Before you speak, I should warn you that you'll be arguing with a very respected lawyer who works in Washington, DC."

Chester's mouth went tight. "I happen to be an attorney as well, and I don't appreciate you trying to intimidate my son. He says you were driving erratically. Maybe you were tired, ma'am, in need of a nap."

Chet spread his arms. "Or mad about the traffic. Ya know, road rage is a thing. Maybe you were angry about the evacuation and started driving crazy. In fact, maybe we need to get out of here before you take out all that rage on us."

Elsie grappled for her phone and opened an app. "I'm live streaming this." She pivoted toward their vehicle. "And I just recorded your license plate, so don't even think about leaving."

Chester shook his head, clapping Chet on the back. "Son, we're going to wait in the car. And I do mean *wait*."

Chet postured like his dad. "Crazy women."

How ironic that they'd just listened to "Mad Woman" by Taylor Swift. What a perfect song to fuel the rage Grammie was about to take out on losers Senior and Junior.

The rolling rumble of the van's side door cut off any response. Chester and Chet turned in tandem just as the wheelchair ramp slid out. The teen's eyes went wide, his face blanching as Rosalynn carefully navigated out with only a couple of inches to spare between her and the grass.

"Oh no. Oh no. Oh-no-oh-no-oh-no," Chet gasped, hyperventilating as it seemed to dawn on him that he'd smashed into a vehicle transporting an individual in a wheelchair. "I hit somebody in a . . . in a . . ."

Elsie wanted to shout at him that he *should* be upset, because that van held her mother and grandmother, the only two people left in the world she could count on.

Chester pulled out his phone, turning pretty pale under his golfer's tan. "We need to make sure EMS is coming too."

Rosalynn set the brakes on her chair. "Let's all take a breath. I'm fine."

Lillian tsked. "Don't say that until we're sure."

Rosalynn sighed. "Stop being a lawyer for five minutes, Mom."

Chet put his hands together, praying pose. "Yes, please. All of you."

As the heat hissed out of the drama, Elsie quit recording. Cars continued to crawl past, with the occasional horn honk. The late-day sun steamed off the pavement, the air heavy with bugs and pressure that made her ears pop. She swallowed hard twice, to clear the ringing. Thank heaven Grammie had taken charge again—handling the exchange of information, snapping photos of documents and damage.

Elsie's teeth started to chatter in the aftermath. She sank to the ground, her phone in one hand, Dusty's leash in the other gripped so tight her fingers started to grow numb. Thinking of her grandmother's stories about trekking to DC all those years ago made her feel like even more of a failure because she didn't have her grandmother's strength to battle through seemingly insurmountable odds. Hadn't Grammie ever just wanted to run away?

Elsie stared at her screen, hoping for some good news. Because right now, it felt like the world was conspiring to keep her from leaving the area.

Only one new text popped through. From her father. With a picture of him eating in a hotel restaurant, slot machines behind him. She shaded the cell from view. Her mom would blow a gasket, getting mad and worried all at once over the gambling.

At least the message wasn't about those awful photos.

Elsie cringed to think of her mother's response if Porter made good on his threat to share more of the pictures. Beyond being hurt, her mom would insist on fighting back. And even though Grammie wasn't a South Carolina lawyer, she would be full of advice on taking legal action.

Willow was supposed to keep her updated if he passed around another photo to anyone else. Except her friend was all wrapped up in the storm and worry for her horses. Which, sure, that was important. But so was this.

She had to stay her course of keeping those images from coming out on her own, because even if she called the police, then *they* would know. *They* would see. A court case would breathe fire into the story.

Her only hope lay in keeping things quiet, while putting distance between her and her high school until they all forgot about her.

Sirens wailed in the distance, lights flashing. Sitting cross-legged in the grass, she swatted away gnats, surrendering to the inevitable.

Their road trip was about to get even longer.

CHAPTER FOURTEEN

Lillian

2026: Winston-Salem, North Carolina

I hated hospitals. With good reason. I'd spent too many terrifying hours in them after Rosalynn's injury. And even while I had faith in the health care professionals we'd chosen, I also understood that some injuries were beyond fixing.

Like my husband's lungs. The transplant had bought him more time, but now we were at the end of the line. My second chance at love was over.

My throat tightened with a grief that could swamp me if I let it. I didn't have that luxury. The hospice manager had assured me that my husband was stable. But the sooner Rosalynn finished in the emergency room, the closer we would be to reaching our destination.

Tasks and routines had always powered me through a crisis, so I shifted my attention onto my daughter while we waited for a nurse to take her for a CT scan. The EMS tech who'd evaluated Rosalynn at the crash site hadn't found anything more than a bruise on her shoulder from the seat belt but still recommended a trip to the emergency room. I didn't even want to consider that the little snot who'd run into us on the interstate could have reinjured my daughter.

At least the police had been clear about fault in writing their report, even though Chet and Chester tried a couple more times to dodge liability. My brief experience with that father reminded me of one of my mama's sayings . . . *He thinks the sun comes up just to hear him crow.*

The van was still drivable, thank heavens, but Chester's insurance would be footing the bill for the repairs and medical expenses. I didn't feel one bit bad about that. If not for him, we would have been at our hotel enjoying supper.

Based on my daughter's pale face, I recognized she was in pain, a level beyond her everyday chronic pain. Dusty refused to leave her side, lying on the floor by the exam table with worried brown eyes. She'd mentioned neuropathy pain before the fender bender, and I hoped that was the only problem.

I'd pushed her too hard and hadn't paid close enough attention, too distracted by Elsie's crisis and all the heartbreak waiting for me at the hospice center. "Rosalynn, would you like something to eat or drink?"

Elsie glanced up from her phone. "I can run to the vending machine if you want. Mom?"

"I'm not hungry. The thought of food makes me a little queasy," she said with a grimace. "I think we're going to need to find a place closer by to stop for the night. I hate to lose our other reservation, but . . ."

The urgency pulsing through me took on a panicked edge. Clearly, forcing the vulnerable words out had been a struggle. But that was my girl. Ever reluctant to cry uncle. Which made her recovery tough in some ways, then and now.

"I agree," I said, before I tapped Elsie on the knee as she sat huddled in a chair with her phone. "Could you start looking up hotels nearby that have an ADA room available? We all need a decent night's sleep."

Rosalynn reached for her cell, tucked under her leg. "Mother, I can manage a Google search. I'm just tired and a little achy, not incapacitated. I'm not sure Elsie would know what to look for anyway." She typed along the keyboard, mumbling, "Why did Elsie think she was ready to leave home?"

Elsie waved without looking up. "I can still hear you. And I'm searching. We can make it a contest to see who finds the best digs for the night."

Their banter made me smile. A wise person cherished pockets of joy. My mama told me that.

My mama also would have been out in the halls pestering the staff. "I wish my mother was here. She would get these folks moving."

Shaking her head, Rosalynn forked a hand through her tangled dark hair. "People didn't tell Della Avery no."

"Wait, are you saying she was scarier than the both of you?" Elsie gave an exaggerated fake shiver. "That's terrifying . . . and a little badass."

"Thank you. I think," Rosalynn said. "I wish you could have met your great-grandmother. Nana Della was one in a million."

I pressed a hand against an ache in my heart that never quite went away. "Mama was special." And before I could stop myself, I admitted, "I was always a little jealous of how close you two were."

Rosalynn frowned. "I didn't know that. How come you never told me?"

"That would have sounded ungrateful," I said, another of Mama's phrases chasing through my mind. *It's a poor frog that won't praise her own pond.*

Elsie set her phone aside for once. "How come?"

I scooted my chair closer to them both. "My mom moved in to help."

"Oh, uh, right." Elsie nodded, sliding to the floor next to Dusty. "She came for a while after Mom's accident."

My granddaughter didn't interfere with Dusty—his vest was on—but she seemed to draw comfort from being near him all the same as she listened.

"Nana Della stayed with us full-time after that, actually, until she passed away the summer before I went to college."

Losing Mama to a surprise heart attack had almost destroyed me. Like someone had cut the umbilical cord too soon and left my spirit to starve.

Then I had refocused myself into action—as usual—and returned to college to pursue a law degree. At first Rosalynn had accused me of enrolling simply to keep track of her.

She'd been wrong.

Okay, not totally wrong, but a person could accomplish two goals at once. Return to college. And watch over my child.

Helicopter parenting can't be eradicated in a day.

Elsie leaned so close to Dusty, she must have been able to feel his body heat, even though the dog kept his focus on Rosalynn. "I knew she was around a lot, but I didn't realize she lived with you for that long. Did she have a remote job?"

Rosalynn laughed wearily. "That wasn't much of a thing in those days—"

Her words were cut short by a nurse coming to wheel her back for a CT scan. Rosalynn passed Dusty's leash to Elsie, giving the dog a release cue. "Take care of my boy for me, please, until I get back."

"Of course." Elsie grabbed the leash. Once the door closed, she scooted closer, plunging her fingers into his fur. "So tell me about your mom's job."

Her voice drew me back to the moment, offering a reprieve from worrying about those tests. "Until Mama moved in with us, she drove a school bus."

"A bus?" Elsie asked, wide-eyed. "For real? How have I never heard this?"

I'd done a poor job passing on the stories of our generations of women, something I needed to rectify. We deserved to be remembered for our resilience, our gift to one another as ingrained as our bright green eyes. "My father died in a car accident when I was three."

Perhaps another reason today's wreck had me so off kilter. On Dad's birthday and every major holiday, we made a pilgrimage to the bridge where the wreck had pushed his car into the water. We threw flowers in the river, and Mama put a fresh coat of white paint on the wooden cross by the road.

"Grammie, I'm sorry. That had to be so hard."

I rubbed my arms to ward away the chill of those Christmases spent tossing red carnations and evergreen into the tide. "They didn't have any savings. They were young, living paycheck to paycheck. Mom drove a bus since she couldn't afford day care. She just strapped me into a booster chair behind her seat."

Elsie gasped. "Isn't that illegal?"

"Not back then where we lived."

"Jeez, you had it rough," Elsie said softly, like a teen who saw no greater tragedy than riding the school bus.

I was thankful for all forms of free transportation growing up. "I didn't see it that way as a kid. I could sleep if I needed to, and Mom bought me earphones so I could listen to music or books on tape."

Elsie rubbed a thumb over her phone, a talisman of sorts. "Too bad you couldn't have an iPad, or whatever you used to watch shows back then."

"In the Dark Ages, you mean?" I laughed, opting not to remind her we only had cartoons on Saturday mornings *back then*. "When you're a kid, perspective can be less complicated."

"How so?" Elsie asked.

"To make extra money, my mother would drive for sporting events, field trips, and concerts. We got in for free. Mom and I would hang out together, watch football games, eat hot dogs and popcorn. And nachos, the kind with oozy cheese that in no way has actual dairy products."

"That sounds pretty cool," Elsie said wistfully, her gaze skirting toward the door.

The simplicity of those days swept through me. "I lived for the halftime show with the marching band. I dreamed of playing the flute and leading the pack once I grew up."

Elsie shifted as Dusty draped himself over her legs. "I never knew you played in the band."

"I didn't."

"Oh, well, the orchestra."

I shook my head. "We didn't have the money for the instrument or lessons. Still somehow Mom always found a way to show me culture for free. I didn't appreciate that when I was young."

But then did a child ever fully appreciate the sacrifices made by a parent? Not while they were small, because they were supposed to be children. Instead, too often, they were in a rush to grow up. Like Elsie and her whole emancipation scheme.

Somehow, I had to make her realize she needed to cherish this last year at home with her mother. For her sake. And yes, for Rosalynn's as well. Because with the wisdom of my mother, I recognized that Rosalynn and Elsie weren't ready to sever that invisible umbilical cord.

Time was precious. All the more reason I didn't want to waste a moment of it by telling my husband about a job offer I absolutely would never consider taking. In no universe did I want to become a Virginia representative in the United States Congress.

CHAPTER FIFTEEN

Rosalynn

2026: Winston-Salem, North Carolina

"Brace," Rosalynn cued Dusty, thankful her emergency room trip had come to an end.

The sturdy Labrador stood, legs stiff so she could rest her hands on him and shift from the exam table back into her chair. Even the minimal movement launched a cascade of nerve pain.

At least she'd been discharged and had a moment to herself while Lillian stepped out to phone the hospice center. Elsie was busy pumping her life's savings into a vending machine.

The CT scan had been necessary—and uneventful, showing no injury. Although the shuffling and stress had only increased the neuropathy pain. She held her tongue, fearing if she spoke out the doctors would admit her for observation. She didn't want to delay her mother, and a hospital wasn't the best place to wade through Elsie's mood.

Heaven help them all when she discovered Seth had drained the college fund. Even though Elsie still had a year left of high school, she would soon be filling out college applications, which would inevitably bring up finances.

Stress swelled inside her.

At least they'd found a hotel. Or rather, they'd found a motel. Elsie had located the lodgings when Rosalynn and Lillian came up empty due to the mass evacuations. They'd even considered regular rooms, but encountered issues with elevator access due to power outages.

The hurricane—still a Category Three—was making its presence felt at home and beyond, stretching limited resources.

A knock sounded on the exam room door.

"Mom," Elsie called, "is it okay to come in?"

"All set," Rosalynn answered, passing Dusty a treat.

Elsie shouldered her way inside, her arms full of soda cans and bags of chips. "I would have helped you change."

"Thanks," she said, caught off guard by the concern in Elsie's eyes. "Dusty and I managed. I didn't want to hold up our departure for the swanky motel you scored."

A rare smile twitched on her daughter's face. "You're welcome."

"Let's hit the road. Grammie's already in the van running the air conditioner."

"Slay," Elsie said, dumping the treats into the canvas bag hanging from the wheelchair. "Would you mind if I help you out to the van? Push your chair, I mean. You look kinda tired."

"Yes, please," she answered. It felt good to connect with her daughter. Rosalynn cued Dusty to trot alongside them as they rolled into the corridor. "It's ironic what my mom said, about being jealous of my relationship with Della. Sometimes I get envious of your closeness with Lillian."

Elsie stayed silent for a couple of heartbeats as they wheeled past the nurses' station. The television mounted on the wall was set to the weather channel, showing depressing videos of home and spouting predictions of heavy storms crawling up the coast. "Grandparents are supposed to be special. Although they can be important in different ways—at least, that's what you told me, right?"

"Since Nana Della lived with us, I naturally spent more time with her." She gripped Dusty's leash tighter.

"Is that why you weren't close to your other grandmother? Because you didn't live together?"

That answer felt like a dodge. "Mimsy and I had a good-enough relationship."

Elsie leaned over her shoulder, her hair sliding forward. "Gaslighting is not cool."

Her daughter had a point. Although were understatements the same as gaslighting? Like how if a Southerner said "under the weather," that could mean anything from a little hungover to recovering from a quadruple bypass.

Had she been covering for her ex-husband for so long she'd allowed herself to gloss over the darker details from other relationships—in the interest of creating the impression of a perfect family?

There was no better time than the present to try a more open approach for her wannabe-adult daughter. "Mimsy would take digs at my mom when she wasn't around."

"Well, that's rude," Elsie said as the sliding doors swooshed open and they stepped into the muggy parking lot. "And stupid."

"You don't know the half of it." Rosalynn glanced back at her daughter. "When I was only seven years old, Mimsy offered me cash for a dance camp if I would help break up my parents' marriage."

Elsie gasped. "You're kidding. Who would do something like that?"

"Well, it backfired." Big-time.

"How so?"

"I saw through her. She thought I would tell them and they would have a fight over it, which would advance her mission to end their relationship."

Elsie stayed silent navigating down the ramp toward the van. "Now I see what you're trying to say."

"What would that be?"

"She never should have put you in that position because kids shouldn't keep secrets from their parents. Except I did that in reverse by expecting Grammie to keep something from you. Sorry about that."

Her daughter's insight surprised her. "I was thinking more along the lines that triangulating is an unhealthy way to handle problems. But I'm fine with your interpretation."

Lillian waved from behind the wheel, motioning to the cell phone in her hand to indicate she was still talking.

Stopping at the side door, Elsie reached for Dusty's leash to help secure him in the van. "Do you think Mimsy cast some kind of bad mojo on you and Dad from the grave that caused you two to split? 'Cause he's definitely not good enough for you."

Rosalynn winced. She couldn't wish for loyalty for herself, then bad-mouth Seth. "You shouldn't say that. Your father loves you and I know you love him."

Sighing, Elsie leaped into the van with Dusty and began buckling his seat belt harness. "Do you have to be so perfect right now? It makes the rest of us humans feel even lower sometimes."

Rosalynn smiled at her daughter, her only child, who had been *so very perfect* to her since that first time she held her and looked into those sweet eyes staring back at her with all the trust in the world. How could Elsie not know her own worth? Rosalynn scavenged for the right answer, but before she could find the words, Lillian finished her call.

"Come on, you two. Let's *hit* the road so we can *hit* the hay." Lillian's voice trembled with an emotion that hinted the call had not gone well.

Rosalynn swallowed down the guilt over delaying them further. But she'd learned years ago the past couldn't be changed. The only thing to do? Move forward.

Once they'd all buckled and Lillian shifted the van into drive, Rosalynn touched her mother's elbow lightly. "Is everything okay?"

Lillian shook her head. "Just some test results that didn't turn out as I would have hoped. There's nothing I can do from here." Her fingers clenched around the wheel. "I'd rather not talk about it now."

The silence weighed heavier with each turn until they pulled into the parking lot for the Magnolia Lodge. Or rather, "ODGE" since the *L* in the sign had burned out. From the storm or from neglect? Tough to tell.

"Well," Elsie said in back as Grammie put the vehicle in park, "it has a pool, and that's where I'll be until they kick me out."

Rosalynn laughed. Lillian didn't. Rosalynn shot a worried glance at her mother as she climbed out of the van. Best to wait until they'd checked in. She started the transfer from the seat to her chair, the traffic roaring on the interstate near the parking lot.

A voice from outside pierced through the night sounds. "What do you think you're doing?"

Lillian's voice.

Elsie looked up fast from unbuckling Dusty and opened the side door.

A red sports car was parked barely an arm's reach away.

Lillian stood at the front bumper, breathing fire. Rosalynn knew from experience the collective stress—of a family member in hospice, an emergency trip to South Carolina, a hurricane evacuation, the wreck, and the ER visit—was about to be unleashed on the individual who'd blocked in a wheelchair-accessible parking spot.

"Hey," Lillian shouted again. "Do you see those blue lines marking the pavement? Oh wait, maybe you can't see them since you parked right on top of them."

"What?" The woman slid from behind the wheel, looking more than a little harried with a Bluetooth in her ear and her wrinkled business suit.

"The lines. And that sign." Lillian pointed. "Those designate this as a parking spot for someone with a disability."

Rosalynn called through the open sliding door. "Mom, it's okay. We can sort this out calmly."

The woman shot a quick glance in Rosalynn's direction, then back at Lillian. "Listen, lady, we're all tired and want to check into our rooms. But my car is not in that spot."

Lillian marched closer. "You're on the lines. That portion is to leave room for my daughter to exit her vehicle. What part of that do you not understand?"

The woman extended a long arm as she skirted past to open her trunk. "We're in a state of emergency." Her leather pumps clicked on asphalt. "The rules are different."

"How so?" Lillian marched after her, the lot lights showcasing her indignation. "Would you like to explain to me how we are supposed to wedge a wheelchair in the three inches of space between your car and ours?"

"You need to calm down," the woman hissed, hitching a paisley duffel from her trunk.

Calm down?

Never in history had a woman ever *calmed down* after being told that.

Rosalynn looked at Elsie and found her daughter's green eyes wide in the overhead dome light. Rosalynn was torn between wanting to intervene and needing to protect her daughter. With tempers running this hot and high . . .

The damaged back hatch creaked open, a painful sound, before Lillian reached inside. She tugged out Rosalynn's walker and stalked back to the thin space between the vehicles.

Elsie scrambled toward the side door, mumbling, "Uh-oh . . ."

Scratch.

Lillian started dragging the walker between the van and the sports car on her way toward the open side door, a metal support bar scraping right along the sports car's shiny red paint job.

The woman shrieked. "You can't do that, bi—"

"Don't you dare." Lillian paused, fury radiating off her, her voice rising with every word. "Since you won't move. And my daughter can't get her wheelchair out. This walker is our only option, even though she'll only be able to take a few steps, albeit painful ones after the long day we've had in this state of emergency situation—"

A security guard jogged through the lot. "What's going on here?"

"Officer," the woman accused, "this crazy lady is trying to damage my car."

Lillian threw back her shoulders. "This *individual* is parked illegally. Give her a ticket."

The sweating security guard eased the walker out of the way. "I'm not a cop, but I'll have to call them if we can't resolve things. I would hate for both of you to get whopping tickets and fines, or worse yet, we end up at the station to file reports and statements."

Sports Car Lady grumbled as she slammed her trunk closed. "Fine. I'll move."

As her engine roared to life and she peeled out to find a new spot, Lillian pivoted slowly toward the van, still holding the walker.

Elsie gaped, her face a mix of shock and a dangerous hint of admiration. Rosalynn gritted her teeth. Frustration—and yes, a hefty dose of anger—swelled. When was her mother going to comprehend that she could fight her own battles?

And in a manner that wouldn't risk them getting arrested. Especially since Elsie was obviously already struggling with how to express herself. She didn't need such a negative example, especially from someone she already idolized.

All the more reason to put the brakes on Elsie's plans to move in with Grammie. Emancipation? The teen needed to understand it wouldn't be all roses, sunshine, and unlimited ice cream sandwiches at Grammie's. Especially when Lillian was faced with losing her partner, a reality Rosalynn wondered if her mother was ready to confront.

And with time running out on their journey, Rosalynn needed to find a way through to her daughter before they reached Alexandria. Tough to do when Elsie was already hotfooting her way to the pool, thumbs flying along her cell phone.

CHAPTER SIXTEEN

Rosalynn

2026: Magnolia Lodge, North Carolina

Rosalynn inched out of the shower, gripping the wobbly railing and praying it would hold. Her legs were on fire but she gritted through the pain long enough to tug on a loose nightgown. Showering had sapped her last bit of energy, even with Dusty's assistance, but she balked at asking her mother or Elsie to help.

She passed Dusty an extra treat.

At least they'd finally settled into their "suite" at the Magnolia Lodge. The space had one room with two double beds. The manager had assured them the bathroom met ADA standards. He'd just bolted the shower's handrail back onto the wall himself and promised a continental breakfast of honey buns and coffee in the morning.

While the mom part of her insisted she should join her daughter at the pool, every other inch of her cried out in pain and exhaustion. So she'd let Elsie go, for now, and taken comfort in having a quiet shower.

Since her accident, privacy was a big deal for Rosalynn. She understood that at times she went overboard, a natural inclination made worse by her accident. Just as she'd begun to hit puberty, her body had become the subject of endless medical procedures. Physical therapy.

Occupational therapy. So many people examined and touched her at a time she already felt her body wasn't her own anymore.

Add to that the loss of control over even the most basic tasks, and she couldn't stop herself from pushing away offers of assistance whenever possible. Heaven help the poor person who offered to bring her a glass of water, because she would bark back how she could do it herself.

"Brace," she cued Dusty and maneuvered into her chair. The air whooshed from the gel cushion. Exhausted, she smoothed her silky caftan into place and motioned to the footrests. "Dusty, plate."

Dusty perked up at his second favorite cue—he did so love working with his paws—and smacked each footrest down for her. After, he stared at her with wide, concerned eyes and rested his head across her feet unasked, but so very needed. The pressure eased the ache ever so slightly. He was so in tune to her, the gift of his devotion humbled her sometimes.

Like today.

She felt like such a failure. As a daughter. As a mom. But she couldn't handle a confrontation with her daughter tonight. A burst of anger surged through her at admitting defeat, that her body was fragile and sometimes slowed her down. People liked to say she was strong. Mentally and emotionally she was. But some days her body wasn't.

There would be time enough to talk tomorrow. Right now, she needed to get in bed and wait for the medications for muscle spasms and nerve pain to kick in so she could drift off to sleep.

"Dusty, tug." She pointed to the fleece rope she'd tied to the handle of the bathroom door. He grabbed it in his mouth and pulled the door open.

She propelled the wheelchair into the main room, stopping by the closest of the two double beds, each covered in a green polyester spread. An identical print of a massive magnolia hung over both headboards in a nod to the motel's name.

Her mother sat at the little table with her tablet open in front of her. Lillian never stopped working, whether for her family or her job.

Typing, she said, “Elsie’s still at the pool. I just checked on her, and if you look through that part in the curtains, you can see her FaceTiming with a friend.”

“Thanks, Mom,” she said as she maneuvered from the chair onto the bed, unable to stifle the grimace as she settled. She patted the space beside her. “Dusty, jump.”

He put a paw on the edge, then another, climbing up in that gentle way of his until he curled against her side. Her sweet, goofy boy.

Lillian shut down her tablet and tucked it into her embroidered bag that doubled as a briefcase. The picture charm swayed, like a pendulum counting down time. “Have you taken something for the neuropathy pain? And the muscle spasms?”

“Yes, Mother. I took gabapentin,” she answered, sagging back into the piled pillows. “And baclofen.”

Lillian steadied the charm, her hand lingering on that long-ago photo of her wedding, with Rosalynn holding a maid of honor bouquet of miniature roses. “One of the toughest parts about parenting is seeing your child in pain and not being able to help.”

Rosalynn’s gaze skated toward the window showcasing Elsie on a lounger with her cell phone. “I hope you realize how much I’ve noticed and appreciated your support over the years.”

“Even when I’m pushy?”

“Even then—mostly,” Rosalynn finished with a grin.

Her mother crossed to the bed and sat on the end. Lillian rested a hand on her daughter’s feet, a routine of theirs over the years. But she waited until Rosalynn nodded. She lifted Rosalynn’s calves onto her lap and began massaging carefully, just as she’d done countless times.

Still, guilt compelled her to say, “Mom, it’s okay. You don’t have to do this. I know you’re tired too—”

“I’m fine.” Her mother rubbed along the length of her calves and thighs in a phantom sensation Rosalynn could only detect in spots, but that still eased the neuropathy. “We’re there for each other. And, uh, maybe I’m trying to make up for the scene I caused in the parking lot.”

Rosalynn was just thankful no one had been hurt—or arrested. Her mother's larger-than-life personality could be overwhelming, but the reaction had been over the top, even for Lillian.

"Are you okay, Mom? Did you get bad news?" She swallowed down the threat of tears. It couldn't be time to say goodbye already? "We *can* leave now. If you're worried about me, I could sleep while you drive. Uh, Elsie can even pull a shift."

"We've both seen what teenagers can do on the road," Lillian said, before they both snickered. "I promise you, we aren't that desperate."

"And about your call to the hospice facility?"

"There's nothing big to share." She turned her attention to the other leg, avoiding Rosalynn's eyes. "Well, nothing unexpected. Just a long-shot idea for a treatment to buy us more time, but his health has deteriorated too much."

"Oh, Mama, I am so sorry." She walled off her own grief over losing him soon and focused on her mother's pain.

"Nothing has changed. Not really. We're still on the same timeline." Her mouth went tight for a moment. "I know it'll lift his spirits to see you and Elsie sooner than planned."

"I'm sorry we haven't traveled up there more."

"You visited last month. You have a job. Elsie has school." Lillian adjusted Rosalynn's gown back over her legs. "Enough about things we can't control."

Rosalynn nodded and sank back deeper into the pillows. "About the incident in the parking lot . . . I could have fought that battle, you know. I'm not a teenager anymore."

"But I'm still your mama." She lifted Rosalynn's hand and massaged, starting at the wrist.

"Of course you are." Her battle for independence then had been fierce. And in many ways, it had carried her through. In others, though, she'd fought back against the very people who were in her corner. "You've always been there for me, more than you ever should have had to be. I realize it was a stressful time for you too, and I'm sorry for that."

"That wasn't your fault." Lillian pressed her thumbs into Rosalynn's calloused palm.

The quiet of the motel space wrapped around her, reminiscent of so many other hotels during trips for dance competitions, then hospital rooms.

She didn't remember the accident itself, which had occurred when she'd starred in a performance of *The Nutcracker*. Her last memory before the fall? She'd soared through the air as Clara. Pure joy, on a cellular level, had filled every corner of her body. Her nerves had come to life with excitement. Then . . .

Nothing.

Until she'd regained consciousness in the hospital in a neck brace, unable to move her legs. Some would have said half her nerves were silenced, but to her twelve-year-old self, it had felt as though her whole world had dimmed.

Since Rosalynn was five years old, her entire life had been focused on dance classes and recitals. Even her friendships were all born in that environment. Her parents had devoted their lives to supporting her dream. Her mother went from sitting outside lessons and rehearsals beaming with pride to sitting outside operating rooms and therapy offices with a rain cloud of worry.

After the accident, her days, weeks, months were filled with appointments and prescriptions. Relearning how to accomplish so many everyday tasks, like putting on her own socks and shifting into the shower.

How bittersweet that in the story where the Nutcracker Prince had been broken, real life had broken her.

In simple terms, she'd experienced an incomplete fracture in the lower lumbar region of her spine. Back then, she'd raged at the people who thought they were consoling her by noting it could have been worse.

Rosalynn tapped her temple. "Up here I understand the problems between you and Dad weren't my fault. But here . . ." She pressed a hand to her heart. She'd been aware of the dreams her parents had shelved for her. "I felt the strain on your marriage, from both of you working overtime to pay for all my lessons, then working even longer hours to cover my medical bills. As a kid, I believed I was responsible for the arguments."

She hadn't intended to confess that part, but the words fell out all the same, born of her worry for Elsie and her own divorce.

"Well, I hope you know that even during the stress, I enjoyed our time together. It's been a long while since we had a sleepover." Lillian tapped Rosalynn's ring finger over the pale stripe where her wedding band had been. "I wish I'd been a bit less of a stage mom."

"Mama," Rosalynn said, flipping her palm to clasp hands and squeezing. "You couldn't have stopped me from chasing that dream. I may not be as outspoken as you are, but I'm just as stubborn."

"You come by it honestly," Lillian said, but her tone was bittersweet.

"That, I do." Rosalynn slid her hand from her mother's. "Thanks for the foot rub and for the talk. Dusty can take over from here with some counterpressure."

"Are you sure?" Lillian eased to her feet.

"Absolutely. I would appreciate it if you could persuade Elsie to come on in for the night." Relinquishing control was tough, especially so close on the heels of Elsie's painful rebuke. But safety had to come first. "She's been out there a long time. Even being able to see her, I'm still nervous. I've heard so many stories about people going missing during evacuations. They get targeted from their posts online about being on the road and check-ins. I try to watch the social media accounts of her and her friends, but it's like that carnival game trying to whack them all. The minute they realize an adult can see them, they go back underground with a new profile."

Just like her mother, she would put the walker through a million vehicles for her girl. Heaven help anyone who tried to hurt Elsie.

"Say no more. I understand." Lillian slid on her sneakers and started toward the door. She pocketed the key card and turned off all the lights except a small lamp. "We'll be quiet when we come back in. Sleep. Grammie's got this."

As the door clicked shut, Rosalynn didn't doubt her mom for a moment—which was the problem. Her mother could so easily take over when it came to Elsie, and right now, with sleep dragging her under, Rosalynn didn't have the energy to resist.

CHAPTER SEVENTEEN

Elsie

2026: Magnolia Lodge, North Carolina

As much as she wanted to find out what had really set Grammie off in the parking lot, Elsie needed some time to herself. Impossible in their rinky-dink motel room with two double beds. One for her mom and Dusty. The other for Grammie and Elsie to share.

Thank goodness they didn't lock the pool gate even though it was long past the 8:00 p.m. closing time. Bugs circled around the halogen lights overhead. The still water glistened. She wanted to jog over to the Denny's restaurant open across the street for a sundae and some fries. But Grammie had left the curtains open to watch her, and she would probably worry Elsie would wander over to the pub rocking out some live music instead.

She scrubbed her toes along the plastic lounger as she listened to Willow. The cell phone connection was kinda spotty, with a roaring in the background.

A shiver rippled through her, in spite of the muggy evening. If only they would let her drive. She had her license. Mom and Grammie could sleep through the night, but no one trusted her.

Ironic. She wasn't the one who'd lost her cool and started to key a car with a walker.

The whole world was upside down.

On the cell phone screen, Willow's face was shadowy in the lantern light. "Lucky thing Jareth went with Porter."

"What do you mean?" Elsie glanced up as a family of five gathered their towels and headed back to their rooms, leaving behind three diving toys at the bottom of the pool.

"Jareth's house already got totally flooded." The connection crackled, then steadied.

"Too bad it couldn't have happened to Porter." Elsie's stomach knotted. She didn't wish him dead. Just maybe feeling some of the same fear she'd experienced because of him. "Are Jareth's parents okay?"

"Yeah, but the Coast Guard had to come rescue them from the attic," she said, bringing the lantern closer.

"The water was that high?" Her anger at her dad doubled, that he would have just left them there. Why wasn't he ever fired up on their behalf, the way Grammie was?

"It's the storm surge." The howling wind almost drowned out her voice. "Some people had to climb on the roof, like the family who lives next door to Jareth."

Elsie felt lower than low for griping about her life when it was so much worse for other people. And her mom would be devastated if their house had been destroyed. "Are your animals okay? Dusty doesn't get freaked out by the weather, but the dog we had before really hated to go to the bathroom in the rain."

"Mom put a kiddie pool on the balcony and dumped the contents of two sandbags into it so the dogs can do their business."

"Ewww." Inventive. But still. Ewww. Restless, she tugged off her shoes and shifted from the lounger to the edge of the pool, dangling her feet into the lukewarm water.

"Definitely gross. She wanted to use scoopable kitty litter, but we didn't have enough, so Dad came up with the sandbag idea. Are y'all having fun hanging out in a hotel? I'm jealous."

"It's not exactly cushy." Elsie scanned the faded paint on the pool fence and the diving board that looked far from trustworthy. "It was hard to find a place with a room left, especially the right kind for Mom. Some of the gas stations have run out of fuel. Others limit how much you can get, and you have to pay cash. The traffic is insane, with all sorts of detours."

"Wow, sounds like a zombie apocalypse out there."

A trio of teens pushed open the gate, laughing as they cannonballed into the deep end. Water sprayed and Elsie shielded her phone with her hands.

"Not quite that bad, but it makes you think. People are cranky. I mean scary cranky. Like the kind that you see in road rage shows."

"Are you guys safe?"

"Whenever we stop, we make sure the area is well lit. As long as nobody tries to pet Dusty, I think we'll be okay." She felt a little more badass about shouting earlier now that she'd seen Grammie lose her cool. Why couldn't people understand? Just because a dog knew some tricks or provided emotional support, that did not make him a service dog. "Respect the vest."

"Dusty's so chill, I forget he's around sometimes," Willow said. "Has it been a pain having to take him along?"

"Not really, other than the regular hassle of dealing with rude people who don't understand about service dogs. There are lots of folks out here with cats and dogs. I even saw a little girl carrying a bowl with her beta fish." There'd been a few folks with farm animals in trailers, but she didn't want to make Willow feel bad. "At one gas station, this guy had a bird that curses like a sailor."

"I wish we'd left." The connection crackled again, worse this time, breaking up. "Gotta . . . Later . . ."

"Bye," she said, but the call had already dropped.

Fear for her friend doubled, along with a loneliness that pinned her down like one of those weighted blankets Willow's little brother used. Elsie eyed the trio of teenagers spraying each other in the pool. Two boys and one girl. They looked like siblings.

Elsie scrolled through her social media feed, relieved no one had tagged her or sent a DM alluding to Porter and the photo he'd flashed around. How pathetic to be happy the world didn't care she'd disappeared.

The splashing grew louder, closer, and she glanced up to find the older of the teenage boys swimming toward her. He stopped beside her legs and grabbed the edge of the pool.

With a flick of his head, he shook his cola-black curls from his face. "Hey, wanna join us?"

She forced herself not to look over her shoulder to see if he was talking to someone else. "I'm not wearing a bathing suit."

"So swim in your shorts and shirt."

Why not enjoy hanging out with people her own age for a change? "Sure. I'm Elsie."

"I'm Kolton," he said. "That's my brother and sister. Kellan and Kyra. We're from Georgia. Evacuating to our aunt's place. How about you?"

"From South Carolina. Going to Grammie's. Same reason." She angled back to place her cell on the lounger, then slid into the pool. The water felt good after sweating all day.

Kolton's brown eyes smiling back at her made her feel even better.

"I saw y'all earlier, when your grandmother lost it with that lady in the sports car. Epic. My sister videoed the whole thing. I bet it goes viral."

Elsie winced. Great. Soon she and Grammie would both be "famous" online. "She's actually a really good lawyer in DC. She came down to help us drive up."

That sounded simpler than going into the whole emancipation saga.

"Cool. Cool." They both held on to the pool edge, almost touching. "How old were you when your mom had the accident? The one that put her in a wheelchair, I mean."

"Why do you assume it was an accident? How do you know she wasn't born that way, with something like spina bifida or cerebral palsy?"

"Uh, was she?"

"No," she conceded. "She did have an accident when she was just a kid."

His brow furrowed in confusion. "Oops. Sorry, I assumed you must have been born already, since . . . I sound stupid here."

"You assumed my mother couldn't have a baby. Well, you're wrong," she snapped back defensively. Look at her and Grammie, scaring off people left and right.

Had the hotel search and the parking lot incident made her more sensitive to comments such as this? Her mom had always been, well, her mom. She hadn't given a lot of thought to those little ways people may have treated her mother differently.

Guilt pinched at the notion she may have been selfish. Even self-centered.

Kolton tapped his foot against hers underwater. "Hey, I'm sorry. I didn't mean to sound like . . . Well, what do I know about that whole childbirth thing?"

"You're forgiven." She nudged back. Her mom had never scrimped on the details. It had been a regular conception—ewww—and a regular delivery. Other than the doctor recommending an epidural—not for pain, but to reduce the additional risk of a sudden increase in blood pressure. Her mother had gone through a lot of extra risk to bring her into the world. "My mom was a really talented ballerina. Like a child prodigy. But there was an accident during a performance. Something to do with lighting not being right and no glow strips on the edge of the stage. She fell off."

He flinched. "That's . . . awful."

Why was she babbling about her mother so much? To a stranger, no less. Because she was nervous. Duh. And she didn't want him to leave. "She still has some sensation in her legs and she can even take a few steps with braces and a walker, but for the most part, she needs her wheelchair."

"And the dog helps, right?" he said, seeming genuinely interested. "I'll let you tell me the details so I don't stuff my big old foot in my mouth again."

"Wow, a guy who learns from his mistakes? I must be dreaming." She could totally talk about Dusty with ease, and enjoyed the opportunity to educate folks so they weren't idiots like at the gas station and the parking lot. "Yeah, he's a mobility service dog. FYI, a service dog helps only one person. That's different from a therapy dog that does things like go to a hospital and comfort lots of folks but isn't allowed inside a place without an invitation—"

The girl shouted from the other side of the pool, "Hey, do you want to play shoulder wars?"

"Shoulder wars?" Elsie called.

"Chicken fights," the sister answered.

Kolton smiled at Elsie. "I'm game if you are."

Nerves tingled. The good kind. But fear made her pause. She'd been so stupid to trust Porter.

Except this wasn't the same. Right? This was just short-term flirting. They would never see each other again.

And she would make sure to keep her top on. No photos allowed.

Elsie nodded.

He slid down in the water so she could climb onto his shoulders. He stood, steadying her with his hands around her ankles.

Squealing, she clung tighter as they charged at the other duo. So fun. So normal. Was this what her days could be like if she succeeded in moving in with Grammie? A regular life. No more feeling mortified every time she met someone's gaze and they snickered or laughed.

Or felt sorry for her.

Even if they hadn't seen the images, she knew they were envisioning her naked. Worse yet, they had a real picture in their minds taken at a summer trip with her classmates going into their senior year, camping and sailing. She'd been in the campground bathhouse showering. And because of the underwear photos she'd sent to Porter earlier, he had told everyone she was into that kind of thing. Which made her wonder all the more if he was responsible for the whole mess.

A jolt startled her back to the present as she slid from Kolton's shoulders, submerged. Water shot up her nose and she spluttered back to the surface. She coughed, pushed her hair from her face, and hacked again. She could feel the snot building. How embarrassing would that be?

"Hold on a minute," she said, keeping her hands over her mouth and nose.

She climbed out of the pool and sprinted for the pile of towels beside her lounger. Dropping down to the edge, she scrubbed the bristly terry cloth over her face until she was in the clear. "I demand a rematch."

The teens in the pool cheered and appeared to be none the wiser. She wadded up the towel and stuffed it under the chair. A chime from her cell phone stopped her halfway.

She thumbed open the text from an unknown number and her heart fell to her stomach. Because even with the anonymous sender, she knew deep in her gut the awful message staring back at her had to be from Porter.

> Pay two thousand dollars to this link or everybody will see the real you.

CHAPTER EIGHTEEN

Lillian

2026: Magnolia Lodge, North Carolina

I welcomed the chance to walk off my nervous energy by retrieving Elsie from the pool. The hospital visit and my daughter's pain would have been enough to rattle me. And my insides still absolutely vibrated with anger from the parking lot encounter, although I was more frustrated with myself than the idiot who'd parked illegally. I'd met plenty of entitled—sometimes simply uninformed—individuals.

But that day, the weight of my burdens had become too much to bear. My husband's latest setback had been far worse than I'd let on. Rosalynn was already suffering enough from exhaustion and stress.

Which I'd increased by losing my cool.

Dragging in deep breaths of night air, I pushed through the pool gate. Three teens climbed the ladder and grabbed towels, calling out "goodbye" and "good luck" and "follow me online." Shoulders slumped, Elsie waved goodbye as she sat on a pool lounger, clutching her phone. She looked at them wistfully as they left. Until her gaze settled on me and the neutral mask slid back into place.

Closing the space between us, I stopped by a table, the umbrella closed for the day. Halogen lights hummed overhead, traffic and music from the pub next door echoing. "Everything okay?"

Elsie placed her cell phone on the nearby table—face down. "I guess *she* sent you to get me."

I decided to ignore—for now—the fact that Elsie hadn't answered my question. "Your mom's worried about you."

"Grammie, I'm seventeen," she said, making a big deal out of squeezing the water from her hair. "And I'm a stone's throw from the room."

"This isn't a normal hotel stop and it's late." I passed her a towel, the bristly fabric a little threadbare. "People take advantage of evacuation situations, snatch up the vulnerable, disappear in the chaos. As for following them online, you can't trust everyone is on the up and up on social media."

Elsie went still as a church mouse.

I guessed I'd finally succeeded in getting through to her about something at least. I patted an empty chair at the plastic table. "We can sit out here together for a minute if you want, while your mom falls asleep."

Elsie wrapped the towel around herself and took the seat, toying with a pair of abandoned goggles. "She looked tired. Today was probably a lot for her."

There. Finally. Empathy. I sat across from her. "She doesn't like for us to make a fuss, but that makes it all the harder for me not to worry. I guess I was a bit over the top about the parking space."

"Today's been a lot for *all* of us. You've always told me we're all entitled to a little grace." She twisted the goggles strap around her water-pruned fingers. "Actually, Grammie, I thought that was pretty badass."

"Thanks, but no it wasn't." Still, I couldn't stop my answering smile. Some of the tension left me and I reached to pat her knee. "What's going on? Really. I know you've let us believe you want to leave because of your mom and dad splitting, but I'm starting to wonder."

"I just want to go." She wrapped the band tighter and tighter. "I hate it at school. They're all so immature. I'm ready to go to college."

"I wouldn't argue with that." I eased the goggles from her grip.

"No joke?" She looked up hopefully. "You think I'm mature?"

"I believe in many ways you're more mature than your peers."

Snorting, Elsie tapped her cell phone. "That's not saying much."

I still wasn't sure I'd gotten the whole story. "You should talk this through with your mom. She's more than a little hurt by your request."

"You're siding with her." She fidgeted with the PopSocket on the back of her phone, clicking it open and closed. "Willow warned me you two would stick together in some kind of parent code that the kid always has to be wrong."

"Maybe it's because parents have already experienced being a teen, so we understand our children and grandchildren don't always get how much we love them and how hard we're trying." I rested a hand on top of hers. "We're human too, you know."

She drew away and went back to clicking the PopSocket. "Your teen years were nothing like mine. Mom's either."

I wanted to snatch that device from her hand and insist she focus on this world. Not the one on the other end of that digital connection.

"Hers were harder," I reminded her gently. Her eyes sheened with tears, but she blinked them away and stayed silent, so I continued, "Your mother is so independent, I realize it's easy for you to minimize the challenges she's tackled. And make no mistake, she's taken them head-on. You could learn something from her, if you would just pay attention."

"Fine," she said, softly but with an edge as she flipped her cell face down on the table. "I'm listening."

"Being honest with each other is important. It helps to have the full picture."

"You talk about the big picture? Well, the way I see it, when have you and Mom ever been anything other than super successful?" Her voice picked up speed and fire. "It's a lot of pressure to live up to. I guess that's why I got so excited to see you yell at that lady in the parking lot."

The conversation wasn't going as I would have hoped, and I needed to connect with her in some way. My instincts nudged me to peel off some of the plaster I'd pasted over my past to the raw bits beneath.

I could show my granddaughter that she wasn't alone. "Okay, so would you like to hear the undiluted version of my first big road trip to DC all those years ago? When I learned the most effective ways to protest for what you want out of life?"

She scrunched her nose. "I assume you're insinuating that me shouting at the children distracting Dusty and you turning the walker into a weapon would be the wrong kind of dissent?"

Dissent. Great word. Pride swelled. This kid had promise. She just lacked confidence. "Well, let's simply say I learned a more effective way."

"I'd like to hear. I mean, it's not like I have anywhere else to be tonight or anyone else to hang out with." She motioned toward the abandoned pool.

The parking lot was quiet. Lights slowly winked off in the windows of the motel. Music from the pub cranked up, masking the sound of the traffic.

We were, for all intents and purposes, alone.

"It was a bit of a journey, so you'll have to pardon me if I take the scenic route." Although hadn't this whole trip taken me on an emotional, bumpy ride to the past? "I was a mess, both from Rosalynn's accident and my marriage falling apart."

"Mom mentioned some of that when she told me she understood how I felt about her and Dad splitting." Her hands clenched. "Except my dad is a loser and she got a fire chief hero for a father."

An image of Grady in his firefighter uniform caught me by surprise. In a bittersweet way. So handsome, and so somber. "He definitely served with honor and saved countless lives over the years. But what made him most honorable? That wasn't his dream job. Not by a long shot."

"Then why did he do it?"

"To pay the bills." My mind filled with memories of him coming home from a shift smelling of soot, his spirit weary. I could sense his longing for the days he'd worked on a deep-sea-fishing charter boat. Yet he'd forged ahead even though each step forward took him further from us as he closed down, drank more, and shut us out. "This trip has brought up a lot of those memories."

"Like the song game in the van?"

"Exactly. And your grandfather's guitar. From the moment I heard your first piano recital, I knew you'd inherited his musical talent." Seeing the acoustic six string had delivered a particularly strong gut punch. "He honed his technique practicing during quiet shifts at the station. On that special trip in particular, he had a whole campground outside of Alexandria, Virginia, singing along."

"So about that undiluted version of your trip to Washington, DC? To march in the protest?"

"*Peaceful* protests and speeches over the span of a few days," I reminded her.

"To bring awareness for the Americans with Disabilities Act, right?" she asked, increasingly engaged. "Except wasn't that passed, like, forever ago?"

"Well, we didn't ride to DC in a horse and buggy," I said, although some days it felt like even longer. "It was 1990, a little over a year after your mother's accident. The protests were in March, and the pressure from those 'wheels of justice' demonstrations led to the president signing the ADA into law on July the twenty-sixth of that year."

"I guess I knew that date in my head. It just didn't register that . . ."

"That it affected your mother so directly." I wished I could say I'd been as aware of the need for such a bill before Rosalynn's accident. How easy it was to be patient waiting for change until the matter became personal.

"I guess I thought it came around just in time for her. Like it was a piece of luck in a tough situation."

Luck? I tamped down the urge to snap at her poor choice of words. The me of those days would have lost my cool. Now? I'd learned to employ a more measured approach, one of education and persuasion.

"It wasn't simply *luck*, Elsie. We were a lot of voices being heard. We were people insisting that the 1968 Architectural Barriers Act and the 1973 Rehabilitation Act weren't enough. It wasn't okay for my child to miss a performance of *The Sleeping Beauty* ballet because her wheelchair was considered a fire hazard. Or how she wasn't eligible for a weekend field trip to Disney due to lack of accommodations."

I still suffered from a bit of regret knowing it wasn't a fight I'd paid much attention to until it affected my own life. Maybe that regret had also pushed me to fight all the harder to become a lawyer.

Somewhere along the line, that personal connection moved me past just fighting for my daughter in a wheelchair. I was protesting for all the children with other disabilities. The adults too, of course, but my heart and my fire were especially focused on the kids.

"Okay, Grammie, sure, but the law passed and there are special parking spots." She paused, then sighed with understanding. "Spots that people ignore."

"Some people. Yes. Because laws don't transform attitudes. And the way I handled things today was a missed opportunity to help change her mind." Although some people would never see outside their own four walls. But I tried to focus on the many who would when shown a perspective they hadn't considered, those who needed us to keep marching in order to recognize someone else's hardship. "So I wish I'd handled the situation differently, but like you reminded me, I should give myself some grace."

"Slay," she said with the slightest of smiles.

I took that to mean something good. It was tough to keep up with the language. "Do you think you could give your mom some grace too, rather than just jumping ship a year early? Going through a divorce is painful. It's more than losing a loved one. It's the death of a million hopes and dreams."

"For me too." Her hand slid to her cell again, covering the pink seashell case.

But she didn't flip it over to check for messages. I saw that as a sign I still had her attention to share my story, while also recognizing I could lose her to a flurry of texts at a moment's notice.

"So you understand," I pressed. "Whatever's going on in your world right now, figure out how to talk to your mother. She's on your side. She's Team Elsie. Just as I've *always* been Team Rosalynn."

CHAPTER NINETEEN

Lillian

1990: Silver Maple Campground, Virginia

While I still hated early mornings, I did appreciate reaching our campground in time to enjoy the sunshine and outdoor cooking. Our KOA was located on the outskirts of Alexandria, Virginia, close enough to drive into DC in the morning. I focused on making the most of this last evening in this little slice of forestry heaven.

Grady had always been the outdoors type. We'd camped often over the years—our affordable vacation mode. Given his choice, he would have lived and worked on a boat, playing his guitar and sleeping under the stars. Life hadn't turned out the way we wanted on a number of fronts.

Now he finished setting up the tent since I had unpacked our food and was catching up on reading in a folding lawn chair. A creek gurgled in the background, a river roaring farther away. There was a chill in the air. Colder than home. But that wasn't a bad thing.

A fire already crackled in the little pit at our site, and I looked forward to cooking over the coals. My mouth watered from the scents drifting from the other campfires. Wind rustled the branches overhead, dappling the ground in nature's lace.

Apparently, we weren't the only ones at the facility planning to attend the march. As we'd followed the markers to our spot, I'd noticed signs propped against campers and bumper stickers on trucks. For the first time in over a year, I didn't feel alone in the fight for my daughter.

Guilt followed on the heels of the thought. Grady was here with me, for Rosalynn. His Rosie, as he often called her. I wasn't alone. For now. When we returned home, however, he would be moving out.

I shook off the morose air and resolved to enjoy this evening, to keep things as uncomplicated as possible.

Grady tapped in the last stake before tossing the small hammer back into his toolbox. The family-size green tent was tall and secure. "What are you reading there?"

"A library book." I saved my place on the page with a finger.

"About what?" He dropped into the other webbed seat. He actually sounded genuinely interested.

I tucked in a bookmark and closed the hardback. "Um, a little constitutional law."

Taking the tome from my hands, he read the dust jacket. "Is this for work?"

While I enjoyed my job as a paralegal, the practice where I worked focused on real estate law. Researching this had been a whole different lane for me, an exciting one. "The focus is more on human rights issues and less on property law. Call it research in preparation for the march."

His brown eyes searched me with an intensity and a curiosity that made me uncomfortable.

My thoughts scrambled and I blurted the first thing that came to mind. "I saw at check-in that they have a bait shop and fishing poles for rent."

"Are you trying to get rid of me already?" he said with a half grin. His smile was lopsided from an accident at work, a falling beam. But he told everyone he'd been hit in the face flipping out of a kayak. He insisted he didn't want Rosalynn worried every time he went to work.

"Get rid of you? That's not nice." I hated the awkwardness between us. "I was actually suggesting that we catch some fish for supper. Together."

"What about the leftovers in the cooler? It still looks pretty full."

"From a crazy amount of PBJs and peanut butter with honey sandwiches that we'll never be able to finish. Most of the rest can be side dishes to go with whatever we catch." I paused, feeling self-conscious. "Never mind. Forget I said anything. It was a silly suggestion."

"Not silly at all. Just surprising."

"You used to live for fishing trips." Many of our teenage dates had taken place on his jon boat, with me reading a book while he threw in a line. I'd loved civics and government even then.

"A lifetime ago." His intense gaze continued to hold me until the air crackled as tangibly as the fire.

My heart thudded and my chest grew tight. Standing, I busied myself with making us a snack. I set the cast iron skillet on the grate and sliced a couple of tablespoons of butter into it. A plan came together for a creative use for the leftovers.

Waste not, want not.

Rosalynn was due to receive a settlement for the accident, but that was her money. We refused to touch it except for surgeries. I would eat peanut butter and jelly until the end of time if it helped my daughter have what she needed.

And that was exactly what we would be having tonight—grilled PBJs. My cuisine was a long way from his mother's dainty Southern classics. "Did you reach your mom? Was she able to stop in to check on Rosalynn and Della?"

His mother lived in the next town over from our West Charleston home, but she'd bowed out of watching Rosalynn, insisting she was worried about injuring her. We all knew it was an excuse. Mimsy was all about the ballet recitals and dress shopping. She'd been less a part of our lives since the accident.

"I called her. She had bridge club today." He scratched the back of his neck, a tic of sorts when he was agitated. "We didn't talk long, since I forgot to bring change and had to call her collect."

And yes, his mother had more money than Midas. Money that she certainly wasn't sharing with folks at a laundromat. I wouldn't miss holiday dinners at her home one bit once Grady moved out.

So many examples of her selfish and rigid ways filled my mind. But top of the list, I was still fuming over this past Christmas, when she'd convinced us to spend the night so Rosalynn could wake up to Santa gifts at Mimsy's house. Rosalynn had an accident in bed and Mimsy lost her temper because I'd used the wrong sheets to remake the mattress. She'd snatched the soiled linens from my hands because I wouldn't wash them to her standards. The anger at me, I could have accepted and withstood. But the way she made my daughter embarrassed about her loss of control over her body?

I would never forgive her. "I refuse to manipulate my daughter the way our mothers have us."

Even as I said the words, I felt guilty for lumping Della in with Mimsy. My mom was never selfish, just passive aggressive at times from having lost such complete control of her world after my father died.

"I hope for both your sakes that's true." He took his guitar from the case and began plucking out a tune while I finished unwrapping a leftover peanut butter sandwich and placed it in the sizzling butter. I added one with honey too, my favorite.

It had been over a year since our last camping trip, and I resolved to make the most of this final one. After the accident, Rosalynn had asked for a family vacation and we'd planned our expedition to a hotel at the beach, only to encounter more obstacles than we could have imagined, even with research. I wondered now why we hadn't thought about taking her camping. As we'd checked in, I had noticed a small arcade with a video game Rosalynn used to enjoy playing at the mall.

Now the time for family vacations had passed.

He segued from Eric Clapton's "Pretending" into Tom Petty's "Free Fallin'." Was he trying to relay something with the lyrics of his choices? "You're getting quite good."

"For someone who's self-taught."

"For anyone, regardless. You have a great ear." And a voice that made my nerves tingle. I flipped the sandwiches, toasting the other side as a hint of peanut butter oozed from between the slices.

"I've more than enough time to practice at the firehouse." His fingers plucked along the strings with art as well as skill. "The guys have started making requests, bringing in sheet music. Helps chase away boredom on the quieter shifts."

"You have a gift, for sure. Why didn't you take lessons as a kid?"

"You've met my parents." He cracked a half smile. "Does my father strike you as the sort who would have paid for music lessons for his boy? Even my fisheries science and management degree seemed frivolous to them. They wanted me to become a doctor."

He'd had to drop out when we'd married. While he may not have become the physician his parents dreamed of, he'd saved lives as a firefighter and through his paramedic training.

A motorhome rumbled past, revealing a mother and son walking along the side of the road, towels over their shoulders after a swim. The boy held one of those new Game Boy devices, his attention totally fixed.

"Well," I said, "your dad sure missed out on some awesome concert material."

"Do you have a request?"

Easy question. "I'm partial to an oldie but a goodie, 'Peaceful Easy Feeling.'"

I'd once told him he reminded me of Glenn Frey from the Eagles. I wondered if he remembered.

The glint in his brown eyes said he did.

Those subtle acoustic tones did things to my insides, turning me as gooey as the sandwiches I was sliding from the pan onto paper towels. I placed one in front of him, while I tasted mine and enjoyed the "concert." We hadn't coexisted in the same space peacefully for years, instead fighting about everything from bills to a wet towel on the floor. Not to mention his mother's interference.

As I took in his innate talent, I realized Rosalynn had inherited her artistic nature and musicality from her father. Why had I never considered it before? Instead of always thinking of my ballerina savant as a changeling child?

The last strains faded, and he set aside his guitar to pick up his dinner. Already I mourned the silence.

"Great idea," he said, biting off a corner. "I love these."

"To be fair, this was one of Mom's recipes from when I was a kid and she took me camping." The honey flavor melted through me, my body humming to life in the quiet.

"Della? The tent, sleeping bags, and all?" He nodded. "Impressive."

"I wanted to join the Girl Scouts and Mom didn't have the money. So she got some gear from the Salvation Army and our adventures began."

"Good for her." He popped the last bite into his mouth and placed the pan back on the grate to cook himself another.

Was he already embracing a bachelor's way of life?

I reached for the jug of sweet tea. "She really is incredible. The way she managed after Dad died . . . That wasn't the easiest time to be a single mom."

"Right now isn't particularly a walk in the park either." He sliced butter into the pan, then dropped in a leftover PBJ. "For you, I mean."

"I have Mom's help."

"And mine," he said softly. "I'll still be in town, and I found an apartment on the first floor so Rosalynn can visit easily."

My stomach knotted and I set down the last half of my dinner. "I'll be fine."

The silence stretched again, no longer easy or peaceful. A log fell and sparks shot upward.

Grady tossed his paper towel into the flames. "I know you can handle whatever life throws at you. I just . . ." His forehead furrowed. "Tomorrow is important. We need to be heard, for Rosie, but it may not make a difference. You'll be careful, right? I don't want you to get hurt."

I knocked on the nearby tree trunk for luck. "I'll be loud but nonviolent."

He studied the sizzling sandwich with exaggerated concentration. "I need you to stay safe. Because I care about you, but also because . . ." His throat moved with emotion. "I can't do this alone."

The words came out so softly, I almost missed them.

A scary hope flickered inside me. "What do you mean?"

"If something happens to you, I won't be able to take care of Rosie on my own." He scrubbed a hand across his chest. "I know that sounds selfish, given how I do a job that could leave you to handle everything on *your* own. And I'm sorry about that."

Divorce was one thing. Thinking of a world without him altogether? Unbearable. I'd spent too many sleepless nights worrying about him battling large blazes.

Those fears had multiplied after a warehouse fire when he'd rescued a fellow firefighter, even needing to perform CPR while battling an injury of his own on that horrible day when a falling beam had hit him, fracturing his cheekbone. If he'd been knocked out . . .

Grady and I had both suffered nightmares after that. "You're more than this career. There are other jobs."

His gaze flicked toward his guitar. Just for an instant before he turned his unflinching attention to me. "What about health insurance?"

The question caught me off guard. Rosalynn and I had always been covered under his policy. Once the divorce was final, though, I'd enrolled in a plan through my office, with our daughter staying on Grady's policy. Including Rosalynn on mine would be tricky because of her preexisting condition. My new coverage might not even accept her at all.

That our child might be without a medical safety net . . .

My hand fluttered to my mouth. "Oh, Grady."

"Exactly." His suntanned face creased with worry and a deep fear. "I can't lose my job, Lillian. Not now. Even if we win a settlement from the theater building, the medical bills are going to be steep."

Except what about him? His health and well-being, physically and emotionally? "But you need to look after yourself."

"I'm careful," he assured me. "I won't risk losing coverage."

I couldn't stop myself from mumbling, "I guess I know what issue I need to make posters for next."

His lopsided smile tucked a dimple into his cheek, and I found myself smiling back.

I reached to clasp his hand in mine, his skin warm, familiar and calloused from hours stroking the guitar strings. He angled toward me and stretched out his other hand to wipe along the corner of my mouth.

"You've got a little peanut butter," he said, "right there."

I flicked my tongue to swipe it away and accidentally licked his finger. His pupils widened, his brown eyes going darker.

Clearing my throat, I eased back and scrambled to pick up the conversational thread where we'd left off. Tough to do with my heart trying to hammer its way out of my chest. "Um, but you promise you'll tell me if you're stressed at work, right? You can always talk to me. Even after."

"I'm taking care of myself—for Rosalynn if nothing else. When I need to decompress, I go out on the water. Paddleboarding. Kayaking. Those bring me peace. Just floating . . ." The stress and exhaustion etched on his face echoed mine. He squeezed my hand. "I'm hoping after we finish the march from the White House to the Capitol that we might camp closer to the river instead. I've already looked into equipment rentals. Wanna join me?"

That simple request stirred me as much as the glide of his thumb across my wrist. My heart pounded so hard against my ribs, I wondered if he could hear it.

Was this pocket of time together about more than peace and making our voices heard for Rosalynn? Our whole marriage had been about supporting her, even before the accident.

Could we also indulge ourselves in one last hurrah, to resurrect the desire that had brought us together in the first place? It hadn't been enough to hold us together when the winds of life tore apart our marriage, but we weren't trying to repair a marriage. We'd turned that page with the divorce. Perhaps after so much heartache, we deserved some time together to say a proper goodbye to our days as husband and wife.

"Yes, Grady, I'd like that very much."

CHAPTER TWENTY

Rosalynn

1989 and 2026

Her parents sat on the front row, their prime-seat tickets comped since she had the starring role. Finally. So many years of work were paying off.

And her parents were smiling for a change, even holding hands instead of arguing over money and everything else under the sun. Behind them, the lead dance instructor from a private school for the arts watched. If she landed that scholarship, her parents would never have to pay for lessons again. They might hold hands more, smile more.

Maybe they wouldn't get the divorce she'd heard them whispering about.

Rosalynn raised her arms in a perfect pirouette, the familiar music and movements bringing her to life. Except she wasn't on a stage. The wooden floor under her became a rubber mat that she couldn't feel, and she wore a plain black leotard for her daily morning yoga, the unadorned Lycra smooth against her body, unlike the itchy costumes of recitals decades ago.

The stretches in the privacy of her home helped with neuropathy. For an hour a day, she could pretend she was still a dancer. She didn't share the time with anyone else for fear their faces would pull her out of the fantasy. The symphony played from the app on her cell phone and she floated her hands through the air, arched upward on her stomach, shifted her weight to swing her legs around in a dance all her own.

Then the past pierced her dream, shifting her performance back to that long-ago stage in the darkest of ways. The lights dimmed and her footing was all wrong.

She grappled through the air, reaching out for something or someone to stop her fall. Her stomach tumbled harder than her body hurtling off the stage. Unexpected and shocking because she never lost her footing during a performance. Never. The shock of it made her heart pound faster as a thousand thoughts raced through her mind.

The embarrassment. The gasps from the crowd. From her parents and the visiting dance instructor.

Already, tears clogged Rosalynn's throat. She'd ruined this once-in-a-lifetime chance that meant as much to her parents as to her.

Then she landed.

Pain exploded through her. The worst she'd ever felt. Even more than when she'd broken her arm during a rehearsal last year because a boy dropped her.

She tried to pick herself up and climb back onstage to recapture the magic and finish the show. She needed to regain control of the performance. But the wooden floor beneath her became the yoga mat again.

Dusty ran toward her, his lopey legs eating up the ground. Yet he never got closer and she needed him. For more than help up. For consolation. He sensed her grief and never faltered.

Except why was he here when she didn't have him back then?

Her dad pushed past Dusty, his voice full of panic as he repeated, "Breathe, Rosie, breathe . . ."

His dear and familiar face morphed into another. One that was decades older, with wrinkles and gray hair. Elsie stood beside him calling out, "Ace, Ace, you can't leave us." Grady became Ace and he was gasping for air, suffocating in spite of the oxygen mask.

Rosalynn snapped awake, even as the fog of sleep still paralyzed her.

"It's my fault," she screamed. "I wasn't focusing and it's my fault."

CHAPTER TWENTY-ONE

Elsie

2026: Magnolia Lodge, North Carolina

"Mom? Mom? Wake up!" *Please, wake up.*

Her mother's nightmarish cries freaked Elsie out. Kneeling by the hotel bed, she shook her mother by the shoulders while Dusty nosed Rosalynn's cheek.

"Mom, you're just having a bad dream." Although from the thrashing, it seemed more like a night terror. One that was still gripping Rosalynn. Her face was contorted with pain and Dusty was trying his best to wake her, gently pawing at her shoulder. "You're okay."

At least Elsie hoped she was. Could she be having leg spasms? Her mother experienced them sometimes, except never with a reaction this extreme.

Rosalynn had seemed restless when she and Grammie had returned from the pool fifteen minutes ago, but they'd assumed it was simply from them opening the door. Elsie rocked back on her heels and wondered if she should get Grammie out of the shower.

Just as Elsie started to stand, Rosalynn's eyes fluttered open. "Elsie? What's going on? Did I oversleep?"

Pain lingered in her mother's voice that amped Elsie's anxiety up another notch when she was already overflowing with hurt of her own, coupled with guilt and shame. She wanted to crawl under the bed and pretend that threatening text hadn't exploded her world.

But her mother needed her. "You didn't oversleep. It's not even midnight. You were having a nightmare."

"Oh, I wonder why Dusty didn't wake me." Her hand drifted to the top of his head. He inched closer, up under her arm.

"He was trying." The pup had a wrinkled brow and concerned brown eyes. "You were dreaming pretty hard."

What worries tormented her mom? Or had it been triggered by pain?

Elsie felt trapped in a nightmare herself, except she couldn't wake up and escape the blackmail message on her phone. How had the drama with Porter and a small group of classmates escalated so massively?

Back at the pool, she'd prayed the text was one of those scams from overseas, like what had happened to Willow's grandparents. They'd been forced to shut down their bank accounts and cancel every credit card.

Sad for them, but Elsie would have preferred that kind of anonymous threat. She only had the hundred dollars left in her checking, plus the cash stored in the guitar case. Her college savings account was safe since that wasn't in her name.

She knew not to call the number, but as she and Grammie had been walking back to the hotel room, Elsie couldn't resist texting the mystery person back with instructions to leave her alone and that she was notifying the cops. Bad move. Whoever it was just doubled down on the threat, even including a photo of her in the campground shower that had made the bottom drop out of her stomach. Sure, the image showed her from the back, with her looking over her shoulder. One of the photos Porter had somehow managed to sneak during their summer camp.

This wasn't some anonymous threat from a keyboard warrior overseas.

She'd clapped a fast palm over the screen and let Grammie keep talking all the way across the parking lot. Because to explain that her anxiety had nothing to do with her parents' splitting meant confessing her dark secret. She could only think of one way out. She had to persuade her mom to free up some of her college funds. Then maybe the person on the other end of that text would leave her alone. Didn't everyone have a price?

Kneeling by her mother's bed, Elsie drew in a shaky breath and prayed her mom wouldn't pick up on her panic.

Rosalynn inched herself up to lean against the headboard, then reached to click on the bedside lamp. "Where's Grammie?"

"She's taking a shower." Elsie nodded toward the bathroom, the sound of running water still echoing. "She said she'll be able to sleep later that way."

"Sounds like my mother."

Elsie shifted to sit cross-legged on the floor. "Do you want to talk about it? The dream?"

Her mom hugged Dusty closer, resting her head on his. "Sometimes I have nightmares about the accident, which is surreal because I don't actually remember it happening."

"That sounds really rough. How often do you have them?" Like were they brought on by stress, maybe? Which only added to her worries about piling trouble on her mom's doorstep.

"Off and on over the years, in different forms. This one was the most specific, though. The other nightmares usually change the outcome or end just as I leap . . ."

Elsie knew the facts of her mother's fall, but right now, the horror saturated the room in a way she'd never felt before.

"Mom, that's a pretty traumatic thing to have gone through. Have you ever talked to anybody about the dreams?" She leaned and clasped her mom's free hand. "Like a counselor?"

"Right after the accident, our health care was iffy about covering a counselor. Mental health care has come a long way." Rosalynn squeezed

Elsie's fingers. "My parents tried to support me with talk and suggestions. But what teenager craves their parents' advice?"

Ouch. Elsie scrunched her nose and accepted the jibe. "You and Nana Della were close, though. Like Grammie and me."

"She had a great way with folksy wisdom, for sure. Although later, yes, I spent time in therapy. I even tried hypnosis." She shook her head. "Nothing has banished the nightmares."

"Do you want me to make you hot tea or something? I think there's decaf over here."

"Yes, thank you," she said, sounding surprised.

Elsie jumped to her feet and walked to the coffee maker by the sink, sifting through the contents in the little basket. She wasn't sure if her mom had agreed to the tea because she really wanted it, or if it was just an attempt to connect. Elsie knew she'd been shutting her mom out, but she wasn't sure how to open up. Even before the whole picture catastrophe, it felt like admitting anything, or being vulnerable, was a threat. Willow would have chalked it up to boundary issues.

To Elsie? It had more to do with struggling to be her own person.

Rosalynn adjusted the covers back over her legs. "Do you want to talk about why you're asking to leave home a year early?"

Elsie paused, then made busy work of riffling through their food stored in a laundry hamper, searching for Grammie's honey. "I wouldn't want to give you more nightmares."

Rosalynn chuckled.

Elsie felt queasy as she forced half a smile in return.

Once the steaming cups were full, she walked back to the bed slowly, careful not to trip in the dim light. She passed one to her mom, then sat on the floor beside the bed again. Keeping her eyes down, she blew on the tea. The silence stretched between them, broken only by the running shower in the bathroom, the air conditioner humming, and the distant music from the pub.

Rosalynn cradled her cup in both hands. "What did you and my mom talk about?"

Elsie weighed her words. She'd hoped Grammie would have the answers to help her. Instead, she'd gone off on some tangent about hanging out at a campground before a demonstration in DC, a story that had felt kinda incomplete. But the sentimental look on her face had kept Elsie quiet. She'd heard that people who got older needed to do life reviews.

Shuddering, she couldn't even imagine what she would do if she couldn't turn to her grandmother anymore. "Grammie told me about when she went to march in some big protest in DC. How cool is that?"

Must be nice to have control of something, to have a voice.

"It was very cool," her mom said softly.

Elsie glanced at her mother. "Did you get to watch her on television?"

"Watch her?" Rosalynn smiled, her eyes gleaming in the dimly lit room. "I was there too. And let me tell you, she was surprised—and not at all pleased—to see me show up unannounced."

"You were *there*? In Washington, DC, in the middle of a protest march?" she asked, surprised.

Rosalynn brushed aside the question. "A story for another day."

Her mother was right. Time was running out for detours. She couldn't afford to wait any longer. "Mom, I need my college fund money."

She snuck a peek at her mother out of the corners of her eyes.

Rosalynn's freaked-out expression didn't offer much hope.

Looking away, Elsie sipped her tea, the sweet, flowery flavor reminding her of peanut butter and honey sandwiches made with love. She was so tired of secrets and complications. She just wanted her old simple life back. She ached to be a part of something happy rather than mired in so much loss and fear.

"Well, Mom," Elsie pushed. "Can I have it?"

Rosalynn set her tea aside. "Oh, Elsie, can we please not discuss that part tonight?"

"We gotta talk about it soon." Like, really soon. Or her life would be over. Beyond being absolutely mortified, what if some university admissions person saw the photos and blacklisted her? Something like that had happened to Willow's older brother when some drunk pictures from a party got posted online, and he didn't get into a military college.

"Elsie, we will hash this out," her mom said. "Later, though, when it's not the middle of the night."

Her chest went tight with panic. "*Why* can't I have the money now?"

Her mother let loose one of those world-weary parental sighs. "It's too late to enroll in college this semester. Besides, you need to finish your senior year—"

"Or I could take my GED and enroll in January." The words tumbled out, powered by fear. "Either way, please let me have *my* money."

Her mother's throat moved in a slow swallow, and for a split second, Elsie thought her mom might relent. Somehow, though, that made her sadder, considering the possibility that her mother would actually let her go. Feeling so upside down and miserable all the time sucked. Elsie just wanted to climb up into bed with her mom and her dog and sleep away all her problems like she did as a kid.

She gripped the bedspread, ready to just surrender and spill everything, only to be stopped short when her grandmother came out of the bathroom, wearing a fluffy bathrobe, her hair slicked back.

"Elsie, did you bring a blow-dryer? The hotel's doesn't work."

She shot to her feet, her courage fleeing just as fast. "Sure. I brought my straightener too. I can style it for you, if you want."

Was that a flash of hurt on her mom's face? Good thing Grammie interrupted them before Elsie caved to the temptation to share all the gory details and shift the weight of her troubles to her mother. The whole reason they'd been having a midnight heart-to-heart was because her mom already had so much on her plate it was giving her nightmares.

Elsie knew that if she wanted to be emancipated, to be labeled an adult, then she needed to take control. Her mom had to grow up fast in a tougher situation. Elsie could surely figure out a way through for herself.

First thing in the morning, she would register for the GED and start looking for a community college near Grammie. Because when push came to shove, Grammie wouldn't turn her away.

With luck, Elsie could get her schooling locked down fast, outrunning whoever was trying to derail her whole future. As for the money part? She would figure that out.

She had no choice.

CHAPTER TWENTY-TWO

Rosalynn

2026: Magnolia Lodge, North Carolina

The next morning, Rosalynn was a mess.

Mostly due to minimal sleep because of the nightmare. She'd dreamed variations of the performance over the years, not just repeats of the accident that ended right as she leaped. In some, she finished the production unharmed, accepting a bouquet from her father as she received a standing ovation.

In others? One of her parents suffered the accident. Or worse yet, one of them died.

The irony of it all? When awake, she couldn't remember anything about that performance over thirty-five years ago beyond her first glide onto the stage for that starring role in *The Nutcracker*. So every incarnation of that evening felt completely real, even if some parts came from other people's recounting.

The horror of her nightmare still burned through her even now as she zipped her vanity bag closed to secure her medications, then tossed her makeup into the matching paisley toiletry kit. Behind her, she heard the rustling of her mom opening and closing the hotel door, going out to pack the van. Her mother had started the day early for once. Of course she would want to get back to the hospice facility as soon as possible.

Rosalynn accidentally dropped a tube of lip gloss on the floor and wondered how much longer it would be until Dusty was back from his walk with Elsie. Reflected in the mirror, she saw Elsie shouldering through the door with the yellow Labrador.

She held the leash in one hand and clutched her cell in the other, speaking to one of her friends. "It stinks that the hurricane hit so soon, but at least you've got a break with the eye of the storm. Right?"

Willow's voice carried from the device softly. "Remind me, where are y'all now?"

Elsie kicked the door closed and untethered Dusty, waving him deeper into the room. "We're in a backwoods motel someplace in North Carolina. The traffic yesterday sucked."

"I'm just happy you're all okay after that wreck."

Dusty trotted over to Rosalynn, checking in with her as he always did when returning. Smiling, she passed him a treat, then hand-signaled him to pick up her lip gloss. She wanted to hear Elsie's conversation and feared her daughter would leave if Rosalynn spoke up.

Elsie flopped back on the bed, her cell held up. "Why are you whispering?"

Willow answered, "I'm not supposed to be on my phone. My mom wants me to save my cell battery."

"Why can't you just recharge it?" Elsie asked.

"The power's officially out now," Willow said, her voice still low. "No more flickering off and on. It's crazy hot already, but we can't open the windows."

Rosalynn zipped her makeup bag closed, thankful they'd left when they had since the storm had made landfall earlier than forecast, then stalled, dumping so much more water. Would she have stayed longer if her mom hadn't come? She certainly wouldn't have gone to Biloxi with Seth.

She and her daughter would have been so isolated and vulnerable. She'd known that intellectually, but hearing the fear in Willow's quiet voice hammered home the gravity.

The danger.

Elsie flipped over onto her stomach. "It looks pretty dark inside. Who else stayed?"

Outside their hotel, a siren wailed, drowning out Willow's answer, fading halfway through Elsie's response.

"—but you're going to be okay, right?" Elsie rolled to her side, her back to Rosalynn. "Just sweaty and bored?"

"I think so." Willow's voice wobbled. "But I'm scared for the horses. I wish I could stay with them in the barn. I hope the cats took shelter in there, because I couldn't catch them."

"I'm sorry I didn't think to ask you to come with us. I was being selfish, all wrapped up in my stuff."

"Relatable," Willow said. "Anything happen with—"

"Hey," Elsie interrupted, sitting up fast. "I should let you save your battery. And we need to hit the road. Text me when you can so I'll know you're all right."

Her daughter disconnected the call. Almost rudely. Maybe the hurricane was overwhelming her even from a distance.

Rosalynn wheeled back from the vanity, turning. Through the part in the curtains, she saw her mom leaning against the bumper of the van, talking into her own phone.

Shifting her attention to her daughter, Rosalynn moved closer. "Elsie, honey, I only caught the tail end of that, but it sounds scary back home. I'm sure you must be worried for your friends."

She searched her daughter's face, the fear in her eyes so intense she wanted to hug her tight. Then, in a blink, Elsie's expression closed off, her walls firmly in place again.

"Yeah, it sounds rough," Elsie said as she swung her feet off the mattress. "The bottom floor of their house has a couple of inches of water, and there's no electricity. The phone connection cut out when we talked last night. I don't know what I would do without my phone."

Rosalynn propelled her chair closer. "Do you want to talk about it?"

"About what?" Eyes wide, Elsie clutched her phone to her chest.

"The hurricane. Worries for your friend. For our house, even."

"Oh, right." She tipped her attention back to her cell and scrolled. "Folks online are already posting some crazy bad video clips."

She held up the screen to show an image of palmetto trees bowing in the torrential rain and wind. In another, the storm plucked apart a dock, one board at a time spiraling up until the rest of the pier floated away. "There are photos all over the internet. It's awful."

Rosalynn skimmed her daughter's damp hair from her face and tucked it behind her ear. "It's incredible—and frightening—how fast information can spread on the web."

Elsie went pale and her gaze dropped to her phone. The silence stretched between them, the kind Rosalynn sensed would bear fruit if she just waited. Elsie sniffled, her eyes glinting with tears. Rosalynn sat unmoving, afraid if she so much as blinked, her daughter would close up again.

Elsie's thumb twitched along her phone case.

The key card chimed from outside an instant before Lillian stepped inside. "I'm about ready to head out. I just need to gather my paperwork and whatever else the two of you have left."

She stopped by the tiny table, unplugging her laptop and wedging it into her oversize embroidered bag. Her bustling presence snapped the fragile connection Rosalynn had finally managed to find with her daughter.

Elsie grabbed her backpack. "I'll wait in the van." She snatched the keys off the bedside table. "I'll start the air conditioner."

The door slammed closed after the teen. Rosalynn deflated, air whooshing from her in disappointment.

Lillian snorted, sliding files into her stitched bag on top of the computer in a tight fit. "Hopefully she doesn't drive off and leave us."

"Stubbornness seems imprinted in our DNA. Quite the legacy," she said. "I'll never forget how mad you were with Nana Della when she brought me to DC without consulting you first."

"Mama and I had quite the argument there in front of the White House."

"Keeping the secret about our travel plans to join you was difficult." Except she'd known if she slipped up and revealed Della's agenda, her mom would never have let her attend the march. Her mother's protectiveness had been smothering back then. It still was.

Pushing the point, though, always seemed to trigger more arguments between her folks. As an adult, she understood a child wasn't responsible for her parents' breakup. As a teen? The guilt about wrecking their marriage had been crushing.

The guilt now weighed just as heavily from making demands on her mother at a heartbreaking time. The stress lines on Lillian's face were deep today. Her mother moved in such a rush an envelope slid free, fluttering to the ground.

Rosalynn pointed toward the fallen letter. "Dusty, get it."

The Labrador pawed at the paper until an end curled up and he gently took it in his mouth. He ambled across the carpet to Rosalynn.

"Drop it," she said. He released the paper onto her lap. She flipped it over to find a logo on the envelope from a US representative from Virginia. "Hey Mom, what big cases are you cooking up?"

She waggled the letter.

Lillian rushed to snatch it from her and stuffed it into her needlepoint bag. "Thanks. I packed on the fly for this trip, so I'm less than organized."

Something in her mother's evasiveness and the way she avoided eye contact made Rosalynn curious. "The congressional return address looked official."

Lillian shook her head, her brown hair smoothed into a low ponytail. A handful of grays glinted, an unspoken testimony to how little free time she had. Lillian had never been one to miss a hairdresser appointment once the silver strands started. She'd always vowed that while she respected Della's bold embrace of graying, she would fight to the end.

With her stylist's help.

"Come on, Mom." Rosalynn hooked her bag onto her chair and closed the distance between them. "Spill the details."

"It's just a follow-up to a meeting," Lillian said dismissively.

"With a US congressman. That's big."

What else had her mom been hiding? Lillian wasn't necessarily humble. She simply insisted she didn't have time to toot her own horn.

Lillian sagged into the rolling chair. "I met with the congressman, his staff, and the party chair a couple of weeks ago. He's retiring. He offered his endorsement if I run for his seat."

"Mom, that's incredible." She slid an arm around her mother in a half hug of congratulations. "Why didn't you say something? Heaven knows we had plenty of time to talk in the van yesterday."

"Because it isn't going to happen." Lillian flattened her hands on top of her bag as if to keep the possibility sealed away. "I would have to commit by the end of this month to receive the financing."

Rosalynn searched for gentle words to make her point. "But the active campaigning wouldn't start until . . . later."

Lillian flinched, her face tight with grief. "I can't accept something because I know my husband would be dead by then."

"I didn't mean that the way it sounded." Thinking of the future sent an answering pain through her. "I'm sorry. The thought of him dying is gut-wrenching. I'll just hush before I make things worse."

"Apology accepted. It's not like I'll be in any shape . . . after . . ." She swallowed, her hands massaging along her throat. "I just won't."

Rosalynn shook her head. "On that point, I disagree. You've always been one to throw yourself into a task or your job as a distraction. I envy you that ability."

Lillian tipped her head to the side, her arched eyebrows pinching together. "Does your work not bring you joy? I was so happy when you landed the marketing director position at the arts center."

No question, her mother was trying to redirect the conversation, but Rosalynn couldn't keep the longing from bubbling up and out. "It doesn't bring me as much joy as what I *should* be doing, what I was born to do."

Her dream still teased at the edges of her mind and heart. The most difficult part of those nightmares was waking up with the sensation of dancing hovering so close in her consciousness, she could still feel the wooden stage under her feet. The air tasted different when she took flight, but that life was over.

Her mom could still pursue a dream opportunity such as this one. And before her return trip home, Rosalynn intended to put all those hardheaded genes to work persuading her mother to go for it.

As for Elsie? Rosalynn would double down on breaking through her daughter's defensive walls, then convince her to come home where she belonged.

CHAPTER TWENTY-THREE

Lillian

1990: Silver Maple Campground, Virginia

Even though I'd known that Grady and I would share a tent that night, I hadn't expected us to share a sleeping bag—or rather, share our two bags zipped into one.

Of course we'd never had much luck resisting each other.

Curled against his side, I rested my cheek against the steady rise and fall of his chest. The thump of his heart mixed with the croak of bullfrogs, interrupted by the sharp call of a nighthawk. The smoky scent of our campfire still clung to the air, but in a pleasing way, reminding me of s'mores and a kiss.

We'd left our shoes outside, a camping superstition that had practical implications. I did worry, though, that the attempt to stay in luck's good graces wouldn't be enough to protect against future conflict. Every moment of this trip tempted fate, and right now, mellow from Grady's touch, I didn't have the will to roll away.

The quiet community of campgrounds had a universal vibe, a sense of connection that I'd never found anywhere else. So many people in one area slept with only the barest barriers between us, no brick walls. I wondered at the trust of us all, strangers drifting off and totally vulnerable. I'd grown less trusting of life in general over the past year. Maybe that was why I needed the old campground peace to give me relief from the unrelenting stress and fear.

A small battery-powered lantern glowed from a hook overhead, the breezy night rustling the nylon. I snuggled against Grady's warmth, the chilly night air giving me an excuse. He skimmed his fingers along my arm with the familiarity of an old married couple who understood the nuances of each other well, so much so it was easy to forget for a moment we were divorced.

"Lillian," he said softly, "I meant to ask how your conversation went with Rosalynn when we got to the campground."

"They didn't answer." But I'd called late, distracted by Grady. I felt guilty over that. "They could have been watching their movies. Earlier, Mom even mentioned taking Rosalynn to the laundromat."

Grady laughed, low and raspy. "Ah, Della's laundromat ministry. I'll be interested to hear what Rosalynn thinks of spending her nana time passing out rolls of quarters and baggies full of detergent powder."

"Since she idolizes my mother, I suspect she'll beg to accompany Mom on a regular basis."

"I can see that," Grady said. "I could call my mother in the morning and have her swing by to check in."

"If you want." I wasn't excited at the notion of Mimsy stopping by without me around. She had a particular talent for subtly hurtful Southern digs. "The neighbors promised to peek in, and they have our itinerary too."

"I should have known you would have everything covered."

"Is that a jab?" Like his mother would have delivered?

"No, ma'am. I'm ever in awe of you." He kissed my forehead.

I tried to play off my need for it to be true, but I didn't dare tip my face to read his expression for fear he would see my vulnerability. "I'm sorry your mother and I don't get along. She never thought I was good enough for her precious prince of a son."

"I know her precious prince of a son has never been good enough for you."

"That's lovely of you to say." My heart all but melted in a way I hadn't felt in so long.

"I'm serious," he said. "You're too good for me. I wondered sometimes if you married me because your mom was struggling and you needed to leave . . ."

Could he be serious? I angled up to my elbow to look into his face, regardless of the risk of him seeing mine. "It's one thing for your mother to think such terrible things about our relationship. But how sad that you would believe that about yourself."

His mouth tipped in that half smile of his, the remnant of nerve damage from that warehouse fire accident. "Chalk it up to my insecurity."

The vulnerability in his voice caught me by surprise. "What do you mean?"

"Forget I said anything." He sat up and reached to turn off the lantern. The sleeping bag slid down around his waist.

My mouth dried up.

I stopped him with a touch to his elbow. "Does this have something to do with our discussion earlier about you staying with the job? I know it's been tough for you since the warehouse fire a couple of years ago. Your drinking got . . ."

"Worse then. Yeah." He scrubbed a hand along his jaw. "Not the wisest coping mechanism."

I'd known he was struggling, but I hadn't grasped how deeply. "I've heard about people getting shell shock from traumatic events or repeated trauma. Such as an attack. Or like on the job for a police officer or firefighter . . ."

"Then you also will have heard about how a problem like that can end a career if word gets out. Which brings me right back to my earlier point about us needing the insurance."

Even though we were no longer a couple, I didn't want him to struggle this way. "We could look into a private counselor, off the books, pay cash."

He cast a sideways glance at me, his brown eyes haunted. "Lillian, even if we had the money for me to see a therapist, there's no amount of counseling that will help me get over what happened the night of Rosalynn's accident."

The worst day of our lives, no question, but I wasn't sure what that had to do with his work stress. So I stayed silent and let him talk.

"When I saw her fall off the stage . . ." His throat moved in a long swallow. "I know in my soul that I handled things correctly in every way. That I stabilized her head without moving her. That I kept others from interfering. My training went on autopilot. Except in my nightmares, I accidentally jostle her and worsen the injury. In my dreams, I'd been drinking that night even though in reality I know I hadn't, since I'd come straight from work to the performance. But I can't escape the gut-sick feeling that I caused her paralysis. The horror of that lingers for days. Then the dream comes again."

Stunned, I held myself still. How had I not realized he blamed himself for Rosalynn's paralysis? To me, it was clear that our daughter's fall from the stage had been a tragic accident, and the only fault lay in the theater staff who hadn't properly marked the edges. Yet hadn't I wrestled with nightmares about that day too? Hadn't I relived those short moments millions of times every day, imagining a different outcome if only one thing had been different?

Knowing the thoughts were toxic didn't make me stop thinking them. It had gotten better, but still . . . I hadn't realized how deeply Grady suffered too.

Elbows on his knees, Grady hung his head. "I realize that job stressors play into my nightmares. Except at work, I can lose myself in the routine. But this? With my child? How could I maintain professional calm?"

The pain and guilt in his voice cut me to the core. I slid an arm around him and rested my head on his shoulder. "I wish there was something I could say, but I don't have a clue how to help. Because I wrestle with the same thing. Blaming myself for enrolling her in lessons. For pushing her to succeed."

"As if anyone could have stopped her from dancing," he reminded me before his smile faltered. "And now she can't."

A new worry took shape inside me, a fear for his hard-won sobriety these past months. "Maybe there's someone at the hospital we can speak with to help us navigate these . . . feelings . . . for Rosalynn's sake." Seeing his face close off, I rushed to add, "Just so we know how hard to push her versus how much to baby her now that we're past the initial crisis . . . past the first-year mark. There seems to be something profound about that point."

His eyes met mine for the first time since his admission. "Well, for one thing, that's how long we agreed to wait before splitting."

A chill crept through me, one that defied the thermal sleeping bag. But he was right. Our divorce had been imminent before the accident because of financial stress, his drinking, my longing to go back to college. We'd only delayed him moving out to give Rosalynn time to heal. Ourselves too, perhaps. As I felt the loss of him all over again, I realized that on some level I'd begun to wonder if his sobriety would bring a change of mind.

And now? I wondered if exactly the opposite was true and if, even stone-cold sober, Grady still welcomed a life separate from me.

CHAPTER TWENTY-FOUR

Lillian

1990: Silver Maple Campground, Virginia

I'd been wrong about a night together being a fitting goodbye for us. Because nothing had changed, except reminding us both how much heartache awaited.

The sun splashed its first rays across our campsite, glowing like the inside of a Georgia peach as we packed our gear without speaking. Grady dismantled the tent while I gathered the trash and tied the plastic bag. I couldn't decide if silence was better than anger. In Grady's case, he was both quiet and grumpy.

Because we'd overslept? Albeit by only a half hour, which was still an hour earlier than I would have preferred. Or because he regretted our impulsive night? The thought hurt.

Swiping up a forgotten napkin, I walked toward the trash bin around the corner. I needed some distance from his broad shoulders showcased to perfection in a fire department T-shirt. Passing the other campsites along the way poured salt on my wounded heart. Families pitched in loading, laughing and working together. Couples, both young and old, shared easy conversation and breakfast by the fire.

So natural. So simple. Why couldn't that happen for me or for my family? I let myself sink so deeply into the pity party I almost missed the voice calling out to me.

"Want some coffee?" a woman shouted from two campsites ahead. A family of four sat around the grated firepit. The father flipped pancakes in a cast iron skillet. "We're Kelly and David. And those two are our daughters."

Their truck sported a Bluegrass State license plate. Protest signs were propped against the tailgate. ACCESS 4 ALL. DISABILITY RIGHTS ARE CIVIL RIGHTS. WHEELS OF JUSTICE.

"Thanks so much. I could use a shot of caffeine. Let me dump the trash first."

Grady would have cautioned me to be careful about approaching strangers, but my heart churned with memories of camping days long ago, of being a part of the campground community. People who'd never met and would likely never cross paths again become temporary friends, sharing company and even food.

Before I could answer, an older couple joined from the neighboring site, carrying a jug of orange juice and a pan of scrambled eggs. They reminded me of Paul Newman and Joanne Woodward, the Hollywood personification of happily ever after.

Forever. What an elusive concept.

The Paul Newman look-alike set down the OJ on the picnic table and spoke to me. "We enjoyed the guitar 'concert' last night, even listening from a distance. Your guy is quite talented. Does he play gigs?"

"Only if you count all the time he spends practicing at work." I tossed one trash bag, then the other, into the silver can hanging from a post. "He's a firefighter. It's not unusual to have a fair amount of downtime between calls."

Kelly served pancakes on paper plates to her teenage twin girls, their permed hair wet. Then she poured coffee into a Styrofoam cup, motioning for me to help myself. "We're here for a protest march in DC to see if we can finally get our government to listen and sign the disability act into law. What brought you two up this way?"

Welcoming the distraction, I accepted the java gratefully, helping myself to cream and sugar to jump-start my morning. "I saw the signs in your truck. We're here for the same reason. Our thirteen-year-old daughter has used a wheelchair since an accident during a ballet performance."

"Where is she?" Kelly looked over her shoulder toward her girls, then back again. "I would love for our twins to meet her and see other kids their age participating."

"Rosalynn's home with my mother. We're still figuring out how to navigate travel with the gear." The excuse, while honest, also felt thin to my own ears. My mind filled with the memory of our sign-making afternoon, with Rosalynn asking me to hold hers extra high. But my fears for her were strong. What if the event turned violent? A thousand other concerns scrolled through my mind beyond just remembering to keep socks on her feet.

Silence settled and I should have just offered my thanks for the coffee and made my way back to our campsite. Still, something made me want to stay in this moment of community awhile longer. Possibly because I wished I could have stayed longer, for more of the speeches and events.

Kelly angled past to grab a stick of margarine from the ice chest. "I bet your daughter's enjoying some spoiling from Grandma."

"No doubt about that. What kind of condition does your child . . . uh . . ." I struggled to find the right words. Had I always been cautious enough about my phrases, realizing how a random expression had the power to hurt?

"Actually," David said, sprinkling chocolate chips into the next batch of pancakes, "I'm the one protesting for my rights. I was diagnosed with multiple sclerosis a couple of years ago. It's under control now, but I'm looking toward the future."

The Paul Newman look-alike poured a glass of OJ for his wife. "We're just here because this moment matters."

That simple.

Those words reminded me of my purpose and what I'd set out to accomplish. As much as I hoped for peace with Grady, I'd taken a step backward by sharing a sleeping bag with him last night. I needed to tread warily in what time we had left. This trip was about our daughter and so many others.

For months, I'd written letters to my congressmen until my fingers cramped, without luck—other than one form letter that left me feeling more hopeless and unseen than before. I'd even telephoned, but never made it past a receptionist who promised to relay my concerns.

Yeah right. As my mama would say, *I didn't just fall off the turnip truck.*

I did mean what I'd told Grady about being careful and keeping my end of the protest peaceful. I had respect for the law and playing by the rules. However, politely playing by the rules from a distance wasn't working.

I'd seen Rosalynn struggle to navigate her new reality, and if there was anything I could do—any mountain to move—I would lean into it for her sake. My daughter was safe in South Carolina, which left me free to grab my megaphone and make some noise.

A couple of hours later, Grady and I had driven into the heart of our nation's capital—my first trip to DC. Growing up, there hadn't been the money. As an adult, there hadn't been the time. Our drive had turned quiet, other than my occasional updates on directions as I followed the map in our worn atlas. No roadside shouting matches this time.

Now, window rolled down, I stuck my head out like an eager puppy and soaked up the landmarks, physical manifestations of the laws I'd studied in my paralegal training. The rumble of bumper-to-bumper traffic was so much louder than even South Carolina's big cities or beach traffic.

If only we could stay longer and tour all the sites—from the majestic Washington Monument to the stunning Rose Garden. My wish list for sightseeing grew longer the more I flipped through the brochures I'd picked up at a rest stop. I would have loved to take my mother to the National Gallery of Art and Rosalynn to the Kennedy Center for the Performing Arts. I could barely contain the urge to ask Grady for an extra loop, but parking was a bear and we'd finally found a spot to wedge our old minivan.

Since there wasn't room to open the back hatch, I had to crawl through to retrieve our supplies. Two backpacks, a pair of signs, and one megaphone later, we started running the winding and long trek to the White House. My steps hammered the pavement as we wove past pedestrians, food trucks, and newspaper stands that were looking to make extra cash off the protestors.

Already I heard voices carrying on the wind. Just the chitter-chatter kind since the protest hadn't begun in earnest. Megaphone in one hand, posters tucked under my other arm, I jogged alongside Grady, leaning forward to balance out the weight of my backpack.

I'd brought sweet tea and snacks. True to my Carolina roots, I knew how to feed a crowd.

There was an urgency here at odds with the laid-back Southern pace, and it went beyond the day's event. But then life had seemed to move faster the farther we drove north, a Southern drawl speeding to a staccato Northern accent. I wanted to slow down and savor every second, but I also didn't want to miss out on even a minute of the main event because of my sluggish approach to mornings.

"Grady, wait," I called, out of breath and trying to keep up. His fitness far outstripped mine, thanks to his firefighter workout regimen. "I don't want to lose you."

The instant the words fell out, they chilled my insides. *I don't want to lose you.*

Now wasn't the time to ask if he'd heard a double meaning, then explain that of course I didn't want to lose what we'd once shared. The good days in the beginning, when Rosalynn had just started sleeping through the night. We had been flat broke, but still enjoyed the simple moments. A day at the lake. A hike in the woods. A late-night video rental.

"Lillian, our destination is in sight." His aviator sunglasses shielded his eyes from view as he stopped at a clogged crosswalk. An overwhelmed police officer was trying to herd people toward the White House. "We're both heading to the same place. I think that's a pretty hefty landmark for a meetup."

Thank heaven for the teasing tone in his voice or I would have taken offense. My emotions were tender. He slid my backpack off and hitched it over his shoulder to ease my burden even as he carried his own.

The stitch in my side faded and I snuck a glance at him. "About last night . . ."

"We're still attracted to each other." He adjusted his ball cap, a sure sign he had more to say but held back. "Let's leave it at that."

I should have been relieved. And I was. But disappointment invaded like kudzu, growing roots with every step. "Yes, I agree. Except when we camp tonight, I don't want either of us to assume anything."

"No worries. I know exactly where we stand." His jaw tensed as he charged forward, the foot traffic growing thicker as we approached the White House.

"Hey Grady?" I clasped his arm to stop him mid-step by the iron security fence.

"Yeah?"

The milling people crowded us. We were so close, the air filled with the scent of his spicy aftershave. His forehead was still furrowed with worry. I wanted to smooth my fingers along the familiar lines of his face and say just the right words to bring that peace I'd sought when starting this trip.

I was coming to realize that after all this time, if there had been a magic phrase, we would have already said it. So since I couldn't fix the larger issue, I opted to offer him reassurance on at least one point.

"I heard what you said yesterday and I'll be careful." But *loud.* Couldn't a person be both? Although even before I completed the thought, I began to wonder. "Is that another reason you came with me? To keep me out of harm's way? I thought you were here because you believe in what we're doing and, yes, because I guilted you into participating."

"I want you and Rosalynn to be safe. That's my most important job in life."

There was an earnestness in his tone, a husky ache that sounded like my spouse from the early days of our marriage. When we could be honest with each other—and ourselves—without fear of vulnerability. I set the megaphone onto a bench and reached to slide his shades up and bask in the warmth of his chocolate-colored eyes.

The sound of traffic, cheers, and chatter faded. How easy it would be to arch up on my toes and kiss him.

"Mom . . . Mom . . ." A shout pierced the bubble and I stepped back, releasing his sunglasses.

That voice sounded familiar. But surely that was just because I missed my daughter. Didn't all mothers turn upon hearing the magical words *mom*, *mother*, *mama*?

Except the shock on Grady's face as he looked over my shoulder gave me only an instant's warning before a pair of shadows stretched past.

Rosalynn stopped her wheelchair and threw her arms wide. "Surprise!"

CHAPTER TWENTY-FIVE

Elsie

2026: Outskirts of Nowheresville, North Carolina

Have I got a surprise for you! The text from her father buzzed into Elsie's cell. Dots scrolled, then the rest of his message appeared. Phone me back. Great news. Miss you, kiddo.

Elsie had ignored two calls from her dad in the past hour rather than explode at him. Great news? Her world currently sucked. Porter's fault. And hers for being gullible. Still, none of that made her dad any less of a jerk, so he could just wait for a response while she figured out how to access her college fund and pay off Porter to delete those photos. Because even though the texter had tried to be "anonymous," she wasn't so easily fooled anymore.

Outside a Podunk repair shop, she kicked the old soda machine that had eaten all her change without releasing a drink. What should have been a short drive from the motel to the hospice facility in Alexandria had already been derailed after less than an hour. They'd barely made it onto the interstate before the van's back hatch had popped open, compliments of the damage from yesterday's accident.

Luckily, no suitcases and none of her mom's equipment had fallen out—three cheers for bungee cords—but Elsie mourned the loss of her favorite pillow, which had been flattened by a passing truck full of chickens.

Rude.

After a frantic pullover on the side of the road to close and secure the hatch—again, cheers for multifunctional bungee cords—they'd been forced to detour to the nearest repair shop.

By the looks of the run-down place, they might never get back on the road again. Her mom and Grammie were arguing with Scooter the Mechanic, who'd insisted he would have to wait for a part to be delivered. Surely the graveyard of wrecked cars behind the cinder-block building had something that would work.

Elsie kicked the old Coke machine again until finally, the *clunk, clunk, clunk* echoed. A bottle rolled into the tray. She wrapped both hands around the cold drink and scouted for a shady spot since the tiny waiting area was packed with sweaty people. Plus somebody had reheated fried fish in the microwave and stunk up the place.

Better to use the time outside in the muggy heat under the shade of a sprawling red maple tree researching community colleges. She'd already registered for the GED and scouted out part-time jobs near Grammie's. Elsie dropped to the ground and leaned back against the trunk, googling options while sipping her cold Coke. Maybe a detailed budget would convince her mom to release the funds. When the time came to actually pay the bill, Elsie could apply for a school loan—

Another text from her father buzzed through.

Then another.

Followed by a simple question mark. Again. And again.

When she'd done that same thing to him, she'd never considered he would use the tactic on her.

A GIF came through this time, of a cartoon character tapping his watch.

GIFs. Ugh.

Something else she'd taught her father and now he used them for everything. Like that little impersonal blip constituted a meaningful exchange.

Sighing, Elsie resisted the urge to send him a GIF of a middle finger and video-called her dad. "Hey, what's the big surprise?"

"Took you long enough to phone me back," he teased, his smile wide as he sat on a hotel bed. He probably had the air conditioner set to subarctic levels.

Just as well to let him see where she was seated by comparison. Did the man have no shame?

She scratched the toe of her shoe over her ankle to dislodge a hungry mosquito. "Where are you?"

"Still in Biloxi." He flipped the phone orientation to showcase the view outside his window. Waterfront. With a riverboat a stone's throw away. "How about you? Did y'all make it up to Lillian's yet?"

Had he missed the car graveyard towering in the background?

"Nope. We're getting the van repaired at some mom-and-pop shop." Her mother wouldn't have had to ask her location. She would have tracked Elsie's cell phone down to the mile marker, every minute of the trip. Such as the time she'd been next to a boat repair shop and her mom had been convinced she was being abducted, like in some episode of *Dexter*.

That had always bugged her. But right now? It seemed kinda caring in light of her dad's neglect. "Do you want to know what's wrong with it?"

He turned the phone back toward his face. "Sure. Do tell."

If he'd really wanted to know, she wouldn't have had to prompt him. And that pissed her off.

"The back hatch flew open on the interstate." The words tumbled out of her mouth fast and furious. "We almost got creamed by a semi."

Sure, she'd exaggerated. Was it so wrong to want him to feel a smidge guilty for hanging out in that icy hotel room while they struggled? They could have met the same fate as her pillow.

"Wow, Elsie, glad you're all okay. Sounds like it could have been worse."

He had a way of minimizing stuff to cut himself slack. Classic loser move.

She needed to remember to fight against those genes, to think of others. She hadn't even asked him about his trip. Not really. "Are y'all getting any bad weather there?"

"Clear skies all around." He adjusted the fluffy pillow behind his head. "The storm seems to be rolling up the coastline following your path. Are you catching any rain?"

"We get little sprinkles every now and again." She'd had it with this superficial conversation. She needed her dad to be *real.* "I'm kinda worried about Mom driving back, though. Hopefully Grammie can convince her to stick around until the storm cleanup is under control and they stop rationing fuel."

"Your mother is strong-willed, but she's also one of the most competent people I've ever known. If she decides to go home, no one can stop her, and she will make the journey in record time."

That felt like another cop-out. Just because a person was an over-achiever didn't mean everyone else could bail on helping. "How much longer are you going to stay there?"

"I had planned to go home tonight, but that brings me to the surprise I wanted to tell you about." His grin spread wider. "I've hit a winning streak. So I think I'm going to stick around awhile longer."

"That's great, Dad." She tried to fake enthusiasm even though she knew his "win" would just cause another argument between her parents. Then an idea tugged at her. One that seemed too good to be true. "How big of a winning streak?"

"Five figures, baby girl," he said with the same overconfidence she'd seen dozens of times. "*High* five figures."

"That's incredible," she said, rather than discourage him. Because right now, she needed a piece of that good fortune. "I was hoping to go ahead and start college early. But Mom keeps changing the subject every time I talk about cashing in the savings. I think she's worried about money with the move."

Twirling a loose lock of hair, she studied his face as she tested the waters. Just before she'd returned his call, she'd spotted a community college that looked affordable. Earlier in the day, she'd made a list of ways she could help her grandmother and Ace.

Her father fidgeted with his college ring, and a twinge of anxiety shot through her. Somebody should let him know that was a "poker tell" that said he probably only had a pair of twos.

"Well, Elsie, I think you should listen to your mother."

She deflated in disappointment, the bark rough against her tank top. She twisted the lock of hair tighter around her finger until it tugged at the roots. But she wasn't accepting defeat. He could bluff all he wanted. She was every bit as stubborn as her mama and grandmother.

"I shouldn't stress her out, what with the divorce and all." Elsie wasn't above applying a little guilt-pressure herself. "I really want to go ahead and start college. I've signed up for the GED—I passed the practice test easy. I've even looked up how to emancipate so y'all won't have to worry about me anymore. I thought I might move up to Alexandria and spend some time with Ace, because he's, you know . . ."

With all the other awful things going on in her life, she couldn't bring herself to say the words. Like if she didn't speak it out loud, then maybe he would live longer.

"Elsie, the last thing your grandmother needs is someone else to take care of right now."

She tried not to bristle. Since when was she a burden?

"Exactly. I will help her. It'll be easier for Mom too, not to have to worry about me. So if you could use some of the money you won to pay for my first semester, I could prove that I'm every bit as determined as she is. How about giving me your account info now so I can go ahead and pass it along to the college."

"This sounds like a mighty big plan. Does your mom know about it?"

"Yes." She nodded fast, wincing at the yank to the strand of hair. "I've talked to both Mom and Grammie."

No need to confess they both hated the idea.

He spun the clunky gold band faster, the red gem flashing like a hazard light. "I'm not sure I should do something like that without checking with your mother first."

Now, of all times, he decided to be a parent rather than a buddy? Where had he been when she would have given anything for fatherly help, guidance, support? What would it be like to have the kind of dad she could trust to fix her colossal problem?

"Daddy, please, just think about it." She hated that she sounded desperate. Even kinda pathetic. But she was so scared. More than she'd ever been in her whole life. "What if your win is a sign?"

His hand fell from his jaw and he nodded. "You may have a point there. I'm a big believer in luck."

Her hopeful heart just about leaped out of her chest. To think her problem could be solved without her mother knowing—without her dad learning her secret either—was more than she could have hoped for. "Then this is my lucky day too."

"Well, baby girl," he said, sitting upright and swinging his legs off the hotel bed, "I need to make hay while the sun's shining."

"What do you mean?" she asked, confused at his shift. "Are you going home? What about the hurricane?"

"Exactly. I'm going back to the casino and make the most of this streak of good fortune." He straightened the collar on his polo shirt. "By tomorrow morning, I bet I'll have enough to cover your whole four-year degree."

Back to the casino. More gambling.

Her heart fell to the pit of her stomach, and all those arguments between her parents played on repeat in her head. Of the time her dad lost their down payment for Rosalynn's new van by betting on a horse race. Or when he'd lied about joining Gamblers Anonymous and her mom found out because of credit card purchases at a pool hall when he was supposed to be at meetings.

As she remembered the aftermath of that rough time, her gaze went to the rotating Goodyear tire sign that held the name of Scooter's garage. Even though her dad wouldn't darken the doorstep of Gamblers Anonymous, her mother had taken Elsie along to some of the support groups for families, which had been totally embarrassing. But also informative enough that Elsie wanted to kick herself for believing that he was serious about cashing in his chips.

By tomorrow morning, he wouldn't have anything left.

There was no easy way out for her. She was going to have to find someone to trust.

And soon.

CHAPTER TWENTY-SIX

Lillian

1990: Washington, DC

Surprised?

More like stunned at my mother and Rosalynn's arrival.

Steadying myself, I grabbed a post on the black metal fence outside the White House for so long I feared my feet would take root clean through the concrete. I still could barely process what my eyes were seeing. Rosalynn and my mother waited an arm's reach away. Here. In front of 1600 Pennsylvania Avenue.

My daughter wore a tie-dyed shirt with *Access 4 All* written in permanent marker. Her green eyes glimmered with excitement, an echo of the exhilaration of the gathering crowd.

Della sported a smile full of chagrin along with a homemade sign with a flag. The stars were shaped like a wheelchair. "I'm glad to see you remembered my megaphone."

In her signature passive-aggressive approach to life, she'd left me no choice but to swallow my anger.

"Rosalynn?" I looked from one to the other. "Mom? What are you two doing here?"

I stepped closer to make way for a pair of power wheelchairs, followed by a woman echoing the protest cries in American Sign Language and a veteran in camo with a vested German shepherd.

Rosalynn propelled her chair forward, her hair in a French braid with a patriotic bow. "This is the adventure I was telling you about on the phone. We're here to join in the demonstration."

That pay-phone conversation at the rest stop yesterday seemed a lifetime ago. "I was thinking more along the lines of you baking a welcome home cake."

"Boring," Rosalynn said with a thumbs-down. "You two don't get to have all the fun. I almost slipped up and told you, which would have spoiled the whole effect. Nana Della caught me just in time."

Of course she had. Because if I'd known, I never would have allowed it. My mother would have realized that. Mama's eyes met mine dead-on, as if daring me to pitch a hissy fit here in the middle of the street.

In front of my daughter, who looked happier than I'd seen her in a year.

Sighing, I backed down. For now. For Rosalynn, I would table the conversation with my mother until my daughter was out of earshot. And there would definitely be a conversation. Because I was madder than a wet hen that my mother had planned all this behind my back when I'd explicitly wanted the emotional security of knowing my daughter was safe at home during the event.

The whole reason we were marching was because people like Rosalynn didn't always have clear paths and safe access to public facilities. Today, the limited access would be all the more stressful for the hundreds crowded into the street who needed adaptive devices for safe navigation.

Rosalynn's gaze tracked the shepherd service dog with longing, before continuing, "Aren't you happy to see us?"

Happy? Not the word I would have chosen. "I'm always happy to see you."

I wrapped her in a hug, so thankful she'd made the trip unscathed. My mind scrolled with dozens of ways the journey could have gone dangerously wrong. My worry for my child went so deep, I couldn't imagine a time it wouldn't motivate my every decision.

Grady knelt beside her chair. "Hello there, Princess. You're a sight for sore eyes. I've missed you."

They'd always been close. She was a daddy's girl. I often wondered if my father had been as sweet with me. I had so few memories of him, since he'd died when I was three—only a vague recollection of him pushing me on a swing at the park. Or was that something I'd created from other people's stories about him?

My heart ached for my daughter and how she would handle news of the divorce. Sure, Grady was often gone for overnight shifts at the firehouse—more since the accident when we needed the money. But they'd grown even closer since he'd stopped drinking, and she'd even started asking to take cookies to him at the fire station sometimes or plan special family meals for when he came home. Having him move out altogether would be painful for her.

For all of us.

"Dad, the airplane ride was awesome. The flight attendant gave me extra snacks and told me about the time the singer Debbie Gibson was on her flight."

"Sounds like you charmed them," he said.

Rosalynn blushed. "I explained we were coming to participate in the protest. They thought I was young, but Nana Della said you're never too young to learn about what's going on in our government."

"Your nana has a point," he agreed, a far-from-subtle dig at our arguments about me sheltering her. "See those two girls over there, the ones about your age with the curly hair? They were at our campground. Would you like to talk with them?"

"Can I, Dad?" She turned toward me. "Mom?"

Her eyes were so hopeful—so hungry—I realized how little time she'd spent with kids her own age in the past year when friends were especially important at this age. All her friendships before the accident had been formed through dance classes and ballet productions. Those children and their parents had visited the hospital often at first, then faded away in the weeks that passed. They'd moved on with their lives and lessons, while our path diverted to surgeries and rehabs.

Standing, Grady touched my arm lightly. "We'll stay within eyesight. I promise."

I remembered his worries for me to be careful and stay safe. Maybe he understood my concerns for Rosalynn better than I'd realized. Reluctantly, I nodded.

Rosalynn grabbed my hand and squeezed hard. "Thanks, Mom." She glanced up at Grady. "Ready when you are."

He grasped the handles on her wheelchair and steered her past a police officer on his walkie-talkie. Someone near us turned up a boom box. The sounds of Bob Dylan's "The Times They Are a-Changin'" earned cheers from a few bystanders. The energy in the crowd was multiplying, but I was still stuck in my head, angry with my mama.

Once Rosalynn and Grady safely reached the twins, I pivoted to face her. "Mother—"

Della cut me off short. "You and Grady look closer, with those old sparks flying."

"That's the last thing on my mind right now," I snapped, not entirely truthfully. "What are you doing here?"

"Rosalynn wanted to participate." My mother shrugged, pushing a wayward cluster of gray curls from her face. "It's a grandmother's job to indulge. I just couldn't tell her no."

After I specifically *had* told my daughter no.

Did Della not understand the risks she'd taken with this "surprise" of hers? Grinding my teeth, I steered her away from a couple passing out rolled-up copies of the Declaration of Independence. Finding a private corner was tough with the growing crowd of protestors, press, and police officers, not to mention service dogs, who reminded me of another subject where my mother had interfered without asking first.

I stepped closer and kept my voice low.

"This isn't like attending a local baseball game or grabbing an extra ice cream sandwich. This . . ." Words failed me when it came to the magnitude of my mother's betrayal. I opted for a simpler question to give myself time to rein in my anger. "How did you even pay for the trip?"

She rested her sign against the iron fence and patted her fanny pack. "Some folks at weekly bingo overheard me talking about wishing Rosalynn could come along. Apparently, I helped someone's grandchild at the laundromat when he was in college. They reached out to others and took up a collection. It was enough to finance both our tickets—first class, no less—and two nights in a hotel suite for all four of us."

"That must have been some very successful college grad to chip in so much," I said dryly, a little enviously too. I'd wanted to finish college, but the cost . . . Graduation was out of reach. Night school to become a paralegal had made more sense.

"Dozens of people contributed. They wanted to be a part of the march in their own way. This is an important moment."

Her words reminded me of the couple at the campground, choosing to participate because it "mattered." My anger at my mom faded a hint even though I could not agree with her method and choices. Not when it affected my child's well-being.

I forced a smile. "Mom, we'll talk more later, all right?"

Sighing, she grasped my arm to stop me. "I understand you're upset with me for bringing Rosalynn, and I have to say I don't really care. Well, I care, but I'm not sorry."

My anger ignited again, and I struggled hard not to lose my temper right then and there. The last thing I needed was to start a fight that would get us all arrested before today's protests even began.

"You're not sorry?" My body vibrated with frustration. "Don't you understand this is a serious breach of trust? You took my medically fragile child on a plane trip, away from her doctors and support, when I specifically set everything up for her to be safe at home while I'm away."

My mother's lips went tight for a moment, like she was taking a draw off one of those menthol cigarettes she'd given up last year. "If you recall, I was the one who accompanied her to her last appointment. And when you and Grady left yesterday, you gave me medical power of attorney—"

"That can certainly be changed." Anger and fear battled inside me. "Think of all the things that could have gone wrong. What if the flight had been delayed? Or if the airport didn't supply transportation? What if she had a crisis mid-flight?" So many more scenarios played out in my mind now, as they had every night as I lay in bed unable to sleep.

"I cleared the trip with her doctor. Lillian, she wanted to come," Mama said. "I don't think you understand how desperate she is to participate."

"Whoa, hold on a minute." I held up a hand as I began to realize my mother wasn't planning some sidelines viewing with a sign. "You can do whatever you want. But if you think, for even an instant, that I'm going to allow Rosalynn to be in the middle of that march—"

"A peaceful protest—"

"That could turn volatile at any moment," I snapped. Even Grady had to realize his concerns for me were minor in comparison to my need to be cautious with Rosalynn. "She's a child. *My* child. Not yours."

"She's thirteen years old and she's had a year that would age anyone." My mother went toe-to-toe with me right there at the fencing in front of the White House, her voice low, but terse enough to draw a few looks from a nearby couple consulting a map. "She has been at the mercy of so many things beyond her control. Even her own body. Is it any wonder she wants to take charge? Rosalynn needs this every bit as much as you do."

I hated to admit it, but my mother had a point. Even from where I stood on the sidewalk, I could see Rosalynn engaged in animated conversation with the other teens, her body language relaxed and happy.

So yes, I understood that maybe this could be a positive experience for her. I just would have appreciated the opportunity to approach the discussion in a different manner, one that added layers of protection for my daughter. I would have studied the schedule of events and chosen the quietest day, making sure she hadn't come over fresh off an exhausting plane ride to participate in a march from the White House to the Capitol.

All moot points now since this had spiraled beyond my control. With Della, Grady, and Rosalynn on the same side against me, I was outnumbered. There was nothing left but to surrender with grace and stick close to my daughter.

"Fine, Mama. Here's your megaphone," I said tightly, thrusting the bright red bullhorn into her free hand. "Let's go make some noise."

CHAPTER TWENTY-SEVEN

Rosalynn

2026: North Carolina / Virginia border

The noise was so deafening in her van with the hatch rattling nonstop, Rosalynn had to take a break at the Virginia state line's welcome center to check the repair. For a moment, she feared that Scooter had lied just to get her out of his hair.

Upon inspection, it appeared he had been true to his word. In fact, she suspected it might never be opened again except with a blowtorch.

Her mother palmed the back window. "We may need earplugs for the rest of the trip, but our luggage is secure."

Rosalynn adjusted her hold on Dusty's leash. "We might as well take a break. Hopefully our last."

Elsie snorted. "I wouldn't bet on that. Luck has *not* been on our side. I'm gonna hit the vending machines."

Lillian frowned, her gaze tracking her granddaughter. "I'm worried about her. Maybe we should consider letting her stay with me—"

"Absolutely not. She's my daughter. If you have extra time on your hands, consider running for Congress." Rosalynn wheeled her chair backward. "I'm taking Dusty over to the grass. The concrete is too hot for his paws."

She and her mother both could use a break from each other. They had their prickly moments on the best of days, and this trip was far from ideal conditions. And truth be told, she was hurt that her mom hadn't shared about the political nod, even if she planned to turn it down. The secrecy made her feel disconnected at a time she needed what bonds she had left in her life.

Even Elsie wanted to box her out.

Seizing a moment to nurse her bruised heart, Rosalynn wheeled along the paved path, in the opposite direction from the dog park. She trusted Dusty's temperament, but she couldn't guarantee other dogs were vaccinated and well mannered.

This should be their last delay and she intended to make the most of it for Dusty. Her dog had great nerve strength, disposition, and endurance, but the hospital, the hotel, and then the body shop had stacked considerable stressors.

On the far side of the brick welcome center, she set the brakes beside a park bench.

"Dusty, brace," she cued, positioning her hands on his shoulders. Her legs trembled but held long enough for her to shift onto the wrought iron seat.

Sure, she could have stayed in her chair, but she was cautious about pressure sores. She would be spending the rest of the day either in the van or in her chair at the hospice facility.

She gave Dusty the full length of his leash so he could sniff to his heart's content, from the lush grass to a cluster of marigolds. His tail wagged, picking up speed. Until she'd had a service dog, she hadn't realized how important exploring smells could be for a dog's mental health. She'd learned so much from her first service dog, Peaches, an apricot-colored standard-size poodle. She'd been paired with Peaches as a high school sophomore after waiting endlessly for the right match.

She'd been surprised to learn the training process took approximately two years. She wouldn't receive her dog until he or she had completed schooling, since well over half of the puppies washed out of the program.

Luckily, Peaches had been picture-perfect, because in those days, Rosalynn had already been struggling to adapt. Becoming a service dog handler had been an additional challenge, beyond learning the dozens of cues. But after she'd begged her parents to investigate an organization, pride kept her from admitting there were days she felt so overwhelmed she couldn't imagine how she would build a future for herself, much less care for this beautiful furry creature.

Thankfully, once her parents made the decision to apply for an assistance animal, they were all in. Her father had even learned to groom Peaches to save money. Rosalynn suspected he also took on the task to steal time for himself with her dog, especially in those early days when Peaches needed to bond with Rosalynn, crucial for their working relationship.

That bond had carried her through the toughest of times during her senior year in high school, on that gut-wrenching day she'd been called out of English class. She knew it had to be serious to pull her from a semester exam. She'd only been called from class once before, when her father had been hurt during a warehouse fire.

This time, though, was far worse.

Her father had been seriously injured on the job during a five-alarm fire in a historic home. The flames engulfed the aged timber. The house collapsed and doctors weren't sure if her father would survive. Peaches's fur had soaked up Rosalynn's tears in the hospital waiting room. By the time she'd cried herself out, Rosalynn understood that their connection was about more than simple movements.

Now her cell phone chimed in the side pouch on her chair, likely Lillian or Elsie looking for her. Rosalynn shook off the weighty past just as Dusty's head popped up from sniffing around the base of an oak. He ambled over and put his paws on the wheelchair seat, nudging his head into the pouch until he came back out with the cell phone in his mouth.

She extended a hand. "Drop."

Dusty released the device onto her palm, then sat waiting for either a treat or direction on what to do next. Maybe both. She fished a piece of kibble from her pocket while checking her screen.

Seth? As much as she wanted to ignore him, he could be phoning about their house or something else in their small beach community. Her chest went tight.

She reached for Dusty with one hand as she cradled her cell in the other and thumbed to activate the FaceTime call. "Seth? Is the house okay?" She hated that he looked so put-together when she had "travel-weary" stamped all over her. "I haven't been able to reach the Realtor."

"I haven't heard anything. I'm still in Biloxi."

Of course he was. Even though he'd positioned himself beside a potted palm near an elevator, she could hear the bells and chimes of slot machines in the background. "Why are you calling?"

She breathed in the scent of late-blooming flowers, struggling to maintain patience.

"Hey, babe, no need to be curt like that. I'm just checking if you got your van fixed."

She hated it when he called her "babe." She should have written that into their divorce decree. *No more infantilizing labels.* "How did you know about the repairs?"

"Elsie told me when I spoke with her this morning."

Rosalynn winced at yet another instance of being shut out by her daughter. Dusty looked up at her with wide chocolate eyes, and she motioned a release cue for him to resume his sniffing.

"All's fine." She hoped.

"The garage looked pretty run-down when Elsie and I FaceTimed. Are you sure you're safe to be on the road?"

She wanted to hang up on him. "It was a small shop, but they got us up and running again quickly for a decent price." Thanks to pulling a part off a wrecked van in their junkyard and some spot welding for good measure. "If that's all, I need to go."

Elsie was sitting on the hood of the van eating a bag of chips while scrolling on her phone. Lillian was on her phone as well. How had people managed to travel back in the day with only pay phones and a prayer?

"Hold on," Seth interjected. "There's actually one more thing."

Of course there was. If he asked for a loan because he'd "come up a little short," she *would* hang up. "What do you need?"

"Something's off with Elsie." His face creased with genuine concern. He did love their daughter. "She's never been a good liar. She has that tell when she's in trouble. You know . . ."

"When she twirls her hair." Rosalynn's gaze shifted to Elsie. She *had* been quiet today, more so than regular teenage sulk.

Her maternal instincts tugged that there was more to Elsie's moods than adjusting to a divorce. There had to be something seriously wrong for Seth to notice.

"Right. That. When I was talking to her, she just about snatched herself bald."

"Do you have any idea why?"

Frowning, Seth thumbed his college ring around and around on his finger, red stone flashing. "She asked me for money."

Rosalynn almost burst out laughing. Then the amusement faded. Her daughter had to know that well was dry. "Why would she do that?"

"I'm, uh, having a winning streak. I told her and she wanted to use some of it. Something about paying for a semester of college. She said she's moving in with Lillian. I can't imagine you're okay with that. But Elsie said she told you."

"Oh, she told me. That doesn't mean I agreed with her." If Elsie thought she would cave on this, her daughter had a rude awakening ahead of her. "About your winning streak. You could earmark some of that for child support."

"If Elsie is moving out . . ."

Seriously?

She'd known he would make excuses not to contribute to Elsie's care, but that he would kick her out of the nest early to dodge paying for school clothes was pathetic. Even for Seth. "You really are a lowlife."

"You can't talk to me that way anymore. We're not married."

"What are you going to do about it? Not pay child support? Oh, that's right. You already don't." That man would be lucky if she restrained herself from running over his feet with her wheelchair the next time she saw him. "Thanks for the heads-up about Elsie. Goodbye."

A deep bark echoed in the distance, growing louder, closer. She disconnected the call and scanned the rest stop area, on guard for an out-of-control critter. Sure enough, a leggy Great Dane galloped past the brick welcome center, leash trailing. A young boy ran after him, elementary age with legs too short to catch up. Panic swelled, increasing like a neuropathy flare.

Dusty popped up from smelling a honeysuckle bush. His head swiveled to the loose dog, then back to Rosalynn.

Her grip tightened on the tether. "Dusty, come."

He hesitated, just for a split second, but one that threw fuel on her fears for him. Images flooded her mind of her sweet boy trapped in a dogfight, and she couldn't protect him.

The Labrador cast one more glance at the animal before trotting back to Rosalynn. She heaved a sigh of relief.

A temporary reprieve.

The Great Dane powered on, closer, closer still. Rosalynn eyed her chair. But there wouldn't be time to make the transfer, and even if she did, that wouldn't keep Dusty out of the other dog's path.

"Mom," she shouted, her voice mixing with barking and the child's squeals to *stop, wait, stop, wait*. "Elsie? Come quick."

Dusty pressed tighter against her, shielding her with his body. His devotion, his selflessness, increased her terror for him just as the Great Dane closed the gap, slamming into her dog.

The leash went taut in Rosalynn's hand.

Her body jerked. Her arms flew out defensively as she tumbled from the bench onto the hard packed earth.

CHAPTER TWENTY-EIGHT

Elsie

2026: North Carolina / Virginia border

Elsie wasn't sure if the cry she heard came from herself or someone else, but no doubt, a shriek was swelling inside her. Sitting on the hood of the van, she gripped her cell phone and stared at the screen in horror. The wind freed a shower of pine needles from the tree shading her, raining on her like pinpricks.

One of those seminude images had been posted on social media. Anonymously. She hadn't been tagged in the image, but Willow had messaged her privately.

It was the same photo she'd been texted with the demand for money, taken in the bathhouse shower, an image from the back. She was smiling over her shoulder. Like she wanted the picture taken, when in fact she'd been totally unaware of the hidden camera.

She understood she'd just been grinning at Willow's joke after a fun day boating at camp. But to anyone seeing the pic? It looked like she'd posed. More than ever, she was certain Porter was behind this, upping the heat to pry money from her.

Sweat beaded on her forehead.

Even knowing the Snapchat message would disappear when seen didn't make her feel one bit better. If even one person took a screenshot before the photo timed out and erased . . .

Another shout split the air.

Definitely not from her this time.

Was that her mom? And barking too, but it didn't sound like Dusty, and the working dog almost never made a sound.

"Elsie, Mom!" Rosalynn's cries carried on the wind. "I need help."

"Mom?" Elsie scrambled off the hood of the van and hopped to the ground.

Her mother shouted again, the cry sweeping aside Elsie's panic over the image on her cell phone. She scanned the rest stop, with no sign of her mom. A handful of tourists wandered back to their cars, glancing toward the far side of the welcome center but keeping their distance.

Losers.

She sprinted toward the sound, tucking her cell phone into her back pocket. She passed the brick center just as Grammie rushed out from the restroom.

"Elsie?" Lillian gasped. "Where's your mother? Did I hear her call out?"

"Yes. This way. Something's wrong," Elsie hollered over her shoulder, her feet pounding the ground as hard as her heart hitting her ribs.

She rounded the corner, behind the welcome center, and blinked in shock at the chaos. Her mom lay on the ground by a bench. Dusty was draped over her, and a big Great Dane–looking dog raced in circles around them.

A kid was clapping his hands. "Juniper, no. Juniper, come, girl, come . . ."

The child's rambling shouts only amped the huge canine into running faster, a frenetic ball of leggy energy. Her paws tore up the earth, sending clods of dirt every which way. Rosalynn had her arms wrapped around Dusty until Elsie couldn't tell for sure who was protecting who. The thought of either of them being injured . . . Elsie ran faster, hopping over a bush and sidestepping a trash can.

She didn't bother wasting time on a plan. Lunging between her mother and Juniper, she grabbed the loose dog by the animal's rhinestone collar. And wow, the big ole beast was strong. Hopefully she wasn't a biter. Elsie shuddered.

"Enough. Sit." She planted her feet firmer and prayed the dog would obey.

Thankfully, Juniper froze, then dropped to her bottom. Although her massive size nearly pulled Elsie over.

The gap-toothed boy scooped up Juniper's loose leash. "Thanks, lady. Sorry. Come on, Juniper."

Elsie kept her hold on the dog, not trusting this child could control such a massive animal. "Where are your parents?"

His eyes went wide. "Please don't tell my mom. Give me the leash. I'll hold on tight this time. I promise."

Elsie understood all too well the fear of parental disapproval. Especially right now. Her cell phone all but burned through her back pocket.

But she couldn't just hand over—

"Juniper," a squeaky, panicked voice called out just before a harried-looking woman sprinted into sight, baggy T-shirt declaring I LOVE MY GREAT DANE.

Apparently, she didn't love her Great Dane enough to keep the dog safe.

The boy's eyes went wider and he whispered, "Please, please don't tell my mother it's my fault."

Grammie jogged up behind her, breathlessly. Lillian's jaw jutted with an expression not too different from when she walker-keyed the car at the hotel.

The mom stopped short, her eyes going wide as she took in Rosalynn and Dusty on the ground, then the wheelchair beside the bench. "Are you okay?"

Rosalynn sat up, an arm still wrapped around Dusty. "We're fine."

"Thank heaven." The mother took the leash from Elsie's hand and glared at the boy. "Tell these ladies you're sorry."

"But Mom, I was just walking Juniper like you—"

"Say. You're. Sorry."

He scuffed his toe along the grass, kicking a dirt clod. "Sorry."

Seemed to Elsie the lady was the one who should be apologizing for not having control of her kid and dog. And maybe all those people in the parking lot who'd ignored calls for help should apologize for being pathetic humans.

The woman rolled her eyes. "Are y'all sure you're okay? Looks like the dogs didn't tussle too hard."

Grammie took a step forward. She had on her lawyer eyes. The ones that had made Elsie confess at four years old when Grammie asked who ate all the cookies she was saving for after dinner.

Even though the look wasn't directed at Elsie now, she had to look away in fear she would blurt out her current secrets—so much worse than stolen peanut butter crinkles.

Rosalynn rested a hand on her mom's arm. "Not now. I don't want this to explode into something that freaks out Dusty."

Dusty was in full-on Velcro-dog mode, pressing against Rosalynn. Her mom was always extra careful about Dusty not being pushed too far for fear the stress might cause him to retire early.

The mother tugged her son by one arm, clutching the leash in her other hand. "Well, we'll get Juniper out of your way."

Once the leggy Great Dane ambled off, Dusty drew in a shuddering sigh.

Same, pup. Same.

Elsie crouched by her mother, trying to find a safe place for her hands to land but needing to check for injuries. "Are you hurt? Don't move too fast."

"I'm fine. I'll have a couple of bruises—including one to my dignity—but I'm not injured. I've taken worse tumbles getting out of bed in the morning."

Her mother was trying to minimize, like always in her Super Mom fashion. Somehow, though, Elsie knew Rosalynn wouldn't be minimizing the sketchy photos and blackmail.

Lillian knelt beside them, her hands skimming Rosalynn's legs and feet. "Where did you hit the ground?"

Rosalynn batted away Grammie's hands. "I said I'm fine. I broke the fall with my arms." She held up her scraped palms as proof, the skin all red and angry.

Elsie winced. "We need to wash those off. Let me help you back into your chair."

Shaking her head, Lillian pulled out her phone. "No, I think we should just call for an ambulance."

"Mother," Rosalynn hissed. "I'm drawing the line. I don't need a second visit from EMS in less than twenty-four hours. Help me get back into the chair. No more delays when we are so close to the end of the trip."

Elsie rocked back on her heels and sat on the grass. "I don't know, Mom. Maybe Grammie is right."

"I'm more concerned for my dog." Rosalynn picked a leaf from his fur. "If there's a problem, I'll have a doctor look me over once we arrive. Fair enough?"

Lillian crossed her arms. "Okay, for now. Although I reserve the right to change my mind."

Elsie sagged in relief the matter had been settled, and that Lillian was there to make the call for help if needed. Then close on the heels of that thought, another iced through her.

What if something like this happened and Rosalynn was alone? Sure, her mom had a red emergency button in her house that was a direct line to 9-1-1, and Dusty knew how to smack it with his paws. But right now, that didn't feel like reassurance enough.

Guilt swamped her for wanting to emancipate, to run away. She should have never put herself in the position where she *had* to leave. It sucked having control over her future stolen.

"Mom," Elsie declared. "If you want to go, then that's what we're doing."

Standing, Elsie slid her arms around her mother's torso and lifted. Grammie clasped one of Rosalynn's hands to add balance. The three of them worked together, hefting and shifting until her mother collapsed back into her seat. Dusty hurried to her side, resting his head on her knee and plastering himself to her thigh again.

Elsie sagged onto the bench, her cell phone pressing into her. At least her mom was okay. One thing to be thankful for in the middle of the doom threatening to swallow her whole. Adrenaline seeped from her as her mind flooded with images of how much worse the loose-dog incident could have turned out.

Posted signs clearly instructed no dogs were allowed off leash around the welcome center. That kid couldn't handle such a large dog and yet the mom had sent him off. Risking his safety too. No one had stepped up to help.

She thought of Grammie's anger at the hotel when the woman boxed in their van, and finally, Elsie really got it. She understood her grandmother's frustration with people who thought the rules didn't apply to them. Folks who didn't consider how those restrictions—hard won—were important to others.

Grammie had spent her life fighting for others, holding people accountable for bad acts. She didn't stand by in a parking lot, looking the other way.

She was brave. She made her voice heard.

Right now, Elsie didn't have a clue how she would find the courage to speak up about the threat on the other side of her cell phone, but she needed to find an opening to tell her mother and Grammie. Soon.

Because time was running out before someone tipped them off.

CHAPTER TWENTY-NINE

Lillian

1990: Washington, DC

"What do we want?" Della shouted through her megaphone.

"Our ADA," I answered with the rest of the marching crowd pushing our way along Pennsylvania Avenue toward the Capitol.

"When do we want it?"

"Now."

The chants continued, like an engine motivating us forward for over an hour as hundreds of people processed toward the Capitol Building, carrying signs declaring . . .

Asking Did Not Work

Equal Access for All

Journalists followed along the outskirts, some even weaving into the crowd, documenting our push for change. Or so we hoped. It could only help our cause to have them capturing us in pictures and videos as we rolled past the National Mall and the Tidal Basin. Past monuments.

Past history.

The air filled with the crackle of hope and frustration. And yes, anger. But there was organization as well, which brought structure to the moment. Momentum grew with each step. The Capitol loomed in the distance, as if on a pedestal with 365 steps leading to the Rotunda.

As far as protest marches went, I'd seen larger on television and in textbooks. But the power of this moment moved me all the same. There was an energy in the air, ignited from being seen as citizens due the same rights as others. Citizens of all ages.

The twins walked on either side of Rosalynn's chair, their teenage voices a high-pitched chorus of cheers. The next generation taking up the cause. The veteran in camo still kept pace ahead of us, his prosthetic leg just barely visible as he walked with his service dog, the German shepherd in its bright yellow vest. A lady wearing a Proud Auntie shirt hooked an arm with a woman wearing sunglasses and using a white cane.

All of us shared a common goal. We needed our country's leaders to understand we were out of patience with their delays. This bill had languished for far too long. We were tired of the feet-dragging. Of complaints about the cost of implementing the changes we asked for and nitpicking over what qualified as a disability.

The time had come to sign the proposed legislation into law. To bring equality. Most of us even had a copy of the Declaration of Independence rolled up, stashed in our pockets.

Grady walked ahead of me, pushing Rosalynn's wheelchair. His shoulders were broad and tempting, reminding me of how easy it had been to share that sleeping bag the night before.

I shook my head to clear my thoughts. There wasn't time to sort through my complicated feelings for Grady right now. Today was all about Rosalynn.

We were near the front of the crowd, so by the time we reached the Capitol, we had a moment to catch our breath until the others joined us, the crowd growing. One speaker after another stepped up to the microphones, motivational, powerful. A pro-ADA congressman even spoke while also communicating with American Sign Language.

"Mom," Rosalynn said, spinning her chair with one hand, her other arm outstretched overhead in pirouette, her face bathed in joy, "this has been the best time of my life since . . ." Her smile wobbled.

I didn't have to ask. The day she'd landed the role of Clara in *The Nutcracker*. And even as I knew I still would have said no to the trip, I resented my mother for being the one to give the experience to Rosalynn.

It seemed good, though, to see the pink in her cheeks from the excitement and the light in her eyes that had been missing for so long.

She took my hand. "Could we please stay an extra day? It's not like we have to rush to catch a plane. Nana Della planned for us to ride back with you. It would mean so much to me to stay for another day. Not just to protest, but to listen to the speeches."

My heart sank at her request.

Yet again, I wished we could stay longer and soak in every single minute. Except sticking around for even one extra day would stretch our budget to the limit, plus the extra time off work.

And if we couldn't stay, Grady and Della would have to tell her.

Was it so wrong of me, though, that I didn't want to be the one to explain the practical realities? I already had to be the bad guy far too often, while Grady was her superman hero. As for my mother? Well, this trip alone proved the lengths she would go to make Rosalynn's wishes come true.

"Maybe," I prevaricated, watching the crowd go around us as more and more protestors arrived at the base of the Capitol steps. "I need to discuss plans with your nana and your dad."

Every superstitious bone in my body cried out to wrap this up and head back to our protective cocoon at home, every inch of our house adapted for her safety. Here? There were so many barriers I'd never noticed before. Not the least of which was that Rosalynn wouldn't even be able to enter the Capitol unless her father carried her up those 365 steps.

Rosalynn grinned. "I'll take that as a yes and leave you to it." She glanced up at her father with hero worship. "Dad, did you see the guy with the service dog? I have so many questions for him. Will you come with me?"

My daughter knew her father would be a softie on the service dog subject. I might as well surrender and go shopping for a food bowl and a better vacuum.

I rested a hand on her shoulder. "Maybe the gentleman doesn't want to be bothered."

"*Mother*, I'll be polite," she said, rolling her eyes. "It's not like I'm disturbing him in a restaurant. This is what we're here for. To shine a light and answer questions."

"Fine." I raised my hands in surrender.

Grady gripped the handles and wheeled her chair toward the veteran sitting on the bottom step of the Capitol and placing a water bowl on the concrete before pouring a drink for his dog.

My mother slid an arm around my waist and drew me to her side. "Now aren't you glad we're here? I wouldn't have missed this for all the benne wafers in Charleston."

Yes, this day had been special. But did my mother really think I could let her off the hook so easily, just because I didn't want to make a scene that would distract from the mission at hand? Right now, my world felt more than a little out of control, with Della and Grady taking my choices away.

"Mama, I can't thank you enough for all you've done for us," I said. "This day is magical. But when we get home, we're gonna need to agree on some ground rules. Your job—as a grandmother—is to spoil her and tell her she's the most special person in the world. My job is to keep her safe and teach her about the dangers in the world."

Della quirked an eyebrow. "So that she's ready to live her own life one day."

That made my throat grow tight. "Sure. Right."

Sniffing, my mother hitched her hands on her hips. "I'm certain there's some book out there about the new and improved parenting techniques. I guess I'll need to make a trip to the library to check it out."

"Mama, I'm not trying to offend you."

"I'm not insulted. I'm trying to tell you that we parents can teach all day long, but experience truly instructs a child. Wouldn't you rather she stretch those wings while she's still under the protection of your roof?"

"It would have been nice if we could have had this conversation before you put my daughter on a plane without asking me."

"Fair point. I've admitted I overstepped. Just as you'll overstep with your grandchild someday. I do understand how difficult it is giving up control." She shot a look at Rosalynn, who was enraptured with the veteran explaining about his service dog. "So are we going to stay? Because I have enough money for an extra night in a hotel."

Control slipped even further away. I gestured toward the crowd. "Given the size of our group, there probably won't be available rooms—"

"No need to worry. Remember? I reserved two nights."

Of course she had. So much for boundaries. "Mom . . ."

"What?" She splayed her hands. "I made the plan before we had our little conversation. Can't we start those new rules next week?"

I surrendered. And likely not for the last time today as I saw the veteran pass Grady a flyer. "It's not like you've left me much choice."

She patted my cheek. "Love you."

"Love you too, Mama." And I meant it. Even when she drove me to the very brink of crazy, I never doubted how much we loved each other.

It just stung that Della was like a second mother to Rosalynn. The *fun* mother—the one in the process of gathering the teens together and passing out tie-dyed headbands and wristbands. My mother had that Pied Piper gift with kids. I saw that even as young as three years old, riding behind her as she drove a school bus. She would pipe music through and have sing-alongs, even popping the clutch like a deep bass beat.

Grady tucked up alongside me. I didn't have to look to confirm it was him.

"Are you and Della okay?" he asked.

"Yeah," I said. Our bond was unbreakable. My gaze lingered on Rosalynn embracing the moment as she helped model and distribute Della's tie-dyed headbands. "I guess it turned out all right in the end."

"You're a great parent, you know that." He slid an arm around my shoulders, his forehead furrowing. "I'm just sorry I didn't make enough money for you to stay home with her so we didn't need Della's help."

There wasn't an argument that would help his pride, so I just rested my head on his shoulder. "We're both pedaling as fast as we can these days."

"Not fast enough," he said, his voice low and husky as his ribs vibrated against me.

"Thank you for this trip and for coming even though I know the time off worries you."

"I *do* want to be here." His gaze skimmed along the groups of people who felt like old friends after just one intense morning. "For you, yes, but for our Rosie."

"Why didn't you insist on bringing her along?" I wondered. "Even though I would have griped, you know I would have caved."

His brown eyes deepened to a darker hue, his pupils widening with emotion. "Because I thought if we had some time alone together, then maybe I wouldn't lose you."

My mouth dried right up.

Such a simple, but loaded, statement. I couldn't quite discern if he was speaking with regret, resignation. Or if he thought there might still be hope. A hope that stirred inside me as well, almost alien because of how long I'd spent painting porch ceilings blue and making sure empty rockers didn't move. Especially this past year.

I touched his bristly jaw and wanted to linger—

"Is there a doctor here . . ." The shriek carried from the direction of the Capitol steps, where a woman knelt beside an older man slumping in a wheelchair. "Or a nurse or someone anywhere? My brother's struggling to breathe. I think he's having a stroke."

Grady straightened, the tender expression on his face wiped away as he went on alert. "I'm a firefighter, with training in emergency medicine."

The woman extended a trembling hand, waving him over. "Please help him."

Grady knelt beside the man, speaking softly and taking his pulse. He slid into work mode, radiating a professionalism that calmed the family standing just behind him. I'd seen Grady at firehouse demonstrations for the public and schoolkids. But I'd never seen him literally on the job . . .

Other than the evening of Rosalynn's accident.

The horror of that time crept over me, catching me unawares. Which felt strange because there wasn't a day I didn't wake up with remembering. But a memory, while gut-wrenching, was in the past. Seeing Grady tending to the man struggling for air made that event from a year ago seem so very present, as if I were viewing it through Grady's eyes for the first time.

Especially after what he'd confided to me on this trip about his dreams of that day.

Standing, he pivoted toward me and the sun streamed over him, his expression unguarded for an instant. I couldn't miss his deep grief and felt it like an echoing blow. Then his face closed off, neutral again. Except in that brief, vulnerable moment, I realized how much wider the gulf between us had grown over this past year as he couldn't quit the job that had begun tearing him apart all the more since the night of Rosalynn's accident.

When he was the first to reach her when she fell off the stage.

CHAPTER THIRTY

ROSALYNN

2026: Alexandria, Virginia

By the time they'd parked at the hospice facility, Rosalynn ached big-time from her fall off the park bench. She was pretty sure she'd been stepped on by the Great Dane before Dusty had shielded her with his body.

Her mother had insisted on driving, and for once, Rosalynn hadn't argued.

The brick facility looked more like a hotel than a hospital, a place for someone to rest for the final leg of their journey. Her throat went tight at the thought and she waved for her mom and Elsie to go on ahead while she took Dusty for a break.

Hopefully the quiet moment would help her muster the nerve to go inside.

She rolled her chair across the parking lot as an ambulance pulled up to the main entrance. A gurney was wheeled out from the lobby with a patient attached to all sorts of IVs and oxygen.

Her wheels jostled along stray rocks on the walkway, and she winced. Finally, she reached the shade of a tulip poplar tree. She gave Dusty the length of his leash, but he stuck close to her, his head swinging back and forth as he scoped the lot. No doubt checking for other animals.

"Dusty-fellow, we're okay," she said, leaning forward to scratch his ears in reassurance. "I'm so sorry I couldn't keep you safe back there. I tried my best to find us a secure spot to relax."

She prayed he would be able to shake off the incident, but she would be watching him all the closer in the days to come and doing her best to keep his workload as light as possible.

"Free time . . ." She made a waving *shoo* gesture with her hand until he inched away, casting frequent baleful looks back at her. That made her heart ache all over again, being reminded that he was more concerned about checking on her than watching out for himself.

At least she'd suffered nothing more than a few bruises. Physically, she was fine. But emotionally? The tumble had taken a toll. As she'd pitched to the ground, her mind had exploded with her most recent nightmare. Of pitching off the stage and the excruciating pain of landing on the front row of seats.

Even if she didn't have an active memory of the event, she'd heard the details. Not from her parents. Even mentioning that night had made their eyes well with tears for years afterward. But her friends? With a juvenile lack of tact, everyone else onstage with her that evening had shared their own vivid memories with her, the horror they'd felt, so much so that over time her mind had created a reality out of their recounting.

How she'd sailed through the air, only to land too close to the edge of the stage. The reflective tape hadn't been placed far enough back.

They'd each told her what they did too . . . The Sugar Plum Fairy, who'd rushed to peer over at her, only to notice how Rosalynn's body had landed at a "freaky weird" angle. The Mouse King, who'd jumped off after her to protect her—or so he'd said. Reports varied on that, some insisting he'd been running down the aisle out of the auditorium.

One thing she did remember with absolute certainty, aside from the worried faces of her parents. When she'd come out of the three-day coma, someone had placed the flowers from her performance in her room—a bouquet of miniature roses from her parents and red carnations with sprigs of holly from Nana Della.

To this day, receiving flowers threatened to give her a panic attack. Something else Seth hadn't ever been able to recall. Like the futility of dumping sugar into his iced tea.

"Mom?" Elsie said softly, shuffling up alongside her.

"Hey there." She looked up sharply. "Where's Grammie?"

Elsie slumped against the fat tree trunk. "She's talking to the guy who runs this place."

"Benjamin Nguyen?"

"Yeah, that's it. Anyway, Ace is off getting a breathing treatment, but he should be back in his room in about fifteen minutes."

"Thanks for letting me know."

Elsie didn't move or scamper off or ask for change for the vending machine.

Strange. "Is everything okay? I mean, other than the obvious here."

Fidgety, Elsie tugged a low-hanging branch. "I know you're busy and probably tired. But do you think after we visit Ace, you and I could have a talk? It's really important."

Rosalynn's exhausted, achy body cried out for a delay until tomorrow, insisting she should take her max allowed dose of gabapentin, curl up in bed with her dog, and sleep for at least twelve hours straight. But how could she say no when she'd spent the past day and a half wanting just this reaction? And of course, Seth's concern about Elsie asking for money piled worry on top of her own.

"Of course, Elsie. Once we have a quick visit, we can leave Grammie to enjoy time with Ace on her own. There's a lovely little garden over there."

Elsie gave a wobbly smile of thanks. "Fresh air rather than hospital air?"

"Exactly." Another swell of dread filled her over passing through those electric doors and seeing the dear man they all loved so much fading away. She tamped down her feelings and focused on her daughter. "We can even raid the vending machine beforehand."

Elsie's eyes welled with tears and she lunged forward, hugging her hard. Rosalynn breathed in the familiar scent of her, the citrus smell now mixing with the memory of the lavender lotion from her babyhood.

For the first time in so very long, Rosalynn had hope when it came to her daughter. They could sort through anything as long as they were communicating. "Come on now. Let's go inside."

Elsie eased away. "Sure." She scrubbed her wrist under her nose, then nodded toward the entrance. "There's Grammie now with that Mr. Nguyen guy."

Rosalynn pivoted her chair enough to see, standing under the covered porch . . .

Whoa. She hadn't expected Benjamin Nguyen to be so . . . unconventional.

So *hot*.

She'd assumed—wrongly—that he would be more her mother's age, that he would be a suit-wearing administrative type. This guy, though, was more casual in his jeans with a T-shirt and a sports jacket. His thick, dark hair brushed his collar.

Purely an objective observation, because of course this would be the weirdest time to feel attracted to a total stranger. She decided to just chalk it up to emotions being raw on so many levels and the sexual dry spell since her divorce.

Her mother waved at her. "Rosalynn? Rosalynn, over here."

Rosalynn cleared her throat and her thoughts, moving closer while Dusty trotted alongside, her daughter trailing. As she drew nearer, her mother's voice drifted on the wind.

"I just wish he was at home. But my husband insists this is where he wants to be because he thinks it's easier on me. Silly."

"Not at all," the director answered, his voice deep and slow. "Many of our patients need to feel in control of what they can."

Rosalynn stopped beside them. "That sounds familiar."

Her mother clutched her stitched bag closer. The afternoon sun glistened off the image of Rosalynn as the young maid of honor beside the bride and groom. "Mr. Nguyen, you've already met Elsie. This is my daughter, Rosalynn, and that's Dusty."

He extended a hand, his brown eyes warm and kind, the perfect eyes for his line of work. "Call me Ben. Nice to meet you. You have a wonderful family."

"Thank you. I've heard great things about your facility from my mother." She pulled her hand back and closed her fingers into a fist as if to hold in all those raw emotions threatening to spill over. "But I don't want to keep you from your work."

"It's no trouble at all. I'm on my break." He turned back to Lillian. "If you're ready, I'll escort you all there to wait until he's finished the breathing treatment."

Starting toward the entrance, Ben smacked the faceplate to open the automatic doors. Dusty cast a baleful look her way at having missed the opportunity to execute his favorite cue. She passed him an extra piece of kibble and a smile of encouragement.

A smile that faded the instant those doors closed behind them. The facility smelled of antiseptic, flowers, and a hint of cafeteria food. Sure, the place sported a wall fountain and soothing colors. But she'd spent so much of her teen years in treatment centers, no amount of floral upholstery could ease the tension building inside her. The past and the present were both tag-teaming her.

Ben waved to the receptionist, waiting by a wall fountain while they signed in and received visitor passes. He continued down the corridor, narrating the perks of the facility and the credentialed staff, but Rosalynn couldn't hear much beyond the ringing in her ears and the squeak of his gym shoes on the tile floor.

They moved deeper into the building, past a small room with a stained-glass window and a dozen pews. A couple knelt at the altar, where a row of candles flickered.

Rosalynn looked back over her shoulder to check on her daughter. Elsie stared ahead, her eyes wide and glazed. She clutched her cell phone to her chest like a lifeline. *She must be missing Willow.* Rosalynn remembered all too well those lonesome days after her accident, when one by one her friends abandoned her. She understood they'd shared little in common once dancing was in her past. But at the time? The loneliness on top of the grief had been overwhelming.

Over time, she'd established relationships again, a more balanced life of professional and personal. But those lonely days stayed with her in the corner of her heart, reminding her how quickly everything familiar could be stripped away.

Maybe that was why she'd stayed with Seth long after their marriage was over on all but paper. Rosalynn forced herself to slow the rambling thoughts, most likely her mind's attempt at distraction from the pain waiting inside that room. Pausing outside the door, she grasped her mother's hand, then took Elsie's as well while keeping the leash steady between their clasped palms. She wasn't sure who was trembling or if they all were.

The hospice director waited to the side until Lillian nodded. He pushed the door open for them to enter, her mother and Elsie first, then Rosalynn with Dusty.

The door closed with a gentle shoosh behind him as he left them in the hospital room, filled with personal touches. A bright quilt was draped over the foot of the bed. A stack of books towered beside the recliner.

Photos lined the windowsill, each one stealing air from Rosalynn's lungs.

A group shot of Elsie, Rosalynn, and Lillian.

A professional photo of him in his firefighter uniform, with Ace stitched in neon yellow—his work nickname, one his granddaughter had overheard and chosen to call him.

An image of Rosalynn as the maid of honor at her parents' remarriage, the same picture on Lillian's purse charm—

The door opened, and Rosalynn sat straighter just as an aide pushed Ace inside in a wheelchair, his shoulders stooped and his skin ashen.

But the love lighting his deep brown eyes burned as bright as ever.

Rosalynn wheeled her chair toe-to-toe with his. “Hi, Daddy.”

CHAPTER THIRTY-ONE

Lillian

2026: Alexandria, Virginia

I hadn't realized until that moment how I'd been holding on by a thread, desperate to have my family all in one place before time ran out. Seeing Rosalynn and her father together now, our granddaughter nearby, felt like the culmination of a journey far bigger than anything our GPS had laid out for us. Adrenaline all but seeped out of my toes, and I palmed the wall.

The nurse's aide backed toward the door, away from my husband's wheelchair. "I'll leave you to your reunion. Just hit the call button if you need anything, Ace."

Back in 1990, Grady and I hadn't dreamed that those accessibility rights we sought for Rosalynn would be necessary for one of us as well. The decades as a firefighter had taken a toll on his lungs. An ultimately lethal toll. These days he was too weak to walk unassisted. His broad shoulders hunched forward, an oxygen cannula hooked around his ears, with the thin tube feeding supplemental air to his nose.

The facility made a valiant effort at appearing homey, with overstuffed furniture and pastel paint, but in my mind, this would always be the place my husband had come to die.

He spread his arms wide, angling forward to hug Rosalynn and Elsie, one after the other. "How are my girls?"

Elsie hung on. "I'm not letting you go."

"I'm doing so much better seeing all of you." He pressed his fingers to the cannula, as if needing additional air to support his words.

"Well, I'm staying for a while, Ace," our granddaughter promised.

His eyes darted to mine with a hint of worry before he looked back at Elsie. "Even though I feel sorry for the people struggling from the storm, I'm glad to see both of you."

Grady's nickname—Ace—had stuck at work after I told everyone at the station about our time in DC. He'd earned the moniker from the protestor who'd overheated. Thanks to Ace's fast action, the gentleman had been stabilized until the EMTs could arrive. Our experience with Rosalynn had made us all too aware of the dangers of autonomic dysreflexia. A wound or stress below the injury site, even too-tight shoes, can trigger a dangerously high spike in blood pressure. Symptoms varied . . . a brutal headache, blurred vision, slow or fast heart rate, goose bumps below the level of injury or sweating above. The list went on.

In that first year, we'd gotten a crash course in so many elements of Rosalynn's care. But the autonomic nervous system, which regulated so many other involuntary functions, concerned me most. That fear never let up. Especially years later when she delivered Elsie. The doctors had recommended an epidural, not because of pain, but to manage the risk of a stroke.

Just as I'd thrown myself into every nuance of Rosalynn's care, I'd searched for a medical solution to keep my husband with me. For once, my beloved books had let me down. They had nothing more to offer me that would keep the love of my life by my side.

We'd come to the end of the road.

"Daddy," Rosalynn answered, waving aside his concern. "We're fine. None the worse for wear after our travel adventures."

"And your house?" he asked our daughter as he reached backward in an unspoken request to hold my hand. "How did it fare with the hurricane? What about the arts center?"

Rosalynn's fingers drifted onto Dusty's head, stroking his ear between her fingers like a talisman. "I spoke to my boss earlier today and the facility won't be reopening anytime soon. As for my home? I hear there's some minor flooding inside. Once conditions are safe for driving, the Realtor will send a company in to vacuum up any water and plug in dehumidifiers."

A fresh surge of anger hit me for the world's worst son-in-law. Why couldn't Seth get his act together like Grady?

"Where's Seth?" Grady asked with barely contained disapproval.

"He evacuated." Rosalynn's smile was as forced as her father's. "But I want to know about you. How are you feeling?"

"Moooom . . ." Elsie rolled her eyes as she hopped onto the corner of the bed and sat cross-legged. "What's he supposed to say to that? Ace, tell me all the scoop about this place. Is the food terrible? Do they have good cable? Or a decent streaming subscription? Is that hot manager dude—Mr. Nguyen—secretly a monster?"

Grady threw back his head, his laugh hoarse but welcome. "Oh, Elsie girl, I have missed you. The baked chicken is not too bad. The creamed spinach is repugnant. We have cable TV, plus a solid internet connection. And Ben Nguyen seems to be doing a top-notch job running a place that has the potential to be depressing."

"Good to hear." Elsie nodded. "I'm gonna have to get you some bling for your wheels."

Something Elsie had asked me to help her do for Rosalynn on Mother's Day a decade ago. The memory brought tears to my eyes.

"Daddy," Rosalynn said, securing her hold on Dusty's leash. "Elsie and I have some things to talk about. And I'm sure you and Mom would like a bit of time on your own. So we'll see you later? Maybe for supper?"

"Out in the courtyard," he declared, his brown eyes wistful.

"A picnic," Elsie promised as she slid off the bed. "I'll bring my guitar. I've started playing, like you."

A blush tinged her cheeks as she admitted her new hobby. I wondered why she'd kept it a secret, but then teenagers could be ferocious about their privacy.

Rosalynn turned to her daughter. "Here are the keys to the van if you want to get the guitar while I find some snacks to tide us over until supper."

She pitched the ring with the fob to Elsie before cuing Dusty toward the door as they disappeared into the corridor, chatting softly.

Even comfortably.

Could this be the time Elsie would finally ease up on her secrets and come clean with her mother about whatever had made her want to run? I hoped so, for their sakes and for my own so I could turn my full attention to my husband as we navigated this bittersweet ache. Although as fast as the thought came to me, a panic started to well at the notion of days full of "lasts."

Last family reunion.

Last time to greet autumn together.

Last kiss.

The magnitude of it all overwhelmed me. Had I rushed to Sullivan's Island as an escape, to give myself something—anything—else to worry about? The thought made me feel small and cowardly.

And most of all? I felt alone.

"Lillian?"

His voice pulled my attention back to the man who would always hold my heart. "Yes, Grady? Do you want help getting back in bed?"

"I'd prefer to sit here, by you."

"So would I." I dragged a chair closer and leaned my head on his shoulder.

"Is she really okay?"

"Rosalynn or Elsie?"

"Both," he said. "But let's start with Elsie. Did you get to the root of why she wants to leave home?"

"She hasn't been forthcoming, but she's softening. I think she and Rosalynn may be talking it through out in the garden—finally."

"I hope so." He rested his head against mine, his breaths shallow. "I'm glad you were there to help her evacuate. I wish I could have—"

"Shhh," I whispered in a kiss against his chest. "I absolutely won't have us wasting time with regrets. We did enough of that in the past before we found our future."

He hmmm-ed in response, wrapping an arm around my shoulders and drawing me closer. "What's this I hear about you being approached to run for Congress?"

How had he found out? I'd been so careful with the calls and correspondence. "Who's been talking?"

"Elsie texted me. She overheard you and Rosalynn talking about it after you left the hotel. She's proud of you." He gave my shoulder a gentle squeeze. "So am I. Care to share details?"

I knew he wouldn't let the subject go until I explained. "The congressman from our district is retiring. The party thinks I would make a competitive candidate. They have some backers."

There had been more, so much more, but the rest didn't matter and I didn't want to give him fodder to press.

"When do you begin putting together your campaign staff?" He paused. "Lillian, you are accepting, aren't you?"

He knew me too well.

"I'm not interested."

He chuckled, then coughed softly before continuing, "Don't try to bs me. I can see right through you. This is the sort of challenge you dreamed of when you went to law school. You want this so much, you're salivating like your mama's in the kitchen frying up some chicken."

I'd flown through undergrad as fast as possible in South Carolina, before going on to finish law school a semester early. I'd already known where I needed to land next. That time in Washington, DC, had imprinted itself on my internal compass. The day I passed the Virginia bar exam, I'd shown Grady the listing for a job on a deep-sea charter boat out of Alexandria. He'd supported my dream, and he deserved his turn, I'd insisted. Rosalynn had graduated and had a marketing job. We were free to leave South Carolina.

He'd lived that dream for over two decades. Except even all that fresh ocean air couldn't erase the damage from years of smoke inhalation.

I swallowed down the grief and thought about his question. We were only ever honest with each other these days. With so little time left, we couldn't waste even a moment on games or avoidance. "I do want it. Someday. Not now."

"Because of me."

I shook my head and breathed in the scent of him, trying to block out the antiseptic medical air. "Because the time isn't right. I need to focus on my family."

"Your family is focused on you too, Lillian. You don't have to carry everything on your own." He angled back and tucked a knuckle under my chin, looking into my eyes. "Let me put it this way. Being a team means sharing the sadness and the joy. Let us be a part of this incredible opportunity."

I could see his point, however . . . "There's no guarantee I would win. It's a long shot."

"There's also a significant chance you could pull this off," he retorted with far more confidence than I had in myself. "And when you're out there standing up for all the Rosies in the world, I would be right there with you. A part of those victories. Even after."

His words stole the air from my lungs until my breathing became as labored as his. I couldn't form words. I could only hold on and listen, as if I might anchor him in the world for a few extra days.

"Understand this, though, Lillian. I'm not finished yet. Sure, the doctor said I might only have weeks left, but he also said I could live for months. I'm bargaining on the latter." He folded my hands in his. "It would be the honor of my life to applaud you when you accept the nomination."

"Grady, I don't know—" My voice cracked.

"You don't have to decide anything today. Just promise me you'll think about it."

I cradled his face in my hands, his skin freshly shaven, and I grieved that someone else had the privilege of helping him today. "I can't think of anything but you."

He kissed me. Not long. Or passionately. But so much more than that. With a connection forged in surviving the storms of life.

Easing back, he asked as if reading my mind, "What are we going to do about Rosalynn's loser ex-husband?"

Anyone else would have thought that question came out of the blue, but we were so in sync these days I wasn't surprised. "Thankfully, he's not our problem, since he's off partying in Biloxi. This time is just about us and our girls."

CHAPTER THIRTY-TWO

Elsie

2026: Alexandria, Virginia

After ditching her mom at the break room, Elsie jogged down the corridor, pausing just long enough for the sliding doors to open out into the parking lot. Her heart hammered louder than her footsteps. She'd only offered to get the guitar as an excuse to buy herself time. The minute she'd seen her grandfather's pale face and sunken eyes, tears had started building up inside her. Any second now, they would overflow.

Outside, she grabbed the back of an empty rocking chair, hung her head, and dragged in gulps of the muggy evening air. Even the scent of honeysuckle couldn't chase away the fear of death. The whole trip—as well as her life this past year—had been too much to bear. But the time had come to speak with her mom, and she wouldn't be able to make it through the conversation if she started out already sobbing her head off. Part of her wanted to use the keys in her fist to crank up the van and escape. After all, she had clothes and a cooler full of food.

Eyes on their vehicle, she straightened, pausing only long enough to still another empty rocker from swaying. Grammie would be proud of her for that. The ritual helped calm the mayhem inside her enough that she could start walking at an even pace. Maybe that was the point of those superstitions, to force a person to stop and regain focus.

She needed to simply retrieve the guitar and go back inside. Maybe she would even sing one of her poems she'd put to music as her gift to Ace. Or ask him about his favorite songs. She wished she'd taken the time in the past to find out those sorts of things, but she'd been so wrapped up in keeping her guitar playing private from her mom. That seemed so silly now.

Rush hour traffic rumbled and honked in the distance. The first buzz of night bugs swelled from the hedges. She thumbed the key fob just as an Uber driver pulled away from the entrance. What a sad state of affairs for the person who had nobody to drive him or her to a hospice center. A twinge of guilt stirred in her gut over feeling so ungrateful for her relatives. Grammie had flown toward a hurricane to help Elsie, even when her own life was teetering on the edge of massive loss.

The sedan sped away, revealing a man pulling a small rolling bag, and she had to blink her eyes twice before she registered . . .

"Dad?"

So much for the power of the stilled rocker. She must have kicked the one beside it into motion to have brought this bad mojo into her life.

Seth stopped, then looked over quickly. "Baby girl, it's so good to see you."

His bag thunked over the curb as he made long strides toward her. An ambulance pulled out of the emergency bay and tore off down the street. Once the siren faded, she blinked and yep, it was still him. She hadn't hallucinated from stress.

"Dad, what are you doing here?" She backed up a step, her calves thumping the van bumper.

"I was worried about you after our conversation earlier." He hauled her in for a quick hug.

His familiar aftershave made her think of happier times getting an extra-large Icee at the gas station . . . while he bought lottery tickets. "How did you get here so fast?"

"I flew."

"At the last minute?" What a freaking big waste of money. While she and Grammie and her mom were rationing out quarters for the vending machines and eating pimento cheese sandwiches, her dad was living it up.

"I used some of my winnings and caught a direct flight. Of course they only had first class left, but nothing except the best when my girl needs me. I really am worried about you."

She blinked back those tears welling up again because for the first time in longer than she could remember, she felt like her father cared about her. "I'm sorry to have scared you so much you would abandon your big winning streak."

He frowned, his forehead crinkling. "Elsie, you're my number one priority. Even in Biloxi, I was only thinking of how I could help you have a better future. Are you upset because your grandfather's dying?"

"In part. Yes, I am sad"—she was heartbroken—"about that. But there's more. I've gotten into trouble and I don't know how to fix it." The words tumbled out like a ball of yarn falling down the steps.

"Hey, hey, now." He took her hand and tugged her toward those two empty rockers. "Have you talked to your mother? Or your grandmother?"

"I . . . I've tried. But they're so worried about Ace." She dropped into the first chair, her throat going tight and the sunset blurring from her tears. "Mom's losing her father. Grammie's gonna . . ."

"*You're* losing your grandfather. It's okay to let people support you. Or even just grieve together." He paused, waiting. Then finally continued, "Are you going to tell me the other part of what's worrying you?"

The confession caught in her throat, but not in the way it had with her mom. She'd struggled to tell her mother for fear of disappointing her. Now she couldn't explain to her father because she didn't trust him. Which sucked. "I'll figure it out."

"What if you can't? Promise me you'll reach out for help, okay?"

Like how her dad had ever asked for help for his gambling addiction? He was one to preach. "I *will* talk to Mom or Grammie soon. In fact, Mom and I have just been waiting for a quiet minute."

Would that even be possible now that her dad had shown up? Her mom would keep her cool over his arrival. But Grammie? She would probably blow a gasket over him swooping in unannounced *after* all the evacuation work.

Right now, Elsie was Team Grammie.

Seth started his rocker in motion. "Whatever you decide, I know it'll be for the best. But about college . . . You really should enjoy your senior year. Why rush leaving the nest? I'll miss you if you're not home."

She wanted to take his reasoning at face value, but she'd caught his act before, all full of advice for how she or her mom should live their lives when he had no interest in putting in the effort to help anyone's dreams come true except his own.

"Dad, the money is mine to go to college," she said, her voice rising enough that even the guy with a hearing aid four rockers down glanced her way. "If I go to court, there's nothing you can do to stop me."

"Elsie . . ." He paused, twisting his class ring. "You can't go to college now."

"You already said that." Exasperated, she forced her voice to stay softer this time.

"No, I mean you *can't*. There's no money." He clasped her wrist, his face full of remorse she'd seen dozens of times in the past.

Like when she'd wanted a car after she'd gotten her driver's license. And when she'd wanted to go on the class field trip to the Florida Keys. Although in hindsight, class trips hadn't turned out too well for her. "What about my college fund . . . ?"

"Divorce is expensive, splitting assets and setting up a second place to live."

The truth was so obvious she couldn't imagine why she hadn't figured it out already. Some pathetic corner of herself had still been holding on to the hope her father would come through for her, that he would protect her. "You gambled it away."

Her stomach sank. She could only imagine how many more times her mother had felt this way, facing someone she loved who made excuses for serving his own ends while robbing his family.

"Only some of it," he rushed to assure her. "The rest went to setting up my new apartment. Then I tried to replace it in Biloxi. I was doing good making some of the money back, but then you called and I dropped everything to come here."

She wasn't buying his excuse for an instant. He'd probably lost the bulk of it ten minutes after he hung up the phone or he'd gotten tossed out of the casino. Even if he'd been on the best winning streak ever, he hadn't raked in enough to replenish her college fund. That he'd *stolen* from her in the first place. "So then you spent whatever winnings you have left paying for a bougie hotel and a first-class plane ticket. All show. No substance."

"Now that's harsh." He clamped a hand on his polo shirt, which reminded her too much of that jerk Chester who'd made excuses for his obnoxious son at the wreck.

"That's not harsh. That's accurate. Mom put money into that account. *My* account." She jabbed a finger on her sternum. "Grammie and Ace even added to it on my birthday and Christmas every year. That was my money. Not yours."

He put on an air of fake guilt—he'd had plenty of practice. He was almost convincing, except he always threw it off like an itchy sweater the minute he left. "You know I'm sorry."

"I know that you're a pathetic loser."

She pushed out of the rocker and didn't even bother stopping it from moving. Bad luck had already taken root in her life with a vengeance. She fished the van key out of her pocket to get the guitar, and maybe even to lock herself inside until he left.

For good.

Except the thought of never seeing him again hurt too, and she hated him for that as well.

"Elsie, honey," her dad called. "Where are you going?"

"To get my guitar," she shouted.

That answer had been true a few minutes ago. Now it just provided a plausible excuse for her to go to the van. Her fist clenched around the key until it bit into her skin.

Once upon a time, she might have given anything to have her dad's undivided attention. Now she knew who the real role models were in her family, and she wouldn't let herself be conned ever again.

CHAPTER THIRTY-THREE

Rosalynn

2026: Alexandria, Virginia

Rosalynn felt trapped in a scenario of "when it rains, it pours." Literally and figuratively. The hurricane. Her father's terminal illness. And now Elsie's drama.

The only way to proceed? One crisis at a time.

Stopping by the family break room, she riffled through a basket of snacks to take along for her talk with Elsie in the meditation garden. Junk food was every teenager's love language. Right? Although Rosalynn suspected it would take more than some gummies and a bag of chips to level out her daughter for their conversation.

After the way Elsie had bolted out of the facility with the excuse of getting the guitar, Rosalynn suspected her daughter was every bit as destroyed over seeing Ace so frail, so close to the end of his life . . . He'd deteriorated drastically since she'd seen him just a few short weeks ago, just before he'd entered the hospice facility. Would he even make it until her planned return visit next month? She'd heard some folks stayed in the place for months and others might only last a couple of days.

That notion would need to stay in the back of her mind until she reached the quiet solitude of a guest room at her parents' home.

She couldn't waste this opening with Elsie. One breath at a time, she willed her heart to regulate as she picked through the goodies. She added a granola bar to her pile, including four packs of gummies, a staple in her daughter's diet that Elsie insisted counted as a daily serving of fruit.

"Can I help you find something?" Ben Nguyen stood in the doorway, leaning a shoulder against the frame. "I have the key to the supply closet. We could raid the extras."

"Thanks, these are great." She appreciated his thoughtfulness, especially at a time she felt her lowest. "Where's the scanner so I can pay?"

"Everything in here has been donated by local groups and families who've used our facility in the past." He opened the refrigerator. "What about something to drink? We have water bottles, water bottles, and more water bottles."

She laughed softly, thankful for the serotonin boost of a little humor. "Thank you, but this will be plenty. We all just refilled our Yetis. I wouldn't want to keep you from your work."

"I'm done for the day." He unclipped his name badge and tucked it into his pocket. "Your father never misses an opportunity to brag about his incredible daughter. I'm glad to have the chance to meet you. And Dusty too. Would he like a bowl for something to drink?"

"Yes, please." People often asked to pet her dog, but few considered his needs. Ben's thoughtfulness touched a corner of her vulnerable heart. "You're sure you don't mind sticking around?"

"No problem at all. My son is with his mom, so I don't need to rush out." He snagged a small paper sack from under the counter and tossed her snacks inside. Next, he picked up a plastic bowl and a water bottle for Dusty. "Where are you headed? I'll carry your stash."

Her gaze dropped to his left hand before she could stop herself. No ring. Not that this was in any way the right time for such thoughts, and a hospice center wasn't exactly a hookup spot. She shrugged off what was probably another subconscious attempt at distraction from all the heartache in her life. "Thanks. I'm meeting my daughter in the meditation garden."

"You're in luck. I know a shortcut." He motioned with flair. "Right this way."

Once in the corridor, she stole a glance at him, wondering at this man who chose to help ease the final stages of people's lives. The facility bustled with activity, a microcosm of everyday events, but with people cherishing every moment. The meal cart rattled down the hall, the scent of some kind of stew lingering. A nurse pushed a teenage boy in a wheelchair, turning into the chapel. In the common gathering room, a woman with a scarf around her head celebrated her birthday while her husband herded three rambunctious boys clamoring for a piece of cake.

Across the corridor, a middle-aged man lay in bed watching television alone, his room bare of any memorabilia, which made her sad. Did Elsie understand how lucky she was to have so many people who cared about her and loved her unconditionally? Just because Seth had let her down didn't mean everyone else would follow suit.

Dusty's nails clicked on the tile floor as they rounded the corner. Glass double doors showcased the side entrance to the garden. Ben leaned toward the electric door opener.

Rosalynn stopped him short. "Hold on. That's Dusty's favorite cue. He becomes seriously depressed if he gets sidelined."

Grinning, he raised his hands. "By all means."

"Dusty," she called, "target."

Her goofy yellow Labrador launched into action, smacking the silver square with both paws. The door swooshed open, and she rolled out into the meditation garden. Walled off from the parking lot, the bricks were covered in vines. Sunset cast a mellow golden glow over the space, adding to the Zen nature. Only a hint of traffic noise leaked into the calm. A fountain gurgled and a handful of patients sat in wheelchairs with staff and visitors. Peaceful and sad at the same time.

She pivoted her chair to face Ben and extended her hand for her snacks. "Thanks for the escort."

"Anytime," he said, passing the paper bag. "Where do you plan to sit? I'll set up Dusty's water bowl."

"How about over . . ." She paused to scan the area for her daughter, landing on . . . Surely her eyes betrayed her. "Seth?"

Her ex-husband stood under a pergola with their daughter, the guitar case on the table beside her. He pivoted fast, his smile flashing bleached white. "Rosalynn. We were just talking about you. Who's this gentleman?"

Ben placed the bowl and water bottle on a nearby table before extending his arm. "Benjamin Nguyen. Facility director."

Nodding, Seth shook hands. "Seth Yates. Elsie's dad and Rosalynn's husband—"

"Ex," Rosalynn snapped back, then winced at the sadness in Elsie's eyes.

Ben cleared his throat. "I'll leave you to your family reunion. Reach out to my staff if you need anything."

Silence echoed as he left, broken only by the trickle of water in the birdbath fountain and the quiet murmurs of the family at the far end.

One look at her daughter clued her in. Something was off between Elsie and Seth. Rosalynn shifted her full, angry focus on her ex-husband. "What brings you up this way? And how did you get here so quickly?"

"Airplane, of course, because I was worried. Things are a mess at home, and the office hasn't opened back up. So I decided to check on my girls."

His girls. The phrase so closely echoed her father's at a time her heart was beyond tender. "Mom's never going to let you stay at her place."

Elsie nodded.

He laughed. "It's okay. I have a little winnings from my time in Biloxi."

Elsie rolled her eyes.

Rosalynn's smile faded. "Elsie mentioned you hit it big."

"Not that big. Win some. Lose some."

The story of Seth in a nutshell.

Elsie watched them out of the corners of her eyes as she twisted the cap off the water bottle and started to fill the bowl for Dusty, only to have it leak. "I'll get another. Be right back."

She snatched up her guitar and bolted away from her parents like she'd stepped on a bed of fire ants. There was no missing the rise in her agitation. But then weren't they all on edge because of Ace?

Seth knelt to scratch Dusty's ears without asking first, an annoying habit of his, even though she'd had a service dog for as long as she'd known him. He refused to listen. Just like the wrongheaded way he poured sugar into iced tea.

Dusty ducked from under his touch and skirted around to the other side of her chair. Smart dog.

Seth dropped into an iron chair at the table, hands clasped between his knees. "What's up with that guy? Ben?"

"You can't seriously think I'm trolling for dates at my father's hospice facility."

He shrugged. "I hope you know I would take you back in a heartbeat, Rosalynn."

Being taken in by Seth once had been plenty. "Hard pass."

"Even if I promise to join Gamblers Anonymous, like you asked?"

That sounded a bit like emotional blackmail, and so poorly timed given what she was going through with her dad. "I sincerely hope you'll go. For your sake and for Elsie's."

"I guess that's a no to getting back together," he said with a wry grin. The sun sank farther and two lightning bugs glinted in the overgrown ferns. "Remember when we went to Congaree National Park in Columbia?"

"To see the fireflies during their mating season." She'd forgotten about that trip until now. Seth had researched the best parks with wheelchair-accessible paths. The Congaree National Park's planked walking trail had gone on for miles with the most beautiful marshy wetlands.

"It wasn't all bad between us," he said in a rare moment of pure honesty, looking more like the charming dreamer she'd fallen for years ago.

His thoughtfulness had touched her then. And truthfully, did so now as well. Sometimes the good memories got buried under the weight of the bad. Even knowing they could never be a couple again, she wanted to find balance, a way to coexist in the same room during those special moments in Elsie's future.

Graduations. Wedding. Grandchildren.

And yes, it also would be nice not to beat herself up over choosing Seth, analyzing every moment of their dating and wondering what signs she'd missed. The thought of shedding that weight from her soul was intoxicating.

Angling back, Seth pushed to his feet. "Well, I'll leave you all to visit. I thought I could pick up some supper for everyone from the cafeteria. I won't stay. I promise."

"That's thoughtful of you." She considered asking him to join her for the conversation with Elsie but feared her daughter would balk at any change in the plan. "How about you take the van to get the food?"

She fished in the side pouch for the keys. Except she'd given them to Elsie earlier. Frowning, she scanned the garden for her daughter, then checked over in the lot.

The van taillights glowed on either side of the smashed rear hatch as Elsie backed out of the parking spot.

CHAPTER THIRTY-FOUR

Lillian

1990: Washington, DC

I sank down on the bottom step of the US Capitol Building, gripping my sign until my knuckles went bloodless as I restrained myself from comforting Grady. His air of professionalism while he spoke with the EMT workers was undeniable. The overheated gentleman would be taken to the nearest hospital for a full assessment, but his medical crisis seemed to have passed. For now. A scary reminder of all the ways we had to look out for Rosalynn.

The siren faded as the ambulance drove away. The crowd broke out in applause, peppered with cheers and blasts from a couple of air horns. Grady just nodded without even a hint of his lopsided smile. I thought of all he'd shared with me about the stressors of his job and of him being the first to reach Rosalynn after her accident. Yes, Grady's calm confidence quieted the crowd, but now I understood the high cost of his composure.

My anxious gaze skimmed the clusters of people until I found my daughter. Already Della lifted her megaphone to renew the rally cry. Rosalynn and her new friends were chanting nearly as loudly as my mother.

"A-D-A, all the way." The chant cycled on repeat.

While I sensed Grady wouldn't accept comfort, I took advantage of the moment to distract him as he stood on the outskirts. How many times had he distanced himself out of pain and I'd assumed he was pulling away? Blaming him.

With determined strides, I closed the space between us and rested a hand on his dependable shoulders. "Isn't our girl something to behold? Before the accident, she was always so expressive, using her dance to tell a story. Today, she's channeling all that power through her voice."

The lines on his forehead relaxed, and he slid an arm along my waist. "I was thinking about showing her my guitar."

"That's an idea." I leaned into the familiarity of him. Of us. Almost daring to hope. "Just don't expect her to sing on key."

He laughed, such a dear sound that rumbled against my ribs. Had he meant it earlier, about hoping our time alone would bring us back together?

That he wouldn't lose me?

His warm brown eyes said he remembered and meant every word. If I dared to trust him.

Grady gave my waist a squeeze, then reached to retrieve his poster. "We should get back to it."

The clatter of a wheelchair split the air. My heart plummeted. The past year had conditioned my body to expect the worst.

I pivoted fast, ready to lend a hand. I even started toward a nearby woman who pitched forward from her chair. Until I saw she wasn't alone. One after another, protestors abandoned their crutches and assistance devices, throwing themselves onto the steps leading to the Capitol Building. Not just to sit on the steps.

They were . . . climbing?

My fingers lifted to my lips at this new demonstration that suddenly took the day's efforts to a whole other level. Even a girl younger than my daughter flung her walker away, collapsing onto those stone stairs to climb with defiance.

Rosalynn propelled her chair forward, a determination stamped on her face that I recognized all too well from her days as a dancer. Another flicker of worry rippled through me, this time from concern for all the ways she could suffer. All those steps. The strain. The heat. The memory of the ambulance that had just driven away.

Emotions were running high, from the protestors to passersby to law enforcement. A kaleidoscope of concerns spun in my mind. I sprinted past Grady, by my mother, my whole attention fixed on my child.

"Let me help you," I said, searching for some kind of way to spare her the risk. "Your father and I can carry you."

Rosalynn pushed my hands away. "I can do it myself."

I turned to Grady for support. He'd expressed concern for my safety. Surely, he would see the dangers of this move for our daughter.

"Grady? Please," I said, gripping his arm. This was his chance to rescue our daughter.

Except he didn't move. He looked at me with an apology that told me I would get no help from him on this. I didn't even bother appealing to my mother.

"Rosalynn . . ." My throat went tight.

"Mama," she answered.

She didn't call me "mama" often. Usually "mom" or "*mother,*" followed by an eye roll or exasperated sigh. But today had been about breaching barriers in our relationship too, as we moved forward in this new direction our life had taken us. She took my hand now. And it almost brought me to my knees to realize she was comforting me.

"I need to do this on my own," Rosalynn continued with a gentle firmness that showed me a facet of the woman she would one day become. "I don't want people feeling sorry for me. I want them to know that nothing, absolutely nothing, will stop me from demanding what I deserve."

Fear tangled up with pride, and a realization of how high a price she would pay if I stopped her from reclaiming her life. I crossed my arms tightly over my chest as if I could hold in all my concerns, and I backed away.

Rosalynn pushed up from her chair, her legs trembling, and I knew she had maybe ten seconds at most to catch herself. She angled forward in a controlled fall onto the top step. I winced. There would be bruises.

Just as there'd been so many bruises over the years of dancing. Each mark had only spurred her to press harder. Then again during her recovery, she'd pushed and pushed. And that same grit was going to drive her to take those steps all the way to the top.

Grady moved alongside her, encouraging. "You've got this, kiddo. One more. I'm here if you need me. I believe in you."

I thought of all the times since the accident that he'd wanted to take her to the beach. To go kayaking. To offer her independence and experiences. Because we wouldn't be around forever. A parent's job was to teach a child self-reliance. Grady was having more luck than I ever had. Truth be told, he probably always would.

If it had been left up to me, my daughter would have missed this chance to fight for herself. To show the world the kind of strength and fortitude that had the power to change hearts and minds.

The thought humbled me silent. I folded her wheelchair and carried it to the top of the steps because I knew she would succeed. My daughter with her indomitable spirit. Grady followed her up, encouraging her one step at a time until sweat plastered her hair to her head.

Della jogged two steps higher, leading call-and-answer chants in her megaphone. "Vote *now*."

"Access *now*."

"Vote *now*."

"Access *now*."

My lips moved in time with the words, and I'm sure I shouted like everyone else. Although I could barely hear over the ringing in my ears. My focus narrowed to my little family until I almost didn't register the news crews filming and photographers crouching down to zoom in on the faces. As much as I wanted to sweep away the prying eyes, I also understood the need for documentation. How many people would open their morning newspaper tomorrow and be motivated?

I became so caught up in thought I almost missed my daughter completing the climb. My mother's whoop of excitement startled me, and my focus widened again. I dropped onto the concrete and shrugged off my backpack. I fished out paper cups and poured water for my daughter . . . then for others too.

Sweat beaded down Rosalynn's face as she gulped the entire drink before swiping her wrist across her mouth. "Did you see me, Mom? I did it."

Her words reminded me of so many other times she'd shown off an accomplishment. But none so powerful as today. I'd never been prouder.

Grady ruffled her hair, his half smile at full wattage and his eyes glinting with restrained tears. "Yes, my girl, you did."

"Okay, I'm ready to go inside the Rotunda with everyone else."

I was all too aware of the police stationed around us, who were looking more and more uncomfortable by the moment. But who was I to tell her no? I opened her wheelchair and set the footplates. She reached toward Grady and me for help standing and settling again.

We swarmed into the Rotunda with the others. My gaze swooped up to the Capitol's magnificent dome overhead. The buzz of excitement quieted into an instant of hushed awe. The history overwhelmed me at a time my mind and senses were already alive from the magnitude of the moment.

Paintings filled the walls. Bronze and marble statues and busts encircled us—Washington, Jefferson, Lincoln. Not just presidents, but figures like Alexander Hamilton and Martin Luther King Jr. My eyes landed on a group sculpture of women, including Susan B. Anthony, called the *Portrait Monument*. I wanted to soak in the efforts of these individuals.

The changes wrought over time by men and women like my daughter. People with strength and vision. People ready to make sacrifices to do good in the world.

As I marveled at those change makers, I felt utterly useless. I knew I needed to find my role, my individual voice for making a difference. Yes, for my daughter and this legislation, but beyond as well. I'd been so zeroed in on this road trip and finding peace for my family, I hadn't given much thought to afterward.

Now? Faint whispers of dreams floated through my mind of what my future, and yes, our future, could hold. More of that hope swelled inside me and I realized why I'd tamped it down for so long.

Hope could be the scariest emotion of all, since it only increased the potential for loss.

CHAPTER THIRTY-FIVE

Elsie

2026: Alexandria, Virginia

Elsie pounded the steering wheel as she waited for the traffic light to change so she could leave the stupid parking lot. Her father's latest betrayal had pushed her over the edge. Without that money to pay off the blackmailer—a.k.a. Porter, hiding behind a burner phone number and a fake Snapchat account—she would be publicly humiliated.

Sure, she had to accept some of the blame too. Hadn't she proved she could botch up her life? Her cell phone buzzed with an incoming text, which she had no intention of reading.

She wished her father could have stayed in Biloxi rather than show up here like he was truly worried about her. She should have guessed, though. He always preferred disappearing during the tough times—like evacuating for a hurricane—then making a big show out of arriving after the fact. As if she and her mom and Grammie didn't have enough heartache.

Cars whizzed past, weaving and bobbing through heavy traffic. Everyone around her was in a hurry, while she sat at a standstill with virtually nowhere else to go. But she sure couldn't stay at that place any longer with her dad lying through his teeth to her mom, pretending he hadn't just pissed away the money she'd counted on to pay off the person trying to extort her.

His selfish greed had killed her very last hope. It wasn't like her mom and Grammie could be any more disappointed in her. Maybe she could just go to her grandparents' bungalow by the shore and eat up all the ice cream in the freezer. Maybe even throw her phone in the river so she wouldn't have to see her life implode on the screen.

A big-ass truck slammed on the brakes nearby, oversize tires squealing as the 4x4 slid halfway into the intersection when the light finally turned for her. Nerves already strung tight, Elsie realized she had no desire to pull into that intense traffic. So much for her big escape. Her breakout would have been much easier in Middle of Nowhere, North Carolina, than rush hour traffic outside the nation's capital. But she wasn't really making great choices recently, so this lined up. It was getting dark and she was tired. The prospect of adding another dent to her mom's van made her feel lower still.

She shifted into reverse and pulled around to the back parking lot, out of sight. Once she calmed down, she would decide what to do next. Stay or bail. For now, she could return Willow's call before her friend blew up her phone with more texts.

Keeping the engine running, she blasted the air conditioner on high, her face still on fire after finding out her dad had stolen her last hope. She pulled up Willow's contact and rested the phone in the hands-free holder. Since the worst of the hurricane had passed, the connection should be better.

"Hey there," Willow answered, the roaring in the background not nearly as bad. She sat in her bedroom closet with an electric lantern, clothes lining the rods over her head. "Did you get the money from your college fund?"

Elsie slouched back in the seat, staring at the ballerina charm on the rearview mirror. "My dad gambled it away. I've decided to come clean to my mom."

"Wow, you're brave." Willow's face paled as she scrubbed her hair back with a scrunchie. "Except don't you think your mom will blow her top?"

"She won't be happy." Her palms went sweaty, and she rubbed them on the seat fabric. "She'll probably want to call the cops on Porter, because he's obviously behind all this. The police will be able to work their internet magic and do stuff like trace his IP address. Maybe even take his phone."

Willow shook her head furiously. "You can't do that. Then the photos will be all over everywhere. *All* of the photos. And maybe Porter is being pressured by somebody and you'll ruin his life."

"Don't you think whoever it is will just keep asking for money again and again?" Panic swelled at the thought. "There will never be any guarantee the pictures won't get out. I don't know what else to do to make this stop. At least I won't have to worry and wait anymore."

"You can't go to the police," Willow whispered, insistent. "Do you really think this is only about you?"

A chilly premonition crept up her spine. "What do you mean?"

"Because the same thing happened to me," Willow cried out.

Her friend's admission shook her all the way to the chipped polish on her toenails. Sadness for her lifelong friend mixed with disillusionment that Willow had stayed quiet while Elsie struggled with fear and shame.

"When? Why didn't you tell me?" They could have been allies. They could have helped each other. Elsie didn't understand. "I didn't know you and Porter had been together."

"It was just a one-time thing. I'm sorry," Willow managed between clenched teeth, hugging her pillow to her face as if trying to muffle the sound of their call.

"Since there are two of us, the police will have to take us more seriously." For the first time since this whole mess began, she felt a tiny sliver of hope. Two voices were stronger than one.

Willow shook her head, her expression hollow. "I can't. I'll get in trouble too." She bit her lip hard and squeezed her eyes shut for a second before blurting, "Porter snuck pictures of me to get in with the cool crowd. Half the starting lineup of the football team are in on it."

Her friend rattled off names that enraged and terrified Elsie all at once.

Willow continued, "They target girls—boys too—to get money in exchange for deleting the images. When I didn't have any money to pay them off, they came up with another way for me to keep them quiet."

For a moment, the words just sat there between them. Willow stared at her. Waiting for her to understand.

Then the pieces came together until the full picture of what had happened exploded in her mind. The worst of the photos had been taken on that school camping trip last summer, right after she'd broken up with Porter. She'd even been talking to Willow in the shower.

Her friend had set her up.

And Elsie felt the last piece of her tattered support network turn to ashes. Her dad's betrayal had sucked, but it hadn't really been a surprise. Her best friend stabbing her in the back? Throwing her to the wolves to save her own skin?

The treachery leveled her.

"How could you?"

Willow leaned in closer to the phone, her face filling the whole screen as she whispered fiercely, "If you say a word, Porter and I will tell the cops it was all your idea."

The line disconnected.

Elsie's ears rang in the aftermath. Her friend's eyes may have been full of tears, but this disloyalty ran too deep for forgiveness. Never in a million years would Elsie have done that to another person, and certainly not for a seat at the cool table. She may have wanted to hide her own humiliation, but she wouldn't have shuffled it onto another person. Her stomach soured, and the pain built. A scream swelled inside her.

A *tap, tap, tap* on the van window startled the shriek from her.

Except it was just her father. She didn't know how much more she could take before she shattered into a million pieces.

Sighing, she rolled the window down. "What now?"

He rested his forearm over the window and leaned toward her. "Are you going or staying?"

"I guess since you found me, I'm staying." She knew she was giving attitude, but she didn't care. She was done trying. "It would suck if you called the cops and reported Mom's van stolen."

A movement in the side mirror snagged her attention. Her mom and Dusty moved closer across the parking lot, halogen streetlights flickering to life as the evening darkened.

Totally busted on the worst moment of her life. Which was saying a lot given her recent history. Her ex-boyfriend had shared underwear photos. Her best friend had set her up to have naked shower pictures. Then she'd received a blackmail offer. Oh, and her father had gambled away her college fund.

Worst of all, her grandpa was dying.

Sighing, Elsie turned off the engine, grabbed the guitar from behind the seat, and hopped out of the vehicle. "I'm not going anywhere. I just needed some time to cool off." She passed the keys to her mother. "The past couple of days have been . . . a lot."

She scowled at her father. At least he had the grace to turn a little red.

Her mom held up the fob. "Seth, how about you use some of those winnings of yours to go get supper for everyone. There's a slew of restaurants nearby."

He scratched the back of his neck. "There's a cafeteria. I could—"

"You could also just leave," Rosalynn snapped, then smiled tightly.

"Right," he said, taking the key chain from her hand. "I saw a fried chicken place up the road."

Elsie shot him her best death glare. "No need to hurry."

Grimacing, Seth clapped a hand over his chest. "Don't worry about thanking me. I can feel the love."

After he drove out of the parking lot into the evening twilight, the silence between her and her mom threatened to swallow Elsie whole. Together, they started back toward the garden, where there would be no more hiding from the truth. She had to tell her mom every mortifying detail.

The Zen garden would need to work overtime to handle the bomb Elsie was about to drop. At least the place was deserted, other than a cardinal flitting from branch to branch and a couple of frogs who'd taken up residence in the fountain.

Rosalynn wheeled her chair up to a wrought iron table and settled Dusty beside her. She tossed a granola bar and some gummy candies on the table. "I'll be glad to have a decent dinner when your dad gets back."

Really? That's what she planned to lead with? "Dad's a loser. He's never there when we really need him. Don't you think I can see how he spends lots of money on himself while you pinch pennies?"

A bucket of chicken wasn't going to fix this.

Her mom fed Dusty a piece of kibble before shifting her full focus to Elsie. "I don't want you to be hurt."

"But I am," she cried, not worrying about her volume since the garden was empty. "All the time. Because I feel like you're gaslighting me by not admitting what a screwup he is."

"Divorce is tough—I don't want you to feel torn between us." She slid a hand on top of Elsie's. "I'm trying to be fair even though there are times I feel let down by Seth too."

"He's not a hero like Ace," Elsie whispered.

At least her mom didn't jump to defend him this time.

Rosalynn squeezed her fingers. "I wish things could be easier for you and that your father could be the hero you need him to be. But most of all, I hope you won't let the hurt take away from the love."

"You did, though, since you split up with Dad," she said, surprised at her own words, ones she hadn't even realized she felt.

"You know that's different."

"I do," she admitted, pushing past the lump in her throat. "You love me no matter what. I think Dad does too. Just sometimes I think he loves himself more."

Her mother didn't answer and Elsie appreciated being given the freedom to sit in her truth for a while. It felt like a validation, but in a way where her mom still held that high ground of not tearing down the other parent to the kid.

Because her mom had integrity. And now, Elsie knew she needed to scrape up some of her own.

She eased her hand from her mother's and tugged her cell phone from her back pocket. She set it face down on the table by the gummies. "Mom, I made a rotten choice and sent some kinda, uh, inappropriate pictures of myself to a boy."

Her mother's eyes blinked fast for a moment, the only sign that she'd registered the information. "Okay. From the look on your face, I'm guessing there's more to this story."

Elsie took comfort from that parental strength she'd always received from her mom. A strength she needed right now, to press through the rest of the awful truth. "He's been showing them to other people."

"Oh, my sweet Elsie," her mom said, holding her arms open wide. "I'm so sorry this has happened to you."

Biting her lip, hard, Elsie slid from her chair and into her mother's hug. Finally, she let her tears flow, with her face hidden. She didn't know how long she let the tears fall, other than at some point she sat on the ground and leaned her head against her mother's knee. Her mom stroked her hair like she did when Elsie was little.

For the first time since she'd been threatened, she had hope that things would turn out okay. She could come to live with Grammie and start over, away from all the bad memories and two-faced people. "I thought you would be mad at me."

"Well, I'm not happy about it," her mother said softly. "But the boy who did this is the one who broke your trust—and the law."

Talk of legal stuff sent her pain spiraling again. She willed even breaths in and out. She needed to share the rest of it before she lost her nerve.

"The pictures I sent to him were just photos of me in my underwear." Her voice trembled as the rest spilled out, even if she couldn't bring herself to name names yet. The thought of facing off against the beloved hometown football stars made her sick to her stomach all over again. "Except, uh, someone else snuck around and took more pictures of me in the shower. Naked. They're, uh, I mean he's gonna post them all over everywhere if I don't give him money. He really means it. That's why I asked for my college fund."

Her mother tucked a hand under Elsie's chin and lifted her head, looking into her eyes. "Elsie, honey, even if you give him money, he will just ask for more and then probably sell the photos online anyway. I need for you to realize how easily this could turn dangerous."

She hadn't even considered the photos might be sold to somebody. But it kinda made sense with the whole blackmail angle.

"I do understand, Mom," she insisted, even more afraid of what her mother might be about to suggest. "That's why I'm telling you, so you'll understand why I need to leave home and move in with Grammie. So I can just put it behind me . . ."

"Elsie, that won't be enough," she said gently. "We have to notify the authorities."

"No, Mom." Her voice squeaked, which was crazy because denial was roaring inside her. "I can't. I won't. I'm not brave like you and Grammie. The police will have to question folks and . . . No. Have Grammie and the lawyers in her firm do their thing. Maybe they know a private detective or something to make this stop. But I just can't."

"Elsie, you know that's not the way things work—"

"Forget I said anything." She would just pitch her cell phone into the water after all before her mom could confiscate it.

Except that wouldn't solve the problem because the photos would still be out there, like her mom said. The awful realization crept through her that she couldn't outrun this and she was probably going to have to do what her mom wanted. Once Grammie heard too, they weren't going to let up. She just needed time to come to peace with that.

A lot of time.

Jumping to her feet, Elsie snatched her phone and the guitar off the table, bolting away from her mom and the unbearable notion of being publicly humiliated. Even hearing her mother call after her didn't slow her footsteps as she sprinted back into the building.

CHAPTER THIRTY-SIX

Rosalynn

2026: Alexandria, Virginia

Rosalynn pushed the wheels on her chair with extra force to ground her trembling hands. This conversation with Elsie was far from over, but she would respect that her daughter needed some space after confessing something so difficult. No wonder Elsie had been a wreck recently. The thought of someone violating her child's trust with those photos . . . It was all she could manage not to sic the cops on anyone even remotely connected.

Her palms slid off the wheels and she stopped just shy of the entrance, giving herself a moment to compose herself before she faced her parents and Elsie. Closing her eyes, she focused on the trickle of the fountain, the croaking of the frogs, the chirping of a bird. Dusty whimpered beside her, pressing his head on her knee, but she was beyond consolation right now.

Her belly filled with rage. She would make sure those responsible paid. She needed a plan, because heaven forbid they get away with what they'd done and prey on someone else.

How odd that in this moment she identified with her mother and grandmother. Their fire and their grit were stamped in her DNA.

She would need Lillian's input at some point. But when? Even if she called South Carolina law enforcement tonight, or in the morning, how could they investigate when the whole Charleston area was in the middle of a natural disaster? Not that Elsie seemed in the least inclined to talk to the authorities.

The sound of the electric door shooshing startled her. Was Elsie back? Rosalynn opened her eyes.

Ben Nguyen stepped through, carrying a couple of fast-food sacks. "Just who I was looking for." He paused, searching her face for a moment. "Is everything okay? Did something happen with your father?"

"He seemed the same when I left his room. Tired, but lucid." She scrubbed a hand over her gritty eyes. "I had some, uh, stressful news on another matter. I'll be all right, though. Thank you for all you've done for my family today. I realize it's your job, but I appreciate the help."

"Don't mention it." He held up the two plastic bags. "I was on my way out and bumped into your ex-husband. He left this at the front desk. It's your supper, I believe, and the keys to your van. He said something about calling an Uber and checking into a hotel."

Was it wrong to feel relieved to have Seth out of her sphere for now?

"Thank you. Message received." She would have to talk to Seth about their daughter soon, but she appreciated the extra time to sort through her thoughts and discuss more with Elsie—after she calmed down.

Her phone chimed with a text from her mother. We'll picnic in the family gathering room instead. Your father's too tired to go outside.

The last sentence broke her heart.

"That's my mother. She wants to have the dinner inside after all. Probably for the best since it's muggy out here." Her hands started shaking again. She wasn't ready to face everyone yet.

"If you need another minute outside, I can drop off the food with them. This place can be rough on the emotions for families. You need to pace yourself."

The show of sympathy eased the pressure cooker inside her. "It's okay. I'm ready."

He waited for Dusty to nail the door opener, his smile lighting his deep brown eyes. Was she drawn to him out of some rebound need to be affirmed? Immaterial since the man was only doing his job. Although was fast food delivery service really a part of his official duties?

Inside, the strains of guitar music, a country tune of some sort, drifted down the corridor. Her father or Elsie? Each strum fanned the turmoil in her gut back to life.

Once Ben set the bags on a table in the common room, she smiled her appreciation. "See you tomorrow."

"Count on it," he said.

And even though she'd only just met the man, something about his quiet, level manner made her think he kept his word on even the small things.

Like her father did.

Ace sat in a recliner by a window with a portable oxygen tank. No hospital gown for him. He sported sweatpants and a button-down Hawaiian shirt. But no guitar. The music came from Elsie sitting on the floor, huddled over the instrument. Making herself smaller? Or channeling her emotion into music? She had her cell phone in front of her as she plucked out a country ballad. "Neon Moon." One of Ace's favorites.

Her daughter played with an unmistakable skill and talent that touched Rosalynn's heart. While also pinching a bit that Elsie had held this back for so long. Technique like hers only came with extensive practice. But then Rosalynn understood all too well how personal art could be to the performer.

She wheeled her chair past a couple playing cards, toward her father. Her mother touched her shoulder lightly before bustling over to the sacks and pulling out containers for their dinner. How many family dinners did they have left?

Rosalynn tapped her father's hand, careful of the bruises from IVs. "Can I get you anything?"

"I'd like to pet Dusty, if he's available for a work break."

Her father knew to ask. Lord love him.

"Of course. He's always had a soft spot for you." She shifted the leash to her other hand. "Dusty, say hello."

The Labrador circled over to her father for a head scratch, leaning into Ace's touch. "Good boy."

"Free time," she cued, releasing Dusty to interact beyond a simple howdy-do. Her dog leaned against her father's leg with his soulful eyes trained on Ace, earning an extra ear rub.

"Is Seth showing up here a sign of reconciliation?"

"No, heavens no," she said without hesitation. "My marriage to Seth is over."

"Are you okay, darlin'?"

As much as she wanted her dad to wade in and make things right, she couldn't tell him about Elsie's troubles. Not now. She settled on a safer struggle to share. "I just feel that I failed. I couldn't pull it off like you and Mom did."

"Totally different situation." He squeezed her fingers.

Was it, though? "You and Mom worked through your drinking problem. I know that addiction is an illness, which makes me feel so . . . wrong for leaving Seth because of his gambling."

His sigh rattled. "I'm not in any way excusing my behavior for all those years, but you understand that I sought treatment and attended AA meetings regularly. I still do—you'd be amazed how many folks here join in. Seth, well, he won't even acknowledge there's a problem. You can't do all the work. He has to want to change."

She understood that in her heart, thanks to attending Al-Anon family groups. But the guilt still lingered for herself and for the pain her child was suffering. Because, yes, right now, she blamed Seth for their daughter seeking the wrong kind of affirmation from a boy. "You're being polite not to call me an enabler for the years he and I were together."

"That's not what I mean at all." He raised their linked hands and put them against his heart. "I'm apologizing to you. I am sorry if my journey created a cycle that led you to him."

"Daddy, don't go there," she said, regretting the sadness in the corners of his eyes but also seeing his need to deal with any regrets. "I shouldn't put this on you right now."

"We need to live our lives. And it has been a great joy and honor to be your father. Thank you for letting me dole out a bit more of that fatherly wisdom."

She leaned her head on his shoulder like a million times before, thankful for this moment now. Outside, a cardinal flitted past the window. Nana Della had always said a cardinal was a deceased loved one coming to visit. What she wouldn't give for time with her grandmother right now.

How would Della have handled Elsie's troubles?

In her best bus driver voice, she would have called in favors from her laundromat ministry friends and had them scare the snot out of everyone involved. She missed Della and would have given anything to fight this battle alongside her. Their bond had been special.

As was Elsie and Grammie's. They shared the kind of connection that would carry them through, no matter how difficult the struggle.

A whimper from Dusty drew her attention, and she wondered if she'd drifted off. Instead, it seemed her father was the one sneaking a cat nap. Dusty nudged his hand for another ear scratch.

Should she let him sleep? Except he'd been so excited about the meal. Her mother bustled around the table, setting places like a formal dinner. Her mom had always been all about the presentation of a meal and the importance of connecting over food.

Rosalynn patted her father on the chest gently. "Daddy, time to eat."

Dusty nudged him more firmly, repeatedly, his behavior so persistent that dread flooded her. Still, her father didn't waken.

"Mom? Mama . . ." Her voice cracked. "There's something wrong."

CHAPTER THIRTY-SEVEN

Elsie

2026: Alexandria, Virginia

Elsie clutched the guitar like a security blanket while doctors and nurses swarmed around Ace. Assessing. Coming faster than buckshot. *Pop, pop, popping.* Each one stung.

"I've got a pulse."

"Bring in a stretcher."

"Sir, can you hear me?"

"He's not responding."

Her heart hammered so hard and fast her ribs hurt. The carpet scratched her legs as she cowered in the corner. All those people in scrubs and lab coats blocked most of her grandfather from sight, except for his feet in slippers and one of his arms hanging limply. His fingers were turning blue.

She sucked in drags of air so fast she went lightheaded from hyperventilating. As if she could somehow compensate for his damaged lungs' struggle for oxygen.

Her mom and Grammie were comforting each other and Elsie could only manage to keep hugging the stupid guitar. Guilt plagued her. She'd dragged all her stress and troubles here when Ace needed peace and rest.

A gurney rattled into the room, pushed by an aide in cheerful scrubs with palm trees and surfboards. Like some Technicolor waves could erase the sadness waiting for her family here. They lifted Ace onto the stretcher and wheeled him out of the common area, across the hall, and into his room.

The silence afterward was deafening. The couple at the other table had gathered their cards and left without a word, as if somehow the crisis were contagious. She just wanted her old life back, when her parents were together and she could spend vacations with her grandparents and see the cherry blossoms.

Elsie hugged the guitar harder. "Why didn't they use those paddles to shock him awake?"

"I'm not sure," Rosalynn said, her voice soft and afraid. "But he does have a pulse. He's just unconscious."

There had to be more they could do. "What if they're wrong and they didn't do CPR?"

Lillian gripped the doorframe, her full attention trained on the treatment room in the distance, crowded with medical staff. "He has a DNR."

"DNR?" Elsie asked.

Rosalynn touched her arm gently, comforting and shushing all at once. "Do not resuscitate."

"Why would he do that?" Elsie cried. "He can't leave us, Grammie."

"He doesn't want to spend his last days on a ventilator." Lillian pushed away from the corridor and charged toward the table full of uneaten food. One container at a time, she refilled the bags.

How could she worry about spoiling fried chicken at a time like this? Elsie wanted to stay quiet. To allow Grammie to react in her own way. But somehow words tumbled out of her mouth anyhow, her fear refusing to shut up.

Elsie blurted, "It's all my fault."

Rosalynn frowned. "What do you mean?"

"I made Grammie come get me." Scooting closer to her mom, she set aside her guitar and rested her hands on Rosalynn's knees. "I brought all my problems with us."

Rosalynn linked fingers with her as if to anchor her. "What happened to you is not your fault. Do you understand me?"

Lillian looked up from storing the food, her face lined with strain. "What are you talking about?"

"Nothing." Elsie shook her head so fast her hair slid out of her messy topknot.

Hadn't she known better than to bring this up now? She should have brought a roll of duct tape for her mouth from the van instead of the guitar, because she definitely needed to work on keeping her thoughts inside.

"Mom," Rosalynn said, "this isn't the right time."

A sad smile flickered across Grammie's face as her gaze shifted toward Elsie. "There is never a perfect moment for tough discussions. You've been hiding what's going on since the moment you called me."

So much for duct tape. She couldn't refuse Grammie now, not when her eyes bored straight into Elsie's soul.

Elsie drew in a shaky breath that did nothing to ease her dizzy head and queasy stomach. "Some embarrassing photos of me are being texted around school. There are, uh, worse ones taken by people I trusted, and somebody tried to get money out of me not to post them everywhere online."

Grammie blinked in surprise, her shoulders braced. "Well, once we take care of your grandfather, we'll make sure those individuals never hurt anyone again."

More guilt and humiliation heaped on top of her. She felt so very small. "Grammie, can we please talk about something else? Should we ask for an update on Ace? Or pray for him?"

"I'm a multitasker. I'm already praying in my mind. The staff will give us updates when they can, and I don't want to pull them from Ace's side while they're helping him. There's nothing more important than my family."

"And I'm *your* family." Elsie stood, her arms hanging uselessly. "What can I do for you?"

"Help distract me," she said.

"I just want to forget it ever happened. Nobody knows who I am up here. It's not like we're famous or some kind of public figures . . ."

Her insides iced as she realized . . . "Grammie, if you run for Congress, people will use the pictures against you." The consequences of her life were so much bigger than she'd ever imagined. Elsie sank to the ground again and put her head between her knees, gasping for air. "You could lose your dream because of me. I'm to blame."

Grammie knelt beside her, rubbing along her back. "Kiddo, I promise you are not responsible. The blame belongs to whoever took the photos and whoever tried to extort you. Your grandfather's health problems are not your fault either."

She wanted to pull herself together. To be strong for everyone else during a tough time instead of falling apart and making everything worse. But the elephant on her chest just settled in deeper.

"Only a loser would let something like this happen to her just to have a boyfriend."

Rosalynn shook her head. "You're just a teenager who's been trying to shoulder a crisis on your own. You're at an incredibly tough age."

Another one of those insights about her mom expanded inside her. Her mother had dealt with so much more as a teen, none of it her fault. Maybe her mom understood more about her struggle for control than Elsie had given her credit for. "Mom . . . Grammie . . . I'm sorry. The last thing I want to do is make this about me."

Grammie knelt beside her, tucking a strand of Elsie's hair behind her ear. "You said you regret calling me with your SOS. But if you hadn't, then you and your mom wouldn't be here today. Your visit might have come too late. I'm so very glad to have you both with me right now."

A cry hitched in Elsie's throat, and she launched into Grammie's arms, extending a hand for her mother too.

She sank into the familiar circle of family. She took strength from them. For the first time, she hoped maybe she would learn how to give some back too. All the while with staff running in and out of her grandfather's room, she knew that Grammie was right.

Family was everything. With the frenzied echo of medical staff working to save Ace, Elsie couldn't escape the single most heartbreaking fact of this trip. *Her* family would never be the same again.

CHAPTER THIRTY-EIGHT

Lillian

1990: Washington, DC

My heart picked up speed as the police walked toward my family. I was more than willing to face arrest for this cause, but what would happen to my daughter if the authorities hauled off all of us? How could my mother not have thought this through when she brought Rosalynn to the protest march?

The officers strode closer to our group. Since the climb up the Capitol steps, there'd been an edge to the authorities. As if they sensed they'd lost control, at least in spirit.

Were they really going to arrest us because we'd parked ourselves in the Rotunda for speeches and sing-alongs? Yes, we were a little noisy—or in my mother's case, a lot noisy—but we weren't impeding anyone or destroying property. How could chanting "access for all" lead to anything negative?

Apparently, that was enough. The authorities first approached the soldier and his German shepherd, instructing him to disperse. The order was ignored. Out came the flex-cuffs. Essentially zip ties, used for larger-scale events. The police had come prepared, expecting to make arrests.

Would they actually detain my daughter? A young teen?

A pair of police officers started our way. Mama shot her arm across my chest like we were in a car and she was saving a child from an impending accident.

Della lowered her megaphone and spoke for my ears only. "This is my moment. You stay with your family."

A mother's worry for her child was the most powerful force of nature, and apparently my mama was protecting *me* so I could protect *Rosalynn.*

"Mama, thank you. For being you."

Della smiled. "Bail me out in the morning so I can come back and protest again. The hotel information and confirmation are in Rosalynn's backpack. The room faces the shore because I know how much Grady adores the water." She patted my face. "He loves it almost as much as he loves you."

Della brought the bullhorn up to her mouth, charging toward the nearest police officer. "With liberty and justice for *all.*"

Sure enough the flex-cuffs came out, and they zip-tied my mother. She made a point of being near a photographer. The entryway framed the shot to perfection. I'd never seen her look happier.

Della wriggled her fingers triumphantly. "Well, I'll be dipped and rolled in cracker crumbs, will you look at that? And if I'm not mistaken, do I hear the diesel rumble of school buses pulling up outside to haul us away?"

A fresh-faced cop guided her by the elbow. "Better access for the wheelchairs."

Della tutted. "Listen to those poor fools grinding the gears. I was made for this moment."

My magnificent mama. How could I ever live up to her legacy?

I only knew I owed it to the next generations to try.

The hotel was swankier than I'd expected, located on the Potomac River. No doubt my frugal mother had wangled her way into that suite upgrade. The day had been long, and everything in me said I should encourage Rosalynn to rest. But she wanted at least a few minutes out by the water.

We splurged on barbecue and fries. Our family outing was filled with hope on a day that had been chock-full of optimism. The sauce was more tomato-based than our South Carolina mustard-based style. Even with the difference, it still carried a taste of home.

Rosalynn's chair was parked on the boardwalk by a picnic table as she polished off her meal. She'd wanted to eat closer to the shore, as we'd done so often in the past, with Grady pointing out all the different kinds of fishing boats. Except there wasn't a wheelchair-accessible path, but maybe that would change if the ADA bill passed. I hoped so. I wasn't done fighting. I'd learned a lot today about never giving up.

My gaze shifted to Grady as he left the table and walked toward the river's rocky shore, hands stuffed in his windbreaker pockets. He'd always been drawn to bodies of water. The breeze rolled off the Potomac River, gentle and calming. The sun slipped lower into the horizon, the chilly March evening growing colder, but we'd bundled up. A couple walked along the dock with a child on the father's shoulders. A woman jogged past with her beagle. In the distance, a sailboat eased toward the pier, a bell clanging. The sounds were every bit as soothing as the crashing waves of home.

I could get used to a place like this.

As if he felt the weight of my gaze, Grady glanced over his shoulder and extended an arm for me. The golden haze of the ending day streamed over his handsome face, his angular jaw peppered with stubble well past a five-o'clock shadow.

Turning to Rosalynn, I nudged the rest of my fries toward her. "I'll be right back. I'm just going to speak with your father."

I picked my way past a tulip poplar, toward Grady, a man I'd loved for most of my adult life.

He slid an arm around my waist, his body warm and solid. "Your mother orchestrated quite a coup today with her moment of fame. I suspect we'll be seeing her photo on the front page of newspapers tomorrow."

I rested my head on his shoulder with an ease I'd missed over the past couple of years as he'd closed himself off from me. Something had shifted in my heart during our journey, culminating in that incredible moment on the Capitol steps.

My family had become whole again. "I believe tomorrow's headliner will be about when Rosalynn and the others took to the Capitol steps. Seeing you encouraging her . . . There aren't words to describe how that moved me."

His throat bobbed in a slow swallow. "It was a powerful moment I'll never forget. Are you going to forgive your mom for showing up unannounced?"

"I already have." And I had. No question, Della would step on my toes a million more times, just as I would with my daughter. But we were all doing our best to care for each other.

"Are you going to forgive *me*?" He tapped my lips in a gentle shush. "Wait. Don't answer yet. I need to say my piece. I've fallen short as a husband over the years. My drinking put a strain on the marriage."

I remembered those times. I'd spent long nights cataloging them in my mind when I'd been telling myself I couldn't possibly stick with him any longer. Yet I couldn't deny things had changed since then.

"You've turned the page." With a year of sobriety and regular AA meetings.

We'd all coped with so much. Following Rosalynn's accident, I remembered a counselor at the hospital encouraging us to attend sessions as a family to deal with some of the fallout from the massive life change. I'd brushed her suggestion aside, overwhelmed with appointments and unable to consider adding more. It struck me now that even though Grady hadn't gone to the counselor then, he had been seeking help in the meetings. I was the one who'd turned my back on probing the deeper emotions.

"I'm trying," he said, his powerful voice cracking with emotion. "I wish I could say it's always easy. There are tough days. I've learned in meetings that recovery is a lifelong process. I promise I'll keep on trying for the rest of my life to be the father Rosalynn deserves, and a man worthy of you."

My heart squeezed for him and his self-doubt. He'd battled his own demons to be there for us. He'd laid his soul bare about the nightmares. He'd finally given me a glimpse into what had made him withdraw in the first place. And this trip had forced me to slow down long enough to ask. To listen.

"Oh, Grady, I am so sorry for all the times I shut you out, the times I charged ahead and didn't let you be a partner in our life. You already are the most honorable man I know."

"Thank you," he said with that perfectly imperfect half smile of his, "but I need to say the rest. Even if you won't take me back, I'm still here for you both, forever. I don't want you to think my sobriety is contingent on us staying together. That's emotional blackmail. It's not fair to you."

"I haven't been blameless." My stubbornness. My pride. My insistence on having my way. I suspected those things would be a lifelong challenge for me, but then Grady and I loved each other. Imperfections and all.

He turned to slide both hands around my waist, resting his forehead against mine. "Do you think we can have a fresh start?"

I gave myself a moment to sink into the joy of knowing we were on the same page, that we still craved the same things in life.

"I want that," I vowed, looping my arms around his neck, tipping my face to his. "So very much."

A sigh of relief shook through him, one echoed inside me. We'd started this journey looking for a peaceful way to remain parted, only to find our way back home to each other. Something I hadn't even believed possible a mere forty-eight hours ago.

He skimmed a kiss across my lips before continuing, "I meant what I said, about hoping you wouldn't leave me. I love you so much, Lillian Barnwell. The mother, professional, incredible person you are . . . You amaze me. And when the time is right for you, I hope you'll become my wife again. Since the first moment I saw you, I knew you would always be the only woman for me."

"Chemistry." I toyed with his hair brushing his collar.

"Yes," he said, brown eyes serious, "but more than that. Connection."

"Yes," I said, to all of it as I arched up on my toes to steal another kiss from my *husband*. My lover. The love of my life. And savored the joy of us having found our way back to one another after such a painful detour.

"Hey," Rosalynn called out from her perch on the boardwalk. "You two get a room." While she teased, her smile reached ear to ear.

"Rosie, girl," Grady called in response, "what do you say we cruise to the end of the pier and dip our toes in the water?"

I started to caution him about the safety and the chill in the spring night air, then paused, thinking of all the times I'd held Rosalynn back. Our girl was meant to soar.

We all were.

And as we dipped our toes into the water, I embraced the wide-open future for our family.

CHAPTER THIRTY-NINE

Rosalynn

2026: Alexandria, Virginia

Rosalynn had already been struggling with the notion of her father dying in a few weeks or a couple of months. But to think of losing him now? When she'd only just arrived?

She wasn't ready.

However, waiting here in the common room with her mother and daughter, Rosalynn understood her role. She needed to be the matriarch now. To be a calm port in the storm for a family in crisis.

"Mama, can I make you some hot tea? I saw little packets of honey."

Lillian smiled her thanks. A wobbly response with tears in her eyes. "That would be nice. Thank you."

Just as Rosalynn started to turn toward the refreshments station, Ben stepped into sight, pausing at the entryway. Did the man ever leave?

Her mother gasped beside her. Rosalynn tucked her own grief to the back burner and clasped her mom's wrist with care. Her mother would be the last to ask for support, but she'd never faced anything like this before. Time to stop assuming she had everything under control.

The facility director smiled. "Mr. Barnwell—"

"Grady," Lillian corrected softly.

"Grady," Ben continued, "has been stabilized."

Her mom's eyes closed in relief, although she looked none too steady on her feet. Elsie rushed to tuck a chair behind her before she fell.

A trembling started deep in Rosalynn's gut, one that threatened to level her at a time she needed to stay strong for her mother. She squeezed Lillian's left hand while Elsie clung to the right.

Ben finished his update.

"His O_2 levels had dipped—"

"He doesn't want a ventilator," Lillian insisted with tears in her eyes.

"And he didn't need one," Ben said in a gentle voice that also held a calm authority. "His oxygen has been increased to a higher saturation, which helped bring him around. For now, he's using a mask instead of the cannula. The doctor is finishing up rounds and will have time to speak with you and Grady at length later about ways to make him comfortable."

Lillian angled forward in her seat. "But he's truly out of immediate danger?"

"He's stable and coherent," Ben reassured. "He asked specifically to see his girls. I'll store your food in the refrigerator. You can go in to see him anytime. All of you."

Elsie hiccuped on a small sob. "Isn't there a rule, like only one or two people at a time in a crisis?"

Rosalynn reached for her daughter with her free hand. "The rules are different in a palliative care facility. It's about Grady living the last days of his life on his terms. Like with the DNR." She turned to her mom. "Are you ready? Do you want us to give you a couple of minutes before we join you?"

"He asked for his girls. Plural." Lillian's smile was steadier, but her green eyes were watery, the color of grass saturated in a storm. "I would really appreciate having you both at my side."

That was as close as her mother would likely ever come to admitting she needed help. Rosalynn secured her hold on Dusty's leash and cued him to tuck into a heel position.

Elsie stopped mid-stride. "Hold on a second." She darted back to the guitar. "I'm going to bring this with me, in case he's up to some music."

Lillian nodded, but her attention was clearly on reaching Grady. Her mom had been so focused on helping Rosalynn and Elsie, the full weight of her worry had been camouflaged. Time to give back some of that unwavering support. Rosalynn snagged her mother's needlepoint bag and settled it on her lap before she wheeled her chair toward the corridor. Dusty's nails clicked on the bleached tiles.

Ben stood at the nurses' station with the carryout bags, writing *Barnwell* on the sacks in fat Sharpie letters. "No one will snitch it here in the staff refrigerator."

Rosalynn slowed her chair to a stop, allowing her mom and Elsie to walk ahead.

"Thank you. I don't know when we'll have time for food, but we'll be glad not to have to expend energy hunting something down."

He jammed the cap back on the permanent marker. "I wish all the families who gather here could have shared moments like the ones you've had today. So easygoing, with guitar music and laughter."

"We have plenty of flaws of our own." She'd barely wrapped her head around her daughter's crisis, and she still had a battle ahead with Seth to ensure he refunded the money he'd taken from Elsie's account. Rosalynn hoped against hope that her ex would pay it back and deal with any fallout from the IRS on taxes, without her involving the courts.

"Sure, but it's how we handle the stressful times that matters."

His words left her feeling a little less like a failure. "That means a lot right now. It's been a rough road trip, to say the least."

"Let me know what we—what I—can do to help."

"You must not have much free time if you offer this kind of personalized service to all the patients and visitors."

"Like I said, there's something special about your crew."

His gaze held hers for a moment, comforting, considerate. Asking for nothing and offering so much. But then that was his job. "Thanks. I hope you can finally call it a day."

By the time Rosalynn reached her father's room, her mother was already perched on the edge of his bed, fussing over him. Lillian skimmed her hands along his brow and adjusted the oxygen mask straps on his face for a better fit.

Some color had returned to his face. A smile lit his eyes. He extended a hand for Dusty and there was no mistaking his request.

"Dusty," she said, "say hello." Her Labrador tucked himself beside the bed for an ear scratch, still watching Rosalynn.

Elsie fidgeted from one foot to the other in the corner, guitar hugged to her chest. Ace waved her over.

Elsie shuffled toward the hospital bed, but she held it together. She drummed along the body of the instrument in a *thud, thud*. "I thought you might want to enjoy some more music. Mom told me this was yours."

He lifted the mask to speak. "I thought I recognized that when we were in the common room earlier. I figured I'd lost it and so I bought another. I must have left it at your place during a visit."

His voice was weak but steady.

Elsie rested the acoustic against the wall, within sight of his bed. "Now you have it back."

He waved her closer and inched aside his mask again. "Those strings look new," he said between breaths.

Elsie touched his wrist. "Please, you don't have to talk."

"I want to visit," he said. "I thought you played the piano. I didn't know you'd started taking guitar lessons. You sounded good earlier, although I was a little out of it then or I would have asked for more."

Elsie looked to Rosalynn for confirmation she could continue to chat. She recalled how Lillian had insisted he wanted to live out his life on his terms. Nodding, Rosalynn edged closer to his bed. She treasured each word from him and every second of their little family gathering.

Easing into a chair, Elsie drew the guitar into her lap. "Maybe I should have told you sooner, but I wanted to make sure I didn't suck. I've watched some videos online." She shrugged. "No formal lessons. Nothing special."

"You definitely don't suck." He trailed a finger along the strings. "I was self-taught, too, during long hours at the firehouse. Play me something now that I'm more awake."

Elsie's hands slid into place on the instrument with a focus and reverence Rosalynn recognized all too well from her time on the stage. Art in all its forms could be transformative. Elsie plucked out a Taylor Swift ballad, beautifully, hauntingly. So much so, Rosalynn held her breath until she grew dizzy. She'd known her daughter was a gifted pianist, but Elsie had pitched such fits about practicing and lessons, Rosalynn had written off the whole musical notion.

About halfway through the tune, Elsie slowed and looked through her lashes. "Sorry I don't know anything by heart from your era, Ace."

Lillian reached toward her granddaughter and smoothed a fold in the guitar strap with a look of nostalgia. "Hey, you're really good. You've got talent."

Elsie blushed. "Do you have a request? I could look up the chords on my phone."

Ace lifted his mask again, elastic straps straining. "Anything's fine as long as you don't play 'Stairway to Heaven' followed by a bunch more songs with the word 'heaven' in the title, because I'm not ready to go."

Silence thudded like a bass drum. Awkward. Then her father's humorous reference to their old family game during trips listing song titles hit just the right note, teasing a chuckle from Rosalynn. "That rules out 'Knockin' on Heaven's Door.'"

A tiny smile even flitted on Lillian's mouth. "Or 'Tears in Heaven.'"

Elsie hugged the guitar upright, the tuning pegs pressed against her cheek. "Or 'Locked Out of Heaven.'" When silence stretched, she added, "By Bruno Mars."

The light laughter felt good, normal, so much better than spending their time together crying. That would come later. For now, they had family memories to make. "What about 'Peaceful Easy Feeling' by the Eagles? Mom told me that's a favorite of yours."

"Perfect," he declared, then drew a deep breath to continue. "Lillian?"

"Yes, my love?" she answered as Elsie began to strum softly, the music chasing away some of the stress and fear of the last hour.

"Lillian, let's go home."

The weight of his simple words hit Rosalynn in the gut. Could he receive the same level of emergency care at home? But she couldn't miss the determination behind his request. He'd made up his mind. Except the decision wasn't up to her.

Her mother nodded, before smoothing a hand over his brow and along his salt-and-pepper hair. Devoted.

Seeing her parents' love, their hard-won fight for family and a life with meaning eased an ache in her heart over her divorce. Family took many shapes, and hers was here. Her parents and her daughter. The people. Not the place.

When she'd set out from Sullivan's Island early yesterday morning, she'd mourned the loss of a marriage, a house, and so many dreams.

Now she knew. She, too, had come home.

CHAPTER FORTY

Lillian

2026: Alexandria, Virginia

Checking Grady out of the facility two days later had been emotional and more difficult than I'd expected. I wanted him in our house, in our place with our family, but a part of me feared no longer having medical professionals at my fingertips. A home health care professional would be coming by regularly. I'd already lined up respite workers. This was a different approach to Grady's illness, but one he clearly wanted.

After a nap in his own bed, Grady had insisted on a picnic supper by the shore. Easy enough to accomplish since our place overlooked the Potomac River.

Once I'd finished law school, we'd sold our little ranch-style home in South Carolina and relocated to Alexandria. The early days were financially tight, but we'd followed our dreams. Grady took a job with a deep-sea fishing charter company. We worked. We saved. He started his own charter fishing business, and we bought a bungalow fixer-upper on the river. Grady's first project had been to install wheelchair-accessible walkways leading to the dock.

We'd been happy here.

We still were happy here, I corrected myself. I knew I had to silence the worries for the future and concentrate on our time together now. I would embrace every precious moment with the man I loved.

While Rosalynn and I polished off our dinner, Grady sat in his wheelchair at the end of the dock. He wore clothes that didn't carry the hospital scent—swim trunks and a T-shirt with the logo of the fishing charter business he'd started.

He'd improved since his scare at the facility and was back to using a cannula for supplemental oxygen. The portable tank gave him more mobility to enjoy our family time.

Like with the picnic by the shore that he'd requested. The food was simple, since we'd only just settled in at home. While he rested, I'd thrown together a meal from the hodgepodge in my refrigerator and pantry.

Even after all these years, the prep work filled me with as much excitement as the actual adventure. Joy multiplied while I packed the cooler full of pimento cheese sandwiches, deviled eggs, some boiled peanuts, and, of course, a jug of sweet tea.

There was an art to making authentic Southern sweet tea, but the most important step? Give the sugar plenty of time to dissolve before adding ice. The truly great things in life just couldn't be rushed.

After supper, Elsie and Rosalynn had parked themselves under a maple tree, talking softly while Elsie practiced plucking out the refrain of another Eagles tune for her grandfather. I appreciated having them close.

Grady looked up at me from his chair, waves lapping at the dock in a gentle rhythm. "Will she be all right? Our little Elsie bug?"

I had a feeling she would, especially now that she was opening up with the details, even when that meant naming her friends and popular athletes at school. While I didn't much like the notion of her returning to Sullivan's Island, where she'd been so betrayed, I trusted the legal experts I'd contacted to fight back against the parents attempting to shield their teens from accountability. Most of all, I had a newfound confidence in my daughter and granddaughter. I wouldn't be keeping my nose out altogether, but I had some breathing room to focus on the man who held my heart in his hands.

"She's talking more to her mama, as she should be. I hate that she tried dealing with such a scare on her own for even a day."

He'd asked me about what had been troubling her, so I'd given him the rough outline, mindful not to upset him since I intended to go scorched earth on the extortionist who'd threatened my family in such a vile way.

I would not relent. "She's on the right path now. She also has Rosalynn and me to help her. You may have noticed that the women in our line can be a bit stubborn."

"A bit?" He chuckled softly, his voice raspy. "I wouldn't have it any other way. Knowing how strong you are—all of you—puts my spirit at ease."

"We built a lasting foundation for our family." Thinking of a world without his physical presence cut clean through me, but I understood he needed reassurance.

"Lillie, my love, we've had quite a journey. I like to believe we've left a mark on the world, you and me." He gripped the arms of his wheelchair and stood, his breathing pumping heavier with the simple exertion. One at a time, he toed off his deck shoes. "And it's not over yet. Let's dip our toes in the water together. All of us."

Like we'd done with Rosalynn after the march. As we'd done countless times over the years, soaking in the last rays of the day.

Kicking off my Crocs, I waved toward the shore, where Elsie and Rosalynn huddled together talking. "Come stick your feet in the water with us."

Elsie set aside her guitar on the picnic table and started toward us. Rosalynn wheeled her chair alongside on the planked walkway that connected to the pier, Dusty's nails tapping.

I wrapped my arm around Grady's waist and together we sank to the edge. He leaned on me more now. But then I'd needed his help before too, all a part of the give-and-take of marriage.

Elsie was already barefoot and Dusty launched into his third favorite cue—tugging off Rosalynn's shoes. He even lined them up, side by side, although I'd heard that part of the skill had taken him much longer to master. During his younger years, he'd preferred to send them airborne.

His playfulness reminded us that fun and laughter made life worth living.

"Brace," Rosalynn cued Dusty, and he assisted in her transfer to sitting on the end of the dock.

I fought back the urge to help, but my daughter and Dusty had it well in hand with Elsie nearby. There was a new awareness about Elsie when it came to making sure her mother's needs were met. Dusty settled close beside Rosalynn, resting his head on her knee.

Things were well under control without my aid.

Grady slid an arm around my shoulders, our feet dangling off the edge as cool water lapped over our toes. An osprey soared low above the surface. A familiar fishing vessel bobbed in the distance, honking a hello to us.

We'd fought hard for our life together, and I didn't regret a moment of the challenge. Not when those times had produced Rosalynn and Elsie. Our stunningly perfect legacy.

Grady was right. He and I had made a mark on the world. With our march to the Capitol and beyond. He'd saved lives through his work. I'd won victories for underdogs with my law practice. But we took the most pride in the family we'd built and the simple moments of everyday routines and joys. Each memory was precious. Like sweet tea on a covered porch with a blue ceiling.

"My girls," he said. He took another breath and turned his whole attention to me. "My girl."

I answered without hesitation. "Always."

EPILOGUE

Rosalynn

September 2027: Alexandria, Virginia

Rosalynn had always dreamed of living on the water. It was funny how hopes took on an unexpected shape that ended up exceeding anything she could have planned. Wind rolled across the Potomac River, sailboats and a fishing vessel dotting the horizon. Great blue herons picked their way along the shallows.

She couldn't imagine a better place to say her final farewell to her father. On the body of water where they'd found healing so long ago after the march. A place she now called home.

Lillian held the box with Ace's ashes, standing between Rosalynn and Elsie at the end of the dock. In a fitting tribute, Elsie plucked out a flawless rendition of "Peaceful Easy Feeling." As the notes washed over them, Lillian knelt and trickled the ashes into the water.

Dusty leaned against Rosalynn, instinctively comforting. Tears stung her eyes, of loss, but also ones of such gratitude for Grady and the honor of being his daughter.

She'd opted to relocate from South Carolina to Virginia to spend more time with her father. Even if her job at the arts center hadn't been put on hold due to hurricane damage, she liked to think she would have come to the same decision. She and Elsie had moved in with her parents. It made sense to pool resources, financially and emotionally, like when Della had come to live with them. Elsie had requested homeschooling for her senior year to spend more time with Ace. She'd also used the flexible schedule to deal with the stress of holding the guilty parties in South Carolina accountable.

They'd made the most of Ace's last months, enjoying a final Christmas together. Best of all, Ace had lived long enough to witness the public announcement of Lillian's candidacy. He'd even scraped up enough strength to be there by her side.

Rosalynn glanced toward Elsie now as she played her grandfather's guitar with focus and intention. Her heart swelled with pride at how her daughter had faced down her fears and made it through the other side of her ordeal.

Lillian had harnessed all her legal influence to recruit a high-powered South Carolina attorney. The dominoes fell from there. Elsie had shared the threats. Willow had turned over evidence against Porter, and she'd received a suspended sentence. Porter had tried to take a plea deal in exchange for implicating the other boys in their school. However, thanks to Elsie's bravery, other girls had stepped forward with accusations.

Freeing Elsie of her ties to Sullivan's Island.

After completing high school, Elsie had enrolled in a local college in Alexandria to pursue a degree in music, surprising all by continuing to live at home with her mom and grandmother. She'd shrugged off their shock and simply noted they deserved time to enjoy being a family.

Rosalynn had suggested Elsie make an appointment with the campus counselor to process the betrayal. Someone neutral since she'd already suffered enough embarrassment during the investigation. The talk therapy seemed to be helping. Elsie had been pushing her grandmother to make bullying and cybercrimes part of her platform. No more hiding in shame for something that had never been her fault.

Seth had driven up to see Elsie once, and their daughter had been warily hopeful. Until Seth let it slip that he was actually on his way to

Atlantic City in New Jersey. Sad. But not unexpected. Making a big change took more than effort. As Ace had shown her, the person had to want the transformation. How thankful she was that her father had chosen to take that step all those years ago.

Rosalynn had given a lot of thought to her own life makeover and had used the small profit from her Sullivan's Island home as seed money toward a loan for a small dance studio. She'd taken her solitary workouts public, with the assistance of two students at a local college. Her studio also offered options in adaptive dance classes, from ballroom to ballet.

And fitness workouts too. Pilates. Yoga. Even doga—yoga with a dog. Turned out, Dusty had a Zen side.

Money was tight. But the rewards were priceless. Dancing again, expressing her art in new and creative ways while helping others to do the same, reignited an empowering fire in her soul.

As the last notes of Elsie's song drifted out over the water, Rosalynn turned to her mother. "Are you ready, Mama?"

Standing, Lillian placed the lid back on the box. "For which part?"

Elsie hugged her grandfather's guitar. "How about all of it?"

Rosalynn glanced over her shoulder at Ben grilling burgers on her mom's back patio. Changes went beyond her professional life to her personal as well. Their friendship had developed into something more. Something fun. As for the future? She enjoyed anticipating the journey, wherever it led them.

A pair of cardinals winged inward to land on the railing like a howdy-do from loved ones. So sweet. But Rosalynn didn't need red birds or superstitions for reminders of her father and Nana Della. She could feel their approval all around her. Elsie was healthy and well on her way to a career in music. Her mother would make an earthshaking addition to Congress.

And Rosalynn? She intended to spend the rest of her days dancing.

ACKNOWLEDGMENTS

I grew up in the days when road trips involved an ice chest full of homemade food and generations piled into my grandma's car on our way to the beach. My siblings, cousins, and I treasure those memories of splashing in the waves and snacking on boiled eggs.

Over the years, I sought to re-create those moments for my own children, even when they lobbied for fast-food restaurants and vending machines. Our most memorable—and nerve-racking—road trips involved evacuating for hurricanes. We would hit the road with our beagle and tabby cat, the hurricane's path dictating which relative we decided to visit. During our first evacuation in particular, my frustrations for myself peeled away as I noticed the barriers others faced.

Those memories stirred in my mind during the early days of plotting *The Sweet Tea Odyssey*. As difficult and frightening as evacuations could be, how much more challenging would it be for someone like my mother? My mom suffered a spinal injury in her fifties that required multiple surgeries. She never made a full recovery due to complications from lupus, diabetes, and neuropathy. She used a walker, then a wheelchair for the remainder of her life, with her faithful Pekingese companion Buster on her lap. While he was not a service dog like Dusty, Buster did supply endless comfort. So much so, I began to investigate ways I could volunteer with service dogs in training. After a decade of volunteering and fostering with the Palmetto Animal Assisted Life Services (PAALS) in Columbia, South Carolina, I've had the enormous honor of watching service dogs train during their two-year journey to graduation. The staff and each of these incredible four-legged life changers served as endless inspiration for Dusty.

My mother's injury occurred after the Americans with Disabilities Act was signed into law, thereby removing some of the barriers to access my mom would have otherwise faced. In honor of her, I knew I wanted to write a story that included the Wheels of Justice March and the pivotal moment later labeled the Capitol Crawl. I've tweaked some details and timelines in the days of demonstrating to fit fictional elements of this story. My characters are not based on any one person in the movement, but together they relay the power of the collective message and the monumental impact.

Endless thanks to all who helped bring this story of my heart into readers' hands: My stellar editor Nancy Holmes, the endlessly insightful Krista Stroever, and the entire incredible Lake Union team. My tenacious literary agent Barbara Collins Rosenberg of the Rosenberg Group. My critique partner and best friend, the talented, award-winning author Joanne Rock. Beta readers Haley Catherine Frank and Marka Danielle Rodgers, who shared professional and personal insights. And thank you to the two gifted physicians—you know who you are—who answered my endless medical questions.

Most of all, my love and thanks to my family. My four miraculous children, their wonderful spouses, and my even more miraculously wonderful grandchildren who've cheered me on as proudly as I've cheered for them. My husband's children and grandchildren, who have shown me a whole new and lovely dimension of family. And to my husband, Jim, my guy. Always.

DISCUSSION QUESTIONS

1. Were you surprised to learn that the Americans with Disabilities Act (ada.gov) wasn't passed until 1990? What did you think of Lillian's and Rosalynn's journeys to support the legislation?
2. *The Sweet Tea Odyssey* is a road trip story, but the characters are all on different journeys in different timelines. What are the three main characters pursuing in the present-day story?
3. Elsie is the victim of two cruel schemes—one at the hands of a former romantic interest, and one because of someone she thought was a friend. Was her predicament believable? What are ways to keep teens safe from similar threats online?
4. Rosalynn's life changed radically as a child. How was her relationship with her grandmother strengthened afterward?
5. Similarly, Elsie chose to reach out to her grandmother when in crisis. What made her seek help from Grammie over her mother?
6. The author makes frequent references to sweet tea and how it should be prepared. What does sweet tea represent, particularly as it relates to adding sugar?
7. Why do you think the author chose to tell Lillian's scenes through first-person point of view? How might the story have been different if told via first person in Rosalynn's or Elsie's point of view?

8. Which character did you relate to the most and why? What are some actions you might take to help those with disabilities live in a more accommodating world? What lessons or insights did you gain from this novel about issues with access?
9. Elsie thinks: "Why couldn't people understand? Just because a dog knew some tricks or provided emotional support, that did not make him a service dog." What elements of service dog training and tasks surprised you? (For more information on service dog standards, laws, and general questions, consider visiting the website for Assistance Dogs International: AssistanceDogsInternational.org.)
10. What are the similarities and differences in Grady and Seth that drove them both toward addiction but allowed only Grady to seek recovery?
11. How did the addictions discussed in the book affect the characters' relationships?
12. Each of the main characters experiences trauma—Rosalynn and Lillian from the accident, Elsie from her friends' betrayal, Grady from both work and Rosalynn's accident. How does each character respond to stress and trauma?
13. What role do secrets play throughout the book?
14. What lessons did you learn about family and togetherness from this story?
15. Where do you think Elsie ends up in fifteen years?
16. Do you believe Ben Nguyen and Rosalynn will form a lasting relationship? If so, how will the road trip have taught her how to have a more balanced partnership?
17. Della, Lillian, Rosalynn, and Elsie all mention their superstitious natures. In what ways are you superstitious? How can those superstitions become self-fulfilling prophecies?

18. Lillian ponders the following: "I'd done a poor job passing on the stories of our generations of women, something I needed to rectify. We deserved to be remembered for our resilience, our gift to one another as ingrained as our bright green eyes." How have the experiences and dynamics of women in your family shaped future generations?

MORE FROM CATHERINE MANN

In South Carolina, a woman discovers her aunt's profound secrets in *Lightning in a Mason Jar*, an emotional novel about trauma, survival, and the bonds of female friendship.

Prologue: 1971

Changing my identity and leaving behind everything familiar should have been difficult. Traumatic, even. Except it wasn't. Because from birth, we women aren't tethered to our names. Marriage may turn a Jane Smith into Jane Brown or Jane Jones. Or into Jane Smith Brown Jones through widowhood or divorce, followed by remarriage.

Even the connection to a first name is tenuous when spoken. "Introducing Mrs. John Smith" would be followed with a whisper like a distorted echo . . .

"Her husband's a *doctor*."

"Her baby d-i-e-d."

"She's barren."

As if a woman's entire worth, her sum total sense of self, were tied into her ring finger and uterus. A Mrs. or a mom.

Could those hushed voices be that oblivious to the world exploding with marches and rallies, bra burnings and sit-ins? I wasn't. I cheered those women on from my living room, images flickering across my new color television set, the wooden cabinet kind that dominated its own corner where once a tiny black and white had rested on an antique tea cart.

This was more than simply incinerating cotton and lace. It was like a broken bottle being melted and reshaped by an emerging sisterhood, a revolutionary sorority.

The world was changing, and that bigger, brighter screen gave me an expanded peek. Decorated with family portraits and silk flowers on top, the Magnavox invited me on a nightly news date to watch *them*. I was proud of *them* and all *they* were battling to achieve. I was also thankful for my safe life that protected *me* from being *them*. What a comfortable place to exist, in that cottony swaddle of complacency.

So yes, I expected the changes that began when my father gave away the bride. Giving *me* away to Phillip, as if I were a possession passed over to a neighbor like a handsaw or a charcoal grill—or the tiny black-and-white television—he no longer needed but still thought of fondly. Although if I'd been a brighter color TV, I might have been wanted. Still objectified, but not discarded.

However, I accepted, and at that time embraced, my new identity as Phillip's wife, even if it meant losing a part of myself. No one forced me to walk down the aisle in my mother's white lace gown that itched, with my hair piled on my head, anchored by Aqua Net that stung my eyes and bobby pins that scarred my scalp. Nobody insisted I put aside completing college to start a family right away. I made my own choices. At least I thought I did.

Then I began doubting even my tiniest of decisions. I forgot to buy slaw for supper, even though Phillip insisted he'd written it on the list I'd anchored to the refrigerator with a banana-shaped magnet—a list I now couldn't locate. But no need to be upset or melodramatic. Didn't I know how much he treasured me?

I thought I'd put the credit card in my wallet as always, except it was in the medicine cabinet. No wonder a husband had to sign the application for a Master Charge card. Perhaps he should keep it from now on. If I wanted extra cash, I only had to ask him and he would increase my household allowance. Money that came from my trust fund.

Maybe I just needed rest. I should cancel the cruise to Mexico with his parents. Send our regrets for my class reunion. Leave behind sad reminders of my dead parents and relocate to the country for fresh air, where we could build my dream studio for glassblowing. Didn't I want to get back to my art? Eventually. Once I was myself again.

Except time went by, feeling more and more strange. And as I lost my bearings, my husband retreated from me in ways that unnerved me. Who was he to become the expert on my mental health? And why did I feel better the days when he traveled for work? The weeks when he left for conferences?

By increments my world grew smaller and smaller, until that day, the worst day, when *I* became one of *them*. My cottony swaddle of complacency split open to reveal a light so blinding it sliced through me like the electroshock therapy that followed. Therapy that Phillip had been quick to suggest. Quick to approve.

In the silence that followed came a soul-deep realization. Phillip intended to keep me institutionalized forever and take what was mine for himself. Who knew when he'd made that decision? Surely not from the start. After the miscarriages? The stillbirth? Or simply because he could. Now that my parents were gone, who would stop him?

Except he underestimated me. Or overestimated himself. He could steal the money, my name, even a piece of my sanity. But he couldn't steal *me*. Which meant I had the most important choice of my life, the first I made completely on my own.

I had to run.

The details of how I managed to escape the hospital aren't important yet. Those secrets are carefully guarded, doled out in increments to only the most trusted in what has become my network—my life's work, you could say. To protect those with the greatest need.

All you have to know for now? I embraced the reality of my own making, being one of *them*. Helping the most vulnerable of *them* when they need to run as well.

Ask me who I am or where I'm from? Eloise Carlisle Curtis is a faint specter, ostracized to the dim recesses of my mind. I rarely think of my life in Mobile, Alabama, anymore, of my marriage, of my art. Of my daughter. In fact, it's better that way since a whisper of that time threatens my present, even my hard-won sanity.

Today? My name is Winnie Ballard. I'm from Bent Oak, South Carolina, where I work in the paper mill.

But tomorrow? Well, like I said, I'm not tethered to something so inconsequential as a name.

ABOUT THE AUTHOR

Photo © 2017 Rob Wilson Photography

Catherine Mann is the *USA Today* bestselling and award-winning author of *Lightning in a Mason Jar* and many other works of contemporary women's fiction and romance that have been published in more than thirty countries. After years of moving around the US, Catherine settled back in her home state of South Carolina with her Harley-riding husband. Empty nesters, they have a blended family of nine children, nine grandchildren, two dogs, and three feral cats, who all provide endless inspiration for new novels. For more information, visit www.catherinemann.com.